Too Many Cooks

Shirley Ann Wilder

A TASTE OF HAPPINESS

"Oh, why did I ask a chef to dinner?" Estelle asked herself.

What had she been thinking? It wasn't that she was a bad cook. She'd certainly garnered her share of compliments over the years, but inviting Gaetano to dinner had not been the best decision she'd made recently. And yet, she'd wanted to thank him.

The doorbell rang and Estelle's heart quickened. When the door opened, it revealed the hugest bouquet she'd ever seen, a riot of color and fragrance. Peeking through lavender irises and yellow roses were two deep brown eyes twinkling with mischief and humor.

"Gaetano, you shouldn't have. They're beautiful." Estelle took the flowers and leaned into the handsome Italian. His lips found hers, and because her hands still held the flowers, she could do nothing but submit. In fact, she not only submitted but responded in such a way that parts of her anatomy suddenly woke with the vigor and enthusiasm of a girl in her twenties. Indeed, for the first time in ages every nerve in her body felt as if it were doing cartwheels and back flips.

Too Many Cooks

Shirley Ann Wilder

www.BOROUGHSPUBLISHINGGROUP.com

TOO MANY COOKS
Copyright © 2015 Shirley Ann Wilder

ISBN 978-1-942886-23-5

To my husband John, who always believed.

ACKNOWLEDGMENTS

No book is ever written by just one person. Though the author may be a single human being, her experiences, her past, the people she's met, the places she's lived and visited all show up between the pages sooner or later. And equally important are the friends who are there cheering the writer on and contributing knowledge, opinions and yes, even helpful criticism.

I am grateful to my family for their encouragement and patience, especially my granddaughter Micaela who is the Italian in our family and the model for Gina. I would be remiss if I didn't list my critique group who listened to this project so many times they began to boycott Italian restaurants. The members in the group who were present from the first sentence are Mary Galusha, Toni Noel and Ann Siracusa, and special thanks to Ann's husband, Luciano, who intrigued me with his Italian phrases, cooking talents and pasta dishes. Sincere thanks also to my San Diego Chapter of Romance Writers of America, who inspired me to keep the faith. Lastly, I want to thank my new friends at Boroughs Publishing Group, Michelle Klayman and my editor, Chris Keeslar.

CONTENTS

Chapter 1

Estelle Bennett hesitated at the door. It was slightly ajar, and the doctor was on the phone. She'd obviously gotten dressed and walked over to his office faster than he'd expected.

She waited out of politeness and debated if she should knock to announce her presence; then the conversation riveted her in place and she couldn't help but listen to every word. Dr. Robert Taylor's voice was not its usual deep, rich baritone. Estelle had known the man for over twenty years and to her he was Dr. Bob, a friend as well as her physician. She could tell he was fighting down emotion.

"You're absolutely sure there's no mistake? It's leukemia for sure? Oh boy, this is not good."

She had come in for a follow-up appointment and to get the results of some tests the physician had taken two weeks ago. She hadn't been sick, just tired. Estelle leaned as close to the crack in the door as she could get without bumping it open.

"She just went through an ordeal not long ago, so if you have no objections I'm not going to tell her yet. God, I feel like the grim reaper. Well, we'll get some meds started and then I'll break it to her. In some cases, I don't think it's unethical to delay delivering a death sentence."

It took Estelle a few minutes to recover after Dr. Taylor hung up. She raised her hand and was just about to knock when he buzzed Nurse Marlow at reception.

"Betty, would you have Mrs. Bennett wait just a few minutes before bringing her to my office? I've just gotten some terrible news, and I need time to compose myself before I see her."

Estelle's heart was in her throat. *Oh, God. That call* was *about me. I have a terrible disease. Leukemia.* She felt her body go from clammy to scorching hot. The urgency to get out of there overwhelmed her. She wanted to run, to hide, to…

Dr. Bob had said he wasn't going to tell her today? Well, too late. She already knew.

Panic commanded her feet to move, and they obeyed. She almost knocked Betty over as she bolted down the hallway, through reception, and out the front door. She heard someone calling her name but didn't stop. She had to be alone.

She scarcely remembered getting in her car, but she must have, because she was driving down the freeway toward home. Suddenly, though, she didn't want to go there. She took the next off-ramp and found herself in the area where her husband's business office had been. If there was ever a time she needed a drink, it was now. But it was only a little past three in the afternoon. Still, what difference did it make if she broke her cardinal rule of no drinks before five o'clock? It had to be five somewhere on the planet.

She pulled into a small strip mall and parked her car in one of the spaces while thoughts of what might be in store for her bounced around in her head. *I'll probably have to give up driving one of these days. Hope it's not too soon. But, why not? The sooner it comes, the sooner I'll be reunited with Marty.*

But, what about Alex? At twenty-nine, her only child was still floundering. He had no clear direction and no real commitments.

Emotion welled up so Estelle pushed it down. She had cried enough, and she certainly wasn't going to break down in public. Leukemia. It wasn't really an ugly name, not for such an ugly disease. It sounded more like a houseplant. *Oh, look how beautiful my leukemias are! Have you ever seen such blooms?*

She was dying though. From a disease that didn't bloom, but instead drained the body of all strength and vigor.

She pulled the car key out of the ignition and then sat for a few minutes. She'd have her drink before phoning the doctor to explain her odd behavior. He'd said he was going to start some meds. They'd probably have instructions stating, "Do not drink alcohol or operate machinery." She'd always been a stickler for rules, but since she hadn't taken the medicine yet, this could be her last drink—or two.

Estelle got out of the car, set the alarm, and walked to the entrance of Gaetano's Ristorante. She'd been by the small Italian restaurant a million times. She and Marty had intended to go there for dinner but never had; it had been the wrong time or he was held up at the office or it had been one of a thousand other excuses for not doing all the things they'd said they would do one day and never did. Typical.

The minute the door closed behind her, scents of basil and garlic bread mixed with the heavy aroma of pasta sauces and cheese, tantalizing her taste buds. Skipping lunch hadn't been a good idea, and now her mouth watered while involuntary growls escaped her stomach. How could she eat after learning that she had so little time left on earth? But if she didn't eat, the glass of wine—or two—would go straight to her head.

She chose a small booth barely large enough for two, but she wasn't a part of a couple anymore so she had plenty of space. Scooting into the seat, she smoothed her skirt over her legs. She'd worked hard at keeping her figure. She'd kept it all right, but for what? For whom? Well, there had been plenty of interest from men, but many of them were her friends' husbands. She'd never felt comfortable around those particular couples afterward. Did the wives know?

Think of this in a positive way, she commanded herself. At least I've been put on notice and can get things in order. How many people get that chance?

She didn't know exactly what the treatment would be, but she'd already decided that she would save Alex the agony of watching the day-by-day dying again. They'd both watched Marty struggle for life. The procedures had been painful, but he'd fought like a tiger. The end had come well over a year ago though…and yet, when she let herself go there, it still hurt.

It bothered her that Dr. Bob couldn't tell her the truth about her condition. Did he think she wasn't woman enough to take it? True, she'd been to hell and back during Marty's illness, so it was logical that their old friend would want to protect her. Marty's death had been hard for him too. They'd been golfing buddies for years. Maybe this was his way of dealing with it.

When Alex finds out, he'll want to hover over me, she realized. I wonder if Dr. Bob will tell him before he tells me. Could he do that? There had to be some ethical rule stating that the patient is always told first. Wasn't there?

She tried to remember if she'd been the first to know about Marty or if the news was given to them both at the same time. Marty's illness had been such a shock. She'd been in a fog for weeks before she came to grips with it, and there were still time segments that remained blocked from her memory.

That made up her mind: She was going to keep her condition a secret for as long as she could. When the effects of the illness became obvious, then she would tell Alex. There was no point in burdening him with this so soon after his father's death.

Of course, she wouldn't wait *too* long, but she needed to get a few specific things in order. Would he want to move into her place? His townhouse was nice but not as large as her house. On the other hand, he'd been away from home a lot and the upkeep of a home the size of hers took considerable attention.

In spite of herself, she felt a lump settle in her throat. The inside of her nose began to burn just like it always did when tears couldn't be held back, so she reached for the bright red napkin on the table in front of her. It had been folded in an intricate manner so that it stood at attention.

A white apron with tomato splotches appeared at her side, and Estelle flinched.

"I'm sorry," a rich, deep voice said. "I didn't mean to startle you. May I get you something? Iced tea, coffee?"

Estelle dabbed at her eyes, then turned to the man wearing the apron. He was fairly tall, and he had beautiful dark hair accented with silver. His deep brown gaze met hers, and she couldn't remember when she'd ever seen such soulful eyes. His face held concern.

"I could also offer you a glass of wine, if you'd prefer. A nice Chianti? Or something white?"

"Yes, that would be wonderful."

"Which?"

"Oh, I'm sorry. I've had quite a day and my head isn't screwed on right I'm afraid. A Chianti will be fine." She needed something heartier than a white to bolster her courage.

The man didn't move. When she looked up he averted his gaze then peered at her with worry in his eyes. When he spoke Estelle detected a slight accent.

"Excuse me, I don't mean to intrude, but…" He flushed. "Never mind. I'll be right back with your wine."

***

Gaetano Lorenzo hurried to the bar and filled one clear glass with his very best Chianti instead of the house brand. This was what his daughter always complained about, really. She said he let his heart rule his head and thus gave away the profits. But, what was wrong with being concerned? That poor lady back there was obviously in some kind of distress. He couldn't help it if he was just naturally curious about people. His restaurant had been the meeting place for many lost souls, and he liked to think he'd helped many of them find each other. He'd made them all a little happier. Too bad he couldn't work the same magic on his daughter. At the rate she was going, he'd be an old man before he got to bounce a grandbaby on his knee.

Young women today. They wanted the big career and waited for marriage until they were almost too old to have babies. Even if Gina fell in love, it could take years before she settled down to matrimony and motherhood. Gaetano wanted that to happen sooner than later. *Mama mia*, it was so much easier in the old country. The parents arranged everything, and everyone was happy. Here in America, his daughter Gina couldn't even cook! Rosie was surely rolling in her grave.

He took the wine back to the table and set it down in front of the woman. She wasn't wearing a wedding band. Not that it was any of his concern, of course, because he certainly never intended to remarry; this was just more of his curiosity. And there was nothing wrong with playing cupid or being interested in people, no matter what Gina said. Rosie had always been a people person too. They'd made quite a team.

Gaetano was so wrapped up in his thoughts he barely heard what the woman said.

"Sir? A menu, please."

"Oh, forgive me. Yes, of course." He fought back embarrassment. *She must think I'm crazy—or worse yet, incompetent.*

He sprinted to the back of the room, took a menu from the stack on the counter, and returned with a smile as he handed it over. At the same moment, his first dinner waitress came through the door.

Good, he thought. Debbie could take over. For some reason this sad lady was making him uneasy. He excused himself and retreated to the kitchen.

***

Estelle pondered the menu. It had been a while since she'd had any real appetite, but just reading about these entrées stirred her taste buds. She took a sip of wine then upended the glass and swallowed the contents in one gulp.

"Did you decide what you'd like?"

The little blonde waitress who'd come to take her order was so perky and cheerful that it was all Estelle could do not to strangle her. Instead, she smiled. "I haven't quite made up my mind. How about bringing me another Chianti?"

"Sure." The young woman took her empty glass.

Estelle looked around at the interior of the restaurant and admired the fact that real plants and not plastic ones adorned the window boxes. The tables were covered with red checkered cloths, and each featured a live centerpiece: a bright red carnation in a bud vase. Before she'd finished her assessment of the room, a full glass of wine appeared. Well, she grudgingly admitted, the service was good. That was important. When you didn't have a lot of time, you needed things done in a hurry. Or, should a person take more time to savor each moment?

From speakers she hadn't quite located, Placido Domingo's beautiful tenor voice filled the room. Estelle listened in silence. Ah, yes, it was his solo from…what? Suddenly she couldn't remember. That must be part of the illness. Loss of memory…and then how much time to the end?

Damn it! It wasn't fair. She didn't deserve this. All her life she'd followed the rules, and in the end none of that mattered. Because the end came, like it or not.

She turned in her seat to get the waitress's attention; she had to go home and get started on her plans. Forget dinner.

"Where *is* that girl?" she muttered.

"Your waitress is seating some customers, but I took it upon myself to make some selections for you."

The voice surprised her, but not as much as the fact that the man who'd seated her was now standing at her table with a fully loaded tray over his head. He lowered the tray and began placing dishes on the table.

"First, a little appetizer. Then salad. Then the entrée, it is one of my masterpieces. Chicken Marsala. And a fresh bottle of wine."

Estelle was speechless and then shocked as the gentleman sat down opposite her. He'd lost the apron, but his eyes were still soulful and staring straight into her.

"Aren't you the chef?" she asked. "When I saw you earlier you were wearing an apron. I just assumed…"

"You were correct. I am one of the chefs."

"Can you leave the kitchen like this?"

"Ah, but I am also the owner. Gaetano Lorenzo." He leaned forward and pressed his lips to her fingertips, his eyes twinkling with mischief. She offered her hand in return to his greeting.

"I called in another chef," he admitted, "so now I can have dinner with you."

Once more Estelle was at a loss for words. She looked around to see who'd witnessed this act of…whatever it was, and she saw that the restaurant had begun to fill up. There was no longer just the one waitress but several, and all of them looked busy. The shades at the windows were lowered, and candles were lighted at each table. She must have zoned out listening to the opera.

"I l-like your music," she stammered, hoping she didn't sound as dumb as she felt.

"I'm glad. This selection is Placido Domingo's aria from La Traviata. Not everyone cares for classical. I think opera is something you must develop a love for."

"Oh, yes, I believe that too. My late husband never took the time. After going alone so often when he couldn't get away I finally let my season tickets lapse."

"What a shame. The opera was my wife's passion, but we also got too busy. We spent so many years getting the restaurant going… Ah, you know how it is."

"Does your wife help out now?"

The minute the words were out of her mouth Estelle instinctively knew she'd put her foot in it. Gaetano's face fell.

"Oh, no. Like you, I am alone. I keep busy—" The man stopped abruptly. He waved his arms in the air and unfurled his napkin. "What are we doing? Our food is getting cold. Eat. Eat!" he scolded.

Estelle smiled and picked up her fork. She couldn't recall when she had such a handsome dinner partner. She squeezed her eyes and blinked, keeping tears at bay while she tried to eat. She didn't have much time left to enjoy meals with anyone, especially someone as nice as this.

A short time later she was saying, "That was absolutely delicious, Gaetano, I can't believe I ate so much!" She really couldn't.

"What are you saying? You eat like a bird."

"Yeah, a *big* bird. I haven't had much of an appetite for a while. It's no fun cooking for one."

"I suppose not. But don't you have any family who visit you?" He seemed genuinely curious.

"I have a son, but I don't want him to feel he has to look after me. Although, he does enjoy a good meal. Here, let me show you his picture."

The restaurateur pulled his wallet out of his hip pocket. "I also have just one child. Let me show you my Gina."

Estelle continued to flip through her bag, finally coming up with a small leather photo case. "This is Alex. He's twenty-nine and still running around the world taking pictures."

"Your son is a photographer?"

"Yes, I guess he makes a fair living with the magazine he works for, but it's time he settled down and got a real job. Stayed in one place. Got married and had a family."

"Ah, I know exactly what you mean," Gaetano said. "My Gina is big-shot attorney, but she's never home either. I spend all my time talking to her answering machine."

They exchanged snapshots.

"Oh, my. Your daughter is very pretty," Estelle realized. It made her think of something else. "Can she cook as well as you?"

The restaurant owner stared intently at the photo of Alex, perhaps seeing a perfect candidate for the beautiful Gina as Estelle had done with Gaetano's daughter for her son. He must have realized that her question was still hanging in mid-air, however, as he spoke in a rush.

"Cook? Gina?" He laughed. Looking once more at the glossy print, he seemed wistful. Maybe he was imagining a little boy or girl with Gina's dark hair and Alex's green eyes and dimpled chin. That's what Estelle was doing. But handing back the photo Gaetano shook his head. "Oh, sure, she can cook up a storm, but she has so little time."

"I think that's the way it is with young people—always rushing," Estelle agreed. A big sigh escaped her lips. "I worry that he doesn't eat properly. He, unlike your daughter, can't even boil water."

Gaetano made a strange face. As if eager to change the subject, he nodded toward Estelle's photo and said, "I think he has your eyes, and maybe your smile?" He handed it back to her.

"Perhaps. I just wish I could be around when he finally settles down. That's not going to happen."

Gaetano seemed amused. "What are you talking about? He's not that old. He will find some lovely lady and pop the question, and you'll be a grand-mama before you know it."

Estelle could no longer hold it in; the tears she'd swallowed came rushing back in a deluge.

Chapter 2

Estelle rolled over in her king-sized bed and checked the clock on the nightstand.

"Nine o'clock!" She bolted upright and immediately felt a stab in her left temple. "Oh, maybe I had a tad too much wine." She sank slowly back onto her pillow and waited for the dagger effect to subside.

Was she hung over? Two drinks was usually her limit. A vague memory of more than one empty bottle being replaced during the dinner she'd shared with Gaetano flitted through her thoughts. But she'd shared a wonderful meal, excellent wine, and beautiful music with a very attractive man. She couldn't remember when she'd had such a pleasant evening. What had started out as the worst day of her life had ended quite the opposite. She'd been the first dinner guest to come into the restaurant and the last one to leave. She'd have to pick her car up later today, of course.

Gaetano had wanted to drive her home, but she'd convinced him that calling a cab made more sense. Last night she'd been concerned how *he* would get home. He'd had more to drink than herself, though he was a fairly tall man. And he'd probably been drinking wine since he was a small child. At least, that's what she'd heard about Italian families. They watered the wine and gave it to their children.

She closed her eyes and tried to remember all that had happened. All that came to mind were flashes of Gaetano's kind eyes, his laughter, his sympathy, and his total understanding of her situation.

Then… *Oh, good Lord.*

He'd scrambled out of his side of the booth and joined her when she began to cry, slipping his arms around her as her head found his shoulder. Between sobs and hiccups—courtesy of the wine—Estelle had somehow gotten out the whole story of her forthcoming demise. His manner had become so comforting and understanding, it was as if he was an old friend instead of a man she'd just met. Had she really spilled her guts to him? She'd never shared private thoughts with anyone, let alone fears and dreams. Not even Marty, really. What was it about this handsome stranger that had made her so comfortable? Or had it been the wine?

It was interesting, though. He had a daughter a year younger than Alex. Pretty, too. They'd whipped out snapshots of their respective offspring as if they were showing off toddlers.

What on earth had she been thinking? Nothing could come of this. She didn't have time for socializing; she had to get her life in order so that she could die. It was just so unfair and cruel. It had taken a long time, but recently she'd decided to accept life as it was, even if that meant a solitary existence. Now—*boom*, just like that— it was going to end. She'd never been particularly religious, but could God be so mean?

Remaining in a horizontal position, she squared her shoulders and lifted her chin. She would be strong and die with dignity. Surely God would understand if she was also a little bit angry.

Still, a thought nagged at her. It would be more comforting if Alex were happily married. It'd be even better if he found a girl like Gina who could cook like her father. In some ways, a good relationship was like a good meal; satisfying, healthy, and comforting. Setting a beautiful table and supplying delicious food was something she'd prided herself on; it was a way she'd supported and cared for her husband. Marty had said many times that it wasn't his business acuity that made his company a success, but rather Estelle's special recipe for pot roast and unusual desserts when they entertained clients. She just knew that being there for him was important.

If I could be sure that Alex wouldn't grieve too much. If he had someone to stand by him, care for him and love him—to *cook* for him—then I could go peacefully, Estelle thought.

She rolled up on one elbow. The throbbing in her head was now just an occasional dull thud, and she sat up and dangled her feet off her bed, not all that tired. Well, that would probably come later: fatigue, weight loss, and the general look of death. Which reminded her, she needed to phone up Dr. Bob to confess to her eavesdropping and let him off the hook. She would do that today…if she had the strength. She collapsed back into bed.

After several minutes she pulled herself to a sitting position and slid her feet into slippers. Commanding herself to stand and walk, she shuffled out to the kitchen to make a pot of much needed coffee. The light on the answering machine was blinking. She pushed the button and listened.

"Estelle, this is Dr. Taylor. We were worried when you ran out of the office this afternoon. I hope it was nothing serious."

Nothing serious? You bet your stethoscope it's serious. But, then, you know that, Dr. Bob! Estelle couldn't believe he was acting so normal.

The doctor's message continued in a very pleasant tone: "There's nothing to worry about right now. You're a little run down, so I've called in a prescription for you at your pharmacy. I'll want to see you in one month. Call the office, and Betty will make you an appointment."

Well, I have at least a month. She couldn't believe he would wait that long to give her the truth, though.

"I'll be on vacation for a couple of weeks. If you have any questions, please feel free to call when I get back. Take good care of yourself, and give my best to Alex when you see him. Bye now."

She fought back surprise at his feigned nonchalance. It was obvious that Dr. Bob needed time to get the courage up to level with her. Mentioning Alex must have been his way of telling her to spend time with him.

The coffeemaker beeped, signaling that the coffee was ready. Estelle poured herself a cup, adding cream and a generous spoonful of sugar. What the hell, she decided, she had dieted for the last time. What did it matter now if she gained weight? With leukemia that probably wouldn't happen no matter how many calories she ingested. She supposed that was the up-side.

***

"Gina, this is your Papa. I need to talk to you as soon as possible. *Please* call me. Why is it I only talk to you through this infernal answering machine? Do you even live there anymore?"

Gaetano slammed the receiver back down into its cradle, frustration pulling the corners of his mouth down and creases lining his forehead. Three times he'd called; three times he'd gotten her machine. It was ridiculous.

Another thing that was ridiculous? How late he was. He was always the first one in the restaurant, every morning but not today. The coffee urns were going, the salads were crisping in the cooler, and Mario and Janet were already in the kitchen preparing several entrées. The news Estelle had shared with him had not made for a restful night—that, and the fact that the two of them had locked up the building hours after everyone else left. She'd looked so sad when he first saw her, and now he knew why. The woman was dying, and her dying wish was to see her son happily married.

By God, that wasn't much to ask, he decided, and he was just the man to help fulfill that dream. Sure, his plan was a little old-fashioned by today's standards, but Gina wasn't exactly a child, and it was time she put her talents to work at home instead of in a courtroom. His lip twitched a bit. He didn't know why he'd lied to the pretty lady about Gina's cooking ability, but he would teach her to cook and introduce her to Alex. Then Estelle would be able to meet her maker in peace.

At the thought of Estelle Bennett's imminent demise, Gaetano felt his heart sink. She was a beautiful lady, much too young to be facing death. She had a great figure, and her shapely legs had not gone unnoticed. He'd looked at few women since he'd lost Rosie, but Estelle had definitely been one. Somehow she'd managed to stir the embers of desire in his heart…and other parts of his body. The feelings were uncomfortable and yet exciting.

By all that was holy, Gaetano would make her last days her happiest. As a bonus, the plan could make him a grandfather.

The whole idea gave his spirits a lift, and whistling he set out to join Mario in the kitchen. Today he would make a special entrée for the lunch crowd, maybe even whip up some fancy desserts. Then he'd give Estelle a call.

The lunch hour was crazy, however, and Gaetano had little time to even think about Estelle let alone call her. If she'd come by, he hadn't noticed. He couldn't have, unless she'd come back to the kitchen. After eleven thirty he was at the range seeing to the pasta, helping Mario create several entrées for a party of twelve, and putting the finishing touches on orders. If business kept improving, he would have to hire another chef and maybe install an additional oven.

Gaetano took off his apron and hung it on the peg in the small hallway separating his office from the kitchen. "Whew, Mario, there is finally a lull. I, for one, am grateful."

His best friend smiled. "Do not complain, it may be slow tonight."

Gaetano shook his head. "No, no, I'm pleased about the business, but I want to see if I can catch Gina at her downtown office." It was his only chance. His daughter usually scheduled her court dates in the morning, so if he timed this right she would be able to see him. He wasn't quite sure what he was going to say, but Gina had to meet Estelle's son. That was as far as he had gotten. It was a beginning.

"You can handle it here, no?"

"You can depend on me, Gaetano. Take all the time you need."

Gaetano was almost to his car when he saw her coming out of the pharmacy next door. Such a petite beauty! Staring, he again noticed her creamy skin. Flawless, and soft as a small child's— peaches and cream his wife would have called it. Rosie's own complexion had been almond, with eyes as dark as midnight and hair to match.

"Estelle. What a wonderful surprise."

"Why, Gaetano, hello. I was just coming to see you. My conscience has been bothering me all night."

"What on earth for?" he asked. His mind searched for a reason. Had he made advances she now found unacceptable? The wine had mellowed him, but he wasn't an amateur; he'd been drinking wine since he was barely able to see over a tabletop.

She looked like a vision from heaven. Her hair danced in the sunlight as if lit by a hundred fires, and as if it were the most natural thing in the world Gaetano took both her hands in his and readied himself to apologize. When he stared into her eyes, they were as green as the moss gathering on sea rocks in tide pools and hypnotic.

"I am almost sure I forgot to pay the bill last night, and I... Gaetano, are you all right?"

"What? I'm sorry, I must have drifted." Embarrassed, he let her hands drop and shoved his own hands into his pants pockets. "You were saying?"

"I owe you for the dinner last night. I'm embarrassed, and I want to make it right." She reached into her purse for her wallet.

Gaetano's hands flew out of his pockets and grasped hers once more. "My dear Estelle. Do you want to insult me? It was my pleasure to serve such a beautiful lady who is now my new friend. Put your money away, I will not hear of it."

"Well, thank you," she began, "but I had no intention of... You don't have to do this, you know, just because you feel sorry for me. About dying, I mean. I'm getting used to the idea, and let's face it, no one lives forever."

Gaetano made a sudden decision, all previous plans flying out of his mind. "The day is too beautiful to think on such sad things. We are going to the beach." Taking her hand, he pulled her toward his car. "We will feed the seagulls and dig our toes into the sand. We'll forget all things unpleasant."

She shook her head. "Oh, that sounds so tempting, but I can't. I need to go see my son. He's leaving town soon for a trip halfway around the world."

Gaetano stopped and turned, not letting go of her hand. "Are you going to tell him?"

She blinked and twisted, and Gaetano knew she was chasing a tear away. He'd known her for such a short time, and yet he read her gestures without effort. He even guessed what she was thinking.

"You don't want to worry him," he said. "If he knew you were ill, he'd not leave town. Am I right?"

"Yes," she admitted. "Alex never left his father's bedside, and I just can't put him through that again. It's too painful."

Too painful for *her*, Gaetano realized.

"How much pain will your son feel when he discovers your deception?" he asked.

"I'm not deceiving him. I will tell him. Later. When the time is right. Not now. It's too much."

"Call him and have him meet us at the beach. I will go for a long walk, and you can have your time together. Then we will all come back here and I'll feed him a good meal. If he decides it is okay to leave town, at least he will have a full belly."

"Oh, I'm not sure that's a good idea…"

"Estelle," Gaetano said, "I should meet your son."

"Why? It's not like we can really expand our friendship to include our children."

"That's exactly what we need to do," Gaetano decided. "Look, what is most important to you? What do you want for him?"

"I want him to be happy. I want him to have someone so that when I'm gone he won't be lonely."

"Exactly," Gaetano said. "I need to meet your son, and so does my Gina. Estelle, this is perfect. We start off slow. We bring the kids together very innocently, we don't want to rush things."

"Gaetano, what are you talking about?"

He saw her confusion, which made sense since this all had popped into his head within the last five seconds. Well, the plan had. But it was a good plan. He felt almost smug about it.

"It is quite simple," he said. "We will arrange a marriage for our children. In my country, in the old days, it was done all the time…and in some cases, it still is. I will meet your son, get my daughter to come into the restaurant, and we'll have a nice meal. Gina is a good girl, and Alex is a smart boy, and before you know it, you'll have the peace you seek and I will be a *gran papá*."

Yes, if Alex was anything like his mother, Gina would fall for the young man just like Rosie had fallen for Gaetano so many years ago. Oh, it was a *wonderful* plan. He would have to remember not to mention cooking, though. Gina couldn't boil an egg without setting off smoke alarms. He would fix that, though. A few lessons and she'd be cooking meals that would make Alex give up his wanderlust.

Estelle still sounded nervous. "Gaetano, Alex is not from your country. He's very independent. If he even gets any hint of matchmaking, he'll run for his life. No, no, this isn't a good idea."

"You worry too much," Gaetano promised. "Now, come on. Where does this wonderful son live? I'll drive."

***

Estelle still couldn't believe that she was letting this crazy, impulsive man talk her into his plan. A short time later she'd called Alex, however, who'd promised to meet them at La Jolla Cove. That too surprised her, since he normally would be busy packing equipment, and it was totally out of character for her to disrupt his routine.

As she'd told Gaetano, she was proud of her son, although galloping all over the world seemed a terrible way to make a living. His apartment was filled with interesting items he'd collected from the far corners of the globe, none of it reflecting who he really was. She'd never presumed to intrude on her son's life since he'd become a man, though, no matter how tempting it was to step in and play a larger role. Estelle was just happy that Alex called her every week and had dinner with her whenever he was in town. She'd never nagged him about getting married, and never found fault with any of the girls he'd brought around, few though they were. No, she was not a controlling mother. So, why in the world was she letting herself be drawn into Gaetano's nutty scheme?

The sun danced along the shoreline, and noisy gulls argued and fussed over the breadcrumbs her companion threw at them. Estelle sat on the bench watching Gaetano tease the birds and waiting for Alex to show up. She'd miss the beach. When Alex was a little boy they spent many hours building sand castles, throwing a Frisbee into the surf, and watching sailboats bob up and down on the water.

"Hello, gorgeous." Alex kissed his mother's cheek and wrapped his arms around her from behind.

"Oh, Alex! You startled me. Come, sit down. How are you? What's new in your life? When do you have to leave?" she asked.

"Whoa, Mom. One question at a time. Sorry, though, I didn't mean to scare you." Alex came around the bench and sat down beside her. "I'm fine, and my trip's been delayed. Something to do with an uprising of some African tribes where I'm supposed to go. And I don't need to ask how *you're* doing. You are absolutely glowing. What did you do, get a lift?"

Estelle stared at her son. "A delay? Oh, Alex, I'm so glad." Perhaps he would be able to meet Gina after all. And his final question she answered in the pseudo-indignant tone she knew he expected. "A lift? How dare you. You know I'd never go under the knife for vanity."

"Just kidding, Mom. You know I like to tease." Alex's eyes twinkled mischievously, and he flashed that grin that melted her heart every time. Yes, he did have her eyes and her smile. But his hair and his face were his father's. Marty had sported a thick head of dark curls up until the chemo treatments.

Would this idea work? She didn't have time to ponder the question. Gaetano stepped up to the bench with his hand outstretched, and Estelle smiled to cover up any nervousness.

"You must be Alex. Your mother has done nothing but talk about you. I'm Gaetano Lorenzo."

Estelle saw the shock on her son's face. It was as if he'd been struck dumb, but after a few minutes he recovered enough to return the handshake and give her a quizzical look. "Well, she's told me nothing about you."

"Well, of course she wouldn't have mentioned me. We are brand-new friends, and when she said that you were leaving town, I told her I would give you a sendoff dinner." Gaetano plopped down on the bench and forced Alex to scoot closer to Estelle. "I own a wonderful restaurant, and we know you are very busy, but a man still has to eat. Is that not right?"

"Gaetano, Alex's trip has been postponed," Estelle reported.

"Well, that's even better. Now we don't have to rush so much. I am going to walk down the beach a bit, and when I come back, we'll all go to my restaurant. Nice to meet you, Alex." Then Gaetano jumped up off the bench. Swinging his plastic bag of bread crumbs, he strolled off in the opposite direction.

Alex gaped. "Mother, who *is* that?"

Her words came out in a rush: "I can see why you'd be confused. Gaetano was right about being my new friend. I just met him. I know he's a bit pushy and very impulsive, but he's a nice man. And I promise you that when you taste his food you will truly think you've died and gone to heaven."

Looking up, she saw Alex was pale. *Died and gone to heaven.* Those words had stung her, too, right after she said them. He was still raw from his father's death. If only he knew what was around the corner, he'd be devastated.

"Oh, honey, I'm sorry. I didn't mean that like it sounded. Heaven in a—"

"Mom, it's okay," Alex interrupted. "I'm glad you're getting back to normal. It's been time enough, and we both need to move on. Please, don't measure your words."

"Please say you'll come to the restaurant," she countered. "It really is fun."

"Of course I will. I'll need to run by my place and change clothes first, but I'd intended to take you to dinner anyway. Now, until your friend comes back, tell me what's been going on with you."

Estelle looked into those eyes that mirrored her own, and she tried to think if this was the right time to level with her child. His grin was captivating, and she couldn't bear to see it fade. So, no, the time wasn't right. Not now. This was to be a night of fun, not sadness. She beamed and pushed all the nagging thoughts from her mind.

"Well, my roses are doing well because I've found a new gardener who's a genius. My cousin Pearl is planning to come out in a month or two, and I just read a wonderful new book. It's a mystery, but the main character is a caterer—and the author included recipes! It's called *Too Many Cooks,* because one of them is the murderer. I thought that quite clever. And you? Are you seeing anyone? Do you still hear from…what was her name? Becky?"

It was the best conversation they'd had in a long time.

Chapter 3

Gina Lorenzo tried to keep her hands steady as she punched in the number on her cell phone. She'd retrieved her messages from her condo, and the three from her father had left her more than a little disturbed. Each was more frantic than the last.

"Hello?"

"Mario, this is Gina. Is Papá there?"

"Hi, Gina, how are you? When are you coming in to see us here at the restaurant? Your father always talks about how long it has been since he's seen you."

"I know, I know," she replied, impatient. Mario had been like an uncle to her, and she loved him as if he were blood kin, but the man could talk. "Mario, just put Papá on."

"Oh, he's not here. He left two, maybe two and a half hours ago. Rushed out like the devil was after him and said he was going to your office."

"He's not there? He never came to my office," Gina promised.

She double-checked the time on her brand-new Rolex. The watch had been an impulse gift for herself when she'd settled the Chambers versus Sullivan case. Her commission on the settlement had been her biggest yet, and Mr. Baxter, the senior partner of Baxter, Baker and Ellis, had even made strong hints that a junior partnership might be in her future. If she'd been a man, she'd already have been promoted, of course, but because Mr. Baxter was afraid she'd get married and start popping out babies, what she deserved had been denied for far too long.

Now Gina was really worried. Her father was a creature of habit. In the twenty-eight years she'd known him, he'd never once been away from his restaurant during the dinner hour. In that way, she was very much like him. She gave all she had to her career. In fact, she had an appointment in ten minutes. It was just a small detail that she needed to present to the judge who would be hearing one of her cases next week, but to her, all details were important.

"It's past four, and he's never late for the beginning of the dinner hour. Where is he?"

Mario seemed at ease. "Don't worry. He'll be in pretty quick, I think."

She'd planned to work on some depositions tonight and map out her strategy for yet another case, but something about her father's voice had made her uneasy. Could he be ill? "Mario, when you see my dad, tell him I'll drop by around six o'clock tonight. I gotta go, though. Just for now."

"Sure, I'll tell him. See you, Gina."

Her dad had been her rock for as long as she could remember. She'd been seven when she'd lost her mother, and her father had stepped right up to the plate and given her a Disneyland existence. When other classes had cupcakes and Kool-Aid for their end-of-the-year parties, hers always feasted on three varieties of pizza, fresh fruit, warm Italian cheese sticks, and Spumoni ice cream. She'd always been the most popular kid in her class.

Guilt flashed through Gina as she remembered all the sacrifices her father had made for her. Now she couldn't remember when she'd last visited him in person. They talked weekly, but mostly he ranted about the fact that she was too skinny and her stupid answering machine that didn't answer any of his questions. "*Mangia, mangia,*" he was always nagging. *Eat, eat.* And what he wanted for her was exactly what Mr. Baxter dreaded.

She couldn't respect her father more, either as a successful businessman or a single father. She'd heard all his stories about his journey to America from his small village near Rome, how he'd been just a small boy of five or six when his family emigrated, and how he'd worked in the restaurant that had been his mama and papa's and that was now his. Gaetano's parents and younger brother were all killed in an auto accident when he was barely out of his teens. He'd had to grow up fast, and he had made that restaurant into one of the most popular Italian joints in the San Diego area. Gina smiled as she remembered her father's stories of meeting her mother and what a help she'd been to him in those early years.

On the other hand, she hadn't been able to make Gaetano understand she appreciated everything he'd done for her. Her successful career was meant as a tribute to him, not a rebellion against his traditions. In spite of the many advantages he'd given her, she'd still had to fight to earn her place. Her job with the law firm was hard and she'd accomplished a great deal. Why couldn't he be proud of her as she was of him?

***

Before meeting his mother and Mr. Pushy Pepperoni for dinner, Alex pushed his duffle bag out of the way and went into the bathroom to take a quick shower. He'd never seen his mother looking so good. Could her new friend be the reason? It was probably a good thing for her to start meeting new people, but this guy? He just wasn't sure he was her type.

He lathered himself with the bar of herbal soap he'd picked up in a small shop in Singapore several months ago. It smelled good, not like the perfumed things he'd sometimes been forced to use when he stayed over at some girl's place. Not that he made a habit of that. He was unattached at the moment, which was totally fine. The life he'd chosen for himself was one of adventure, freedom and independence. He'd watched his dad slave away at a desk all his life and then *poof*, dead at fifty-nine. Well, that wasn't going to happen to him. He kept himself in shape, watched the carbs, took vitamins, and went easy on the booze. If he wasn't in such good condition, he couldn't do what he did for a living. He was one of the several photojournalists and scientists who made up the expedition team for *World Wide Weekly*. One month he could be hiking the Andes to capture evidence of a lost society, a few months later he was tramping across the Gobi to document some rare vegetation being studied as a possible new medicine. It was an exciting life, and he was paid well. But there were drawbacks. He couldn't have any pets, plants, or permanent females. No woman could, or would, put up with his lifestyle—at least, no woman he'd ever met. At least, not one that he found attractive. The world just didn't seem to make them feisty enough. Or tolerant enough. Or at least he didn't meet that type of woman.

Speaking of not-feisty, he worried about his mother quite a bit. Since his father passed, she hadn't seemed to connect to anything. Her husband had been her entire world, even if he'd never made much room in his own world for her. Estelle was pretty remarkable, though. Alex appreciated that she'd allowed him to explore and lead his life exactly as he wanted to lead it. And she'd certainly been a wonderful mother while he was growing up.

He changed into a pair of white twill shorts, slid a braided belt into the loops, and pulled a knitted collared shirt over his head. Grabbing up his wallet, he checked the slip of paper on which his mother had written their destination. Gaetano's Ristorante. Then he slid his bare feet into a pair of sandals he'd picked up on one of his journeys and headed out.

Locking the door to his townhouse, he took the stairs to the underground parking lot where his latest purchase awaited: an only slightly used bright red Ferrari 612 Scaglietti. It was an extravagance he couldn't really justify, but the fact that the insurance cost more than a king's ransom failed to dampen his joy whenever he slid behind the wheel onto the soft, buttery leather seats. The car was everything to him. It was the coolest thing he'd ever owned.

He inserted the key, and like always, the engine responded with a roar of power that simultaneously thrilled and terrified him. The fact that this machine obeyed his commands was a bit intoxicating. He'd been known to take risks when he felt like this and never knew when he'd push it too far. But as long as he kept the thrills in check, there was nothing to fear.

Ah, freedom. There was plenty of time for him to settle down like his mother wanted. Not now, though. Right now it was time to fly.

***

Gina sped up and squeaked through the yellow light just as it turned red. Cameras had been installed at many of the busiest intersections in the area, so she knew she'd been tempting fate lately. Her name was becoming well known in local legal arenas, but traffic court was one place she wanted to avoid. She hoped no one would notice that a certain bright, up-and-coming female attorney had a penchant for speeding.

She pulled her Toyota Camry into the parking lot of her father's restaurant in a slot next to a bright red Italian sports car. As she did, she realized what had happened. "Oh my God. Papá is going through his mid-life crisis. He's bought himself his dream car. Way to go, Pop." It was time the man did something nice for himself.

Smoothing down her skirt, she suddenly wished she'd gone home and changed into something more comfortable. The Michael Kors cotton weave she wore had been a bargain on E-bay at forty percent off the retail price, but white was not a real smart choice, especially when she'd most likely be eating pasta. She tugged it into place and shed her black linen blazer, tossing the latter across the passenger seat. Getting out of the car, she clicked her alarm remote, tucked her black and white striped blouse into her waistband, and made her way to the entrance of her father's restaurant.

Inside, Gina scanned the dining room and nodded at a couple of the waitresses before spotting her father at the large half-circular booth across the room. He was standing but leaning over a woman seated next to a young, good-looking guy.

This was why her father's restaurant was successful. The food made loyal patrons, but Gaetano was the heart of the business. Her dad tried to make everyone feel special. He would go out of his way to make sure everyone had a good time—and he seemed to be succeeding now, too. The woman was laughing and the young man was smiling.

Good grief, the woman couldn't be with that gorgeous hunk, could she? They weren't a couple, were they? If so, the woman was in for a shock, because the notably younger man was definitely looking in Gina's direction. Gina enjoyed the toe to head gaze he gave her, and then she directed her attention back to her father...only to see that he wasn't even aware she'd arrived.

Gina's jaw dropped. Her father had just traced the older woman's cheek and jaw with his knuckles then let his hand rest on her shoulder. And even from this distance, Gina caught his expression. Oh, it was subtle, but she'd seen the tenderness.

So had the hunk. A shadow of annoyance crossed his face, and Gina processed that. The woman was obviously the object of her father's affection, and the young man was not pleased.

Gina was surprised by conflicting emotions, both disappointment and relief. While she wanted her father to be happy, she couldn't understand why she'd never gotten a hint of someone entering his life. She'd always shared with him who she was seeing. Not that she'd had a lot to share lately. While she'd achieved success in her career, her luck with men left much to be desired. She'd always managed to say the wrong thing, and so relationships ended early. Since an early few debacles she'd buried herself in work rather than admit that she was inept at the art of romance. What did she need a relationship for, though, anyway? It wasn't like she needed a man to make her life complete, some Prince Charming without whom she couldn't exist. Life was already pretty good. Wasn't it?

She continued to observe her father and the redhead and saw the two were clearly close, so they must have known each other for some time. Oh, she realized. This was the reason for the phone calls. Her father had a girlfriend. Oh, God, she wasn't ready for this, she admitted to herself. It wasn't that she'd never imagined such a scenario; lots of women had made plays for her dad. But though he dated from time to time, nothing had ever seemed to click. This time appeared different.

Her impulse was to run, but several waitresses had already seen her. For that reason, the best option was to join the group, be pleasant, and then get the hell out of there as soon as possible. Also, if the two were involved, Gina needed to find out about the woman's character.

She squared her shoulders, tilted her chin, and walked over to the booth. "Hello, Papá."

Her father turned. "Gina, you did come!" He beamed and gave her a big hug then kissed her on each cheek. "Mario told me you would be here, but I didn't hold my breath."

"Papá, I come as often as I can." It irritated Gina whenever her father implied she neglected him. However, maybe he wouldn't be turning his attention to this attractive middle-aged woman if she'd spent more time with him.

"Estelle, Alex, I'd like you to meet my beautiful and brilliant daughter. Gina, my friend Estelle Bennett and her son Alex."

Her *son*. That made more sense.

The young man rose from his seat and reached across the table to grasp Gina's hand in a firm shake. He was taller than her father. Once more he gave her a thorough appraisal, and he seemed to approve of what he saw. Up close she saw a family resemblance in the eyes, though his dark hair sharply contrasted with Estelle's auburn locks.

He was still drop-dead gorgeous. He was also *built*. His gaze held hers as his lips moved, but Gina couldn't decipher his words. She had to assume he was saying the normal words of greeting, so she nodded and mumbled an appropriate response, all the while smiling like an idiot and extending the handshake longer than necessary. It was ridiculous, but the touch of those long fingers sent a wave of pleasure up her arm, around the nape of her neck, and into her scalp. She stood motionless and only returned to reality at the sound of her father's irritation.

"Gina, say hello to Alex's mother."

Embarrassed that her father was treating her like a child, Gina immediately made it worse by acting like one. She dropped Alex's hand and hastily greeted the woman. "Of c-course," she stammered. "It's nice to meet you, Mrs....er, uh, Ms. Bennett." Turning back to the son she said, "And you too, Alex."

"The pleasure is ours, dear," Estelle said, but Gina caught the frown she directed at her son. Evidently Gina wasn't the only one with a parent who still hadn't realized their offspring had made the transition from child to adult.

The woman sighed audibly. "Alex, you're acting like an eighth-grader. My goodness, you should be used to meeting people with all your world travels. Scoot back and let Gina into the booth. Gaetano, would you like to sit by your daughter?"

Alex was still standing and looked totally uncomfortable.

Gaetano beamed at Estelle. "No, no. I'll be fine here at the end."

Gina marveled at how easily Estelle maneuvered everyone into their seats. The men were soon on the outside, like bookends, and the women were in the middle. The booth was large and circular, yet it seemed much too small at the moment. The scent of whatever aftershave Alex wore drifted in Gina's direction. Shivers ran up and down her spine like fingers on piano keys, but she tried her best to ignore them.

"So, this is nice, isn't it? Two sets of new friends." Gaetano smiled like he'd won the lottery, reaching past Estelle to fill Gina's wine glass. Estelle took a sip herself, but her quick look at the younger pair did not go unnoticed.

The parents started off conversation with an update on how they met. Then there were the usual questions about the children's jobs and the places they had been. Alex's job was by far the most fascinating. Gina loved her work, but trying a case and the accompanying hours and hours of preparation in an office paled in comparison with traveling to exotic places, meeting people from other countries, and seeing wild creatures in their natural habitat. Part of her wished she'd taken a job like that. But only part of her.

Food soon arrived. Two of the waitresses brought two large trays, one filled with entrées, and another with salads and side dishes. A busboy carried folding racks and helped the girls place the trays on them.

As the entrées were settled and the salads distributed, Gaetano stood up. "I hope you all will forgive me, but I ordered for everyone. After all, it is my restaurant and I know what is best." He winked at Estelle and added, "Which is everything. There is calamari, chicken Marsala and of course pasta, pasta, and more pasta." He and Estelle began to laugh.

Gina glanced at Alex. He looked as dumbfounded as she felt. She searched her mind to come up with an explanation that would excuse her father's outlandish behavior, but she had nothing. She wanted to say something to Alex. Anything. But words failed to materialize as her focus zeroed in on Alex's incredible green eyes and those dark, wispy curls gathered at his temples and sideburns.

Gosh, he was handsome. She supposed she was lucky to be sitting next to a handsome guy. As desperate as her father was to marry her off, he might have paired her up with anyone.

Is it really so important for me to get married? she asked herself. *I do want to get married and have a family someday, no matter how silly it is to believe in Prince Charming or white knights or anything.* She did want that. Just not right now.

She stole another glance at Alex and was surprised and pleased that she caught him eyeing her at the same time. Well, she supposed having a good relationship with someone smart, handsome, and interesting wouldn't be the worst thing. Maybe it would calm her papa down.

Wait a minute. Had Alex been eyeing her earrings?

Chapter 4

Somehow she got through the meal. Gina felt she indulged way too much, but eating kept her from having to talk. Mostly she watched her father and Estelle, as they seemed to be thoroughly enjoying the meal and each other's company. Alex seemed to be eating and watching as well. He didn't seem to be watching her. She'd been mistaken earlier.

At one point, Gaetano whispered something into Estelle's ear. Immediately afterward, Estelle made an attempt to draw both Alex and Gina into a conversation. The exchange became four-way and lively for a brief period but eventually lapsed back into a dialogue between the older couple.

Gina certainly appreciated being close to such an attractive man during dinner, but it was a limited pleasure. Alex Bennett was obviously spoken for. Or, maybe he was gay. He hadn't sent any vibes in her direction after their initial meeting. He just really likes my earrings, she consoled herself; she'd caught him eyeing them multiple times now. She should have stayed home and worked on those depositions after all. Her worries for her father looked unfounded, unless this lady was some kind of gold-digger or wound up breaking his heart. But if the size of the rock in her dinner ring was any indication, Estelle Bennett was not hurting for bucks.

She made a decision. "Papá, thanks so much for dinner, and it was nice meeting you, Estelle, and you too, Alex, but I really have to leave."

"What?" Gaetano's eyes were wide and he began to protest. "You can't leave yet. We haven't had dessert, and I'll personally prepare your favorite latte."

Help came from another quarter. Alex stood and pulled on his belt as if he'd like to loosen it. "I really should be going too."

"Oh, honey, don't go. We've not had a chance to talk," his mother pleaded.

But nothing the two parents said made a difference. Gina and Alex were able to escape together, leaving their parents alone at the table, though they each carried a bag of Styrofoam boxes of food Gaetano had insisted they take.

The two exited the restaurant and walked toward their cars. For several minutes they were both quiet, until Alex finally broke the silence.

"The food was wonderful."

"It always is," Gina agreed. She stole a sideways glance at the man, feeling a moment of regret that she'd failed to pique his interest. "I don't dare come too often or I'd end up buying my clothes from Omar the Tentmaker and driving a wide-body Hummer." Not that she was really worried. While her appearance fell short of exotic, she was confident that she looked good in a bikini. Maybe he just didn't like brunettes?

"Your father and my mother seemed to have a lot to talk about. They certainly looked comfortable with each other."

Ah. He really wasn't interested. He hadn't picked up on her reference to her body at all. Gina refrained from releasing the sigh she felt sitting on her chest and said, "Yes. Yes, they did."

She paused and turned, deciding to address the parental issue up front. "Look, this must have been as awkward for you as it was for me. Gaetano…well, it isn't like him not to tell me if he's seeing someone. He must be going through the mid-life crazies, because I think he just bought that bright red sports car."

When she pointed to the car parked under the overhead light post, Alex shook his head. "No, he didn't. That's my Ferrari."

"Oh," she said, taken aback. "It's beautiful."

It was the best reaction she'd got from him all night, apart from the first. Alex Bennett smiled with pride and launched into a detailed description of the car's performance capabilities. Gina hadn't the faintest idea what any of it meant.

"It's just that my father is acting so weird," she explained. "When I saw the car, I assumed…"

She didn't try to complete the sentence. What she really wanted to know was how long her dad had been seeing Alex's mother. Why had he kept something so important from her, and how much did Alex know? After a moment's consideration, it seemed best just to jump in and ask.

"I had no idea my dad was dating. How long have he and your mom been seeing each other?"

Alex shrugged. "I don't know. I just met your father today. But I do know my mother hasn't looked this happy in a long time."

Gina laughed, pleased. "Well, it's hard to be sad around my dad. He has this incurable happy gene that keeps everything sunny side up." She fished in her purse for her keys. "Looks like I parked right next to you. Don't worry, though, I didn't ding your door." Then she punched in her alarm code. Juggling her purse and the bag of food, she pulled her car door open—to crash it into the Ferrari with a solid bang.

She'd misjudged her strength. Gina felt her stomach sink.

"Oh, my God. I can't believe I just did that! I mean, I just said I'd been so careful, and it's like…you know, when you say something and then it happens. Like déjà vu backwards, it isn't imagined but really is real?"

The more Gina babbled and tried to make sense, the worse it got. Not that Alex was listening. He'd dropped his doggie bag and rushed around the car, pushing her door away from his Ferrari and scrunching Gina in the process.

"For crying out loud," Gina scolded, "let me put my stuff down and I'll shut it."

"Sorry, but you don't understand. This paint can't be matched. I had it specially blended to get this exact shade." He was crouching down, running his fingers along the side of his vehicle. Gina heard him groan.

"I'm sure we can find something close, though. Is it really bad?" Gina asked. She tossed her paper bag and purse into the back seat of her Camry then squeezed into the small area beside Alex. She felt awful.

"I can't tell. The light isn't bright enough. I think I have a flashlight somewhere."

Alex got up and went around to the driver's side of the sports car, and in a few minutes he was back carrying a small pen-sized flashlight. Gina leaned over his shoulder and tried to see the damage as he flashed the beam across the door. The paint was scraped off an area measuring about a half inch.

"Well, *that* doesn't look too bad," she offered.

"There's a dent," Alex countered. "A damn dent!"

"Where? Let me feel." Gina leaned over, and Alex took her fingers and guided them along a small crease. There was a definite dent.

She laughed nervously. "Guess we're lucky we have insurance, huh? Send me a bill, and I'll forward it on to my agent."

He stared at her a moment, fire in his eyes, and then he sighed. "I suppose that's probably the best way to handle it. Sorry I overreacted," he added. "I haven't had the car very long, and I'm still a bit paranoid about it."

"Gosh, I don't blame you," she replied. And she didn't. He'd only sworn once. In his position she might have done a lot more. "I really am *so* sorry. I'll give you my card, and I'll write my home and cell numbers down for you. Call me when you get an estimate to turn in to the insurance."

He took her business card and fished one of his own out of his wallet. Handing it over he said, "You can reach me here for the next week or so. I was supposed to be leaving the country, but the trip's been delayed. If you don't mind, I'd like to get this taken care of before I have to leave."

"I understand," Gina said. She smiled and looked at Alex then his card. She tried to think of something clever or funny to say, something that would ease the tension a bit, but her mind really wasn't working. He was absolutely gorgeous. Why had she gone and crushed the door of his car? Why couldn't he have been interested in her? Why didn't things ever come easy?

"So, I guess you have a girl in every port. Since you travel so much," she suggested.

"No," he said. "No, I really don't have the time when I'm working expeditions. Besides, the women in the places I visit aren't exactly off the pages of *Vogue*."

"*Vogue*?" she repeated. "So you like models. Thin and tall for you, huh? Or do you like boys? I mean men. Uh, males. Because there's nothing wrong with that." The words were out before she could stop them.

"Excuse me?" Alex looked shocked, then embarrassed. "Oh, God, was it my behavior about the scratch? I mean, I have nothing against homosexuals, and I work with a few of them, but oh, Lord, if you think… Wait. Why are you asking that? I am *not* gay."

He ran his fingers through that glorious head of curls, and Gina smiled inwardly. He wasn't gay? Well, he had a bit of that babbling thing himself. Unless he'd caught it from her. Was babbling sort of like yawning? She'd never been able to see anyone yawn without picking it up herself.

"Sorry, I don't know why I said that," she said. Apart from the fact that she'd wanted him to hit on her and hadn't. "I guess the thought crossed my mind because you're really good-looking. Most gay guys I've met are, too, and you said you don't have a girlfriend."

"I didn't say I didn't have a girlfriend," he pointed out. "I said I don't have a girl in every port."

"Oh, so you do have a girlfriend. How nice. Is she a model?"

"No," he replied. "I don't have a girlfriend. Well, I did, but now I don't. And yes, she was a model, but she isn't now."

"Why did she give it up?"

"What? Our relationship? I don't know exactly. I think she got tired of my being gone all the time. Actually, I know she did."

"Oh." Gina made a face. "I would have thought modeling would keep her busy while you were away. Didn't she get to travel? Couldn't she go with you?"

"Modeling filled her time," Alex agreed, "but not enough, I guess. And no, she couldn't go with me. The places I travel seldom come with five-star hotel accommodations. She wasn't into that."

"So, she gave up her career to spend more time with you and then the relationship went belly up," Gina said. The comments were rolling off her tongue as if she were grilling a witness on the stand, but she couldn't seem to help herself. "You must be hard to get along with."

Alex looked shell-shocked. "What in the hell are you talking about?"

"Don't yell at me." Gina crossed her arms, knowing full well that her body language was doing nothing to defuse a sticky situation, but that didn't matter. She was using courtroom tactics to put him on the defensive, because she wanted to know the truth. "I'm talking about your girlfriend who gave up a modeling career to be with you and you dumped her anyway. You may be handsome, but you really aren't that nice. I don't blame your girlfriend for wanting to get away."

"Wait a minute," Alex growled. He grasped both her upper arms as if that would hold her in place and said, "I don't know what page you're on, lady, but I'm reading a whole different book. Is this some sort of act to make me feel guilty? You're the one who hit my car."

Gina's breath caught. He was strong, though his grip was gentle. If she closed her eyes, she could almost imagine his lips crashing down to meet hers. Tingles flashed up her arms and everywhere through her body.

He released her suddenly. "I'm sorry. I didn't mean to grab you like that. Please accept my apology."

That brought Gina out of her daydream. She gazed up into Alex's jade-green eyes, momentarily speechless, then blurted, "It's okay. I apologize for what I said. I talk like this sometimes. I'm sure you had reasons for ending the relationship."

Alex grinned and shook his head, as if exasperated. "I'm really not sure we're having the same conversation. Weren't we just talking about how she was bored with me gone all the time? I told you, *she* ended it. She dumped me for the guy who sold me my car insurance."

"Really? An *insurance salesman?*" Gina hoped her disbelief wasn't too obvious, but it didn't seem that Alex was going to expand on the subject, so she stammered, "Hmmm. W-well, I guess people have different tastes."

"Honestly, I just don't think we were a good match. She was used to getting a lot of attention, and I don't know, I just like a woman who is secure and confident and not always looking for my approval. Take you, for instance. I get the sense that you know who you are and you don't need anyone to validate you."

"That kind of makes me sound a bit hard and inflexible," she said.

"Oh." He looked surprised. "I didn't mean it like that. Trust me, you look very soft and flexible."

"What? Now I sound like a marshmallow."

"Oh God, why am I sounding like such an idiot? Or are you messing with me? What I meant was…you're very pretty and obviously smart. Your self-confidence appears strong."

"Oh. Well, I've just proved my physical strength, too," she joked. "I am really sorry about this. I had no idea the door would swing so far out."

Alex scratched the back of his head. "Yeah, that surprised me too."

It seemed they'd hit a wall in the conversation. Neither of them said anything more. The silence stretched. Finally, Gina gave up. If he wasn't interested, he wasn't interested. Weren't guys supposed to do the work in picking up a girl? She'd been doing all the talking.

As she started to open her car door, Alex quickly flattened himself against the side of his Ferrari. He gave a nervous laugh. It annoyed her.

"Relax, Alex, I'll be careful," she said. Why couldn't he have just asked her out? "So, you'll call me when you get the estimates?"

"Sure thing," he said. But he stayed right where he was.

Gina shrugged. Getting into her car, she backed out of the parking spot. Giving him one final wave as she pulled away, she decided his ex-girlfriend was nuts. Alex seemed like he might be one heck of a guy if a girl could ever connect with him, and apparently some girl had and then thrown it away. She couldn't believe that his ex-gal pal had settled for someone who thought rates and deductibles.

Oh well. Different strokes for different folks.

Chapter 5

Estelle wandered over to the window in the front of the restaurant while Gaetano gave instructions to his staff. Her eyes scanned the parking lot but stopped on Gina and Alex with their heads together. What were they doing?

Gaetano appeared behind her and pressed his hand to the small of her back. "Are you ready to leave, Estelle?" She'd driven her car home after they'd come back from the beach, as Gaetano had insisted on driving. He'd said he wouldn't hear of her showing up at the restaurant alone.

"Look," she said. "Our children are engaged in what appears to be a lively conversation."

"What did I tell you?" he replied. "You thought our experiment failed. I told you they were perfect for each other."

"Oh, but look, they're each leaving in their own car."

"Wow. Is that Alex's Ferrari?" Gaetano asked. He gave Estelle a sly look. "He is definitely a perfect match for my Gina. Do you think his future father-in-law might borrow his car sometime? I could take his mother for a ride in the country."

Estelle giggled. The idea of a long ride in the country with Gaetano was tempting and romantic, but the thought also went through her mind that she was acting younger than either of their children. *What on earth is wrong with me?* She gave herself a mental shake. Why should Gaetano's hand on her body make all her senses spring to life? Their friendship was innocent and harmless. She didn't have time for anything more. She was dying.

A short time later she was leaning back against the leather headrest in Gaetano's car. His vehicle wasn't a latest model, but it was spotless and still had that new car smell. She found the ride extremely pleasant.

Estelle closed her eyes and let herself be lulled into total relaxation by the songs on the radio. This golden oldies station played all the tunes that had been popular when she and Marty first married, and each brought a fond memory. She'd loved to dance when she was younger, and in the beginning she and Marty had gone dancing every weekend. Then Alex arrived and Marty's business boomed. There had become very little time for dancing—or for anything else.

Gaetano removed one hand from the steering wheel and gently patted her knee. "So, you think our children are a good match? I do."

His voice stirred her, not to mention the touch on her leg. Ordinarily she would have considered such an action forward and out of place, but tonight it felt natural and sweet. It took her out of her comfort zone, but that wasn't entirely bad.

Regarding the match? Gina was a pretty girl, petite and feminine in every way, and there was something about her that definitely had her father's stamp. The scene between her and Alex in the restaurant parking lot still puzzled Estelle, however. They'd hardly exchanged more than a few words all through dinner, then standing by their vehicles it looked as if they'd had quite a discussion.

"Of course," Gaetano continued, as if reading her mind, "we couldn't hear what they were saying, but they had their heads together. That's a good sign, isn't it?"

"It would seem so," Estelle answered. "They certainly make an attractive couple."

She glanced over at Gaetano and once more admired his profile. We look pretty good together too, she thought. No doubt about it, he was a handsome man. Besides handsome, he was kind, funny…and though she tried to dismiss it from her thoughts, he was damn sexy. So, why he hadn't remarried—or at least been swept up into some sort of long-term relationship?

His hand made parts of her body tingle with excitement and anticipation. Anticipation? What was *that* all about? She couldn't anticipate anything truly, not when the next day might bring failing health. When would the illness rob her of strength? How long would it be until she was confined to her bed and gasping for her last breath? How could she engage in any relationship that was going to be cruelly cut short at its very beginning?

"I think we were right in getting them together," Gaetano remarked. "Gina needs to think about starting a family. Does Alex like children?"

"You know, I really don't know," Estelle admitted. "It's odd that he and I have never discussed it. Probably that's because he's never been in a relationship long enough for it to progress to the subject."

Gaetano's tone was suddenly sharp. "What are you saying? Is Alex a love-'em-and-leave-'em type? You should have told me. I don't want him breaking Gina's heart."

"He most certainly is not that kind of person," Estelle snapped. "You know his job takes him out of the country. There aren't many girls who can handle that. So how do I know Gina isn't like the rest and Alex won't end up with a broken heart?"

"Because I tell you she isn't. She's a good girl, and she doesn't go into things lightly."

"Well," Estelle said, "Alex is an honest and decent—"

Gaetano cut her off. "Stop, Estelle. Listen to us. We're having a spat."

She eyed him, ready to continue her spiel on what a wonderful person her son was when she caught the hint of a grin tugging at the corners of his mouth. He was even more handsome when he wore that expression.

"We don't know each other well enough to have a spat," she remarked. Then she smiled, and they both let gales of laughter bubble out.

"We are something," Gaetano said. "Here we are fighting over whose kid is the prize, over who will jilt who, and we don't even know if they really clicked or not. Are we foolish old people?"

"I hope we're neither of those things. I may not have a lot of time left, and I don't want to waste any of it being foolish. And, truthfully, I don't think getting old is an option for me."

She saw sadness cloud Gaetano's eyes and wished she hadn't brought up her illness. It was easy to forget when she was with him; in the two days they'd been together, she'd never laughed more or felt better. Even Alex had said she looked radiant. Had she ever laughed like this with Marty? Surely she must have in the more than thirty years they'd been married. But, for the life of her, she couldn't remember when.

When she'd first overheard her doctor on the phone and guessed the dreadful news was about her, she hadn't been all that sad. It had been more shock. She'd have followed Marty and not complained too much, except about Alex, whom she wanted to see settled. But now? For some reason, everything had changed. She felt alive and vibrant and...happy? Yes, happy. Happier, in fact, than she'd been in years.

"You must not think of that," Gaetano said. "We had a great time tonight, and tomorrow we will do something special. Maybe we'll even invite the children."

Leave it to this dear, kind man to attempt to pull her out of the glooms. A surge of anger rose in her at being doomed. It wasn't fair. She was finally having fun and enjoying the attention of a nice man again, and it would soon be taken away. How soon? That was a question she needed to ask the doctor. Maybe there would even be some new drugs or treatments that would change things.

"Gaetano, what are you planning?" Estelle forced her somber thoughts aside to focus on the man beside her. A wave of tenderness and gratitude rose up in her chest. But while he was determined to make her happy in the time she had left, she knew she couldn't take advantage of him. She couldn't let him focus on her like he was doing. "I'm sure you need to attend to your business. You can't let my problems become yours."

"Don't you worry about my business," Gaetano commanded, waving away her protests as if swatting a pesky insect. "I am the boss. I can do anything I want. And tomorrow I want to take you on an adventure. Maybe we won't invite the kids after all."

He grinned, and Estelle's mouth tilted up at each corner in response. The heaviness in her chest disappeared, and she was sorry to see that they had arrived at her house. For just a moment she considered asking Gaetano in for a nightcap; then she pushed the thought from her mind. She didn't even agree to go on the adventure with him tomorrow.

Gaetano turned the key and the engine fell silent. The radio, too. Before Estelle could collect her purse and undo her seat belt, he had her door open and his hand outstretched to assist her from the car. Then he leaned down, kissed her fingertips, and tucked her arm securely in his as he walked her to the front door.

That hint of Old World charm was so much a part of him, and it didn't fail to tug at Estelle's heartstrings. He didn't ask to be invited inside.

※ ※ ※

Gaetano drove by his restaurant after dropping Estelle off. He knew it probably wasn't necessary, but he wanted to check to be sure his crew had remembered to turn on the courtesy lights inside the building and extinguish the neon sign outside. When he was satisfied his business was safe and no one had left a door unlocked or a burner on, he turned back onto the parkway and began his short drive home.

The closer he got to his small bungalow, the more he dreaded going into the empty house. It was a strange feeling, and one that brought back old memories. Right after Rosie died, it had been hard going home, but he'd had to because of Gina. His cousin Maria had been a good babysitter, but his child needed her daddy. As time went on, he'd eventually grown eager to get home just to spend time with her. But now the old feelings of loneliness were back. Puttering around the garden wasn't the same with Gina gone.

Tonight, it had been all he could do to leave Estelle at her doorstep and not kiss her for real. That kiss on the hand was just something he did out of habit; the female patrons at his restaurant all seemed to like it. Of course, he didn't ever attempt it until they'd established themselves as regulars, but the kiss made for good business—and to be honest, Gaetano enjoyed it too. It made him feel young again. It was fun to flirt, though he'd never gotten seriously involved with any woman since Rosie died.

Was that all this was with Estelle? Harmless flirting? That's how it had started out. She was a sick lady and so sad. He'd just wanted to make her feel better. To give her some laughs and fun. That wasn't a crime.

And yet, there was this unsettled feeling in the pit of his belly every time he was near her. Whenever she laughed, his heart jumped. Whenever she touched his arm or put her hand on his, shivers skated up and down his spine. Last night, when he'd fallen asleep, her face was the one he saw before he closed his eyes. It was the first image he'd thought of upon awakening.

Gaetano had just pulled into his driveway as his anger boiled up and spilled over. He shouted at the top of his lungs, "It's not fair. She shouldn't have to die!"

That rage went unnoticed, as his car windows were tightly shut and no lights were on in his neighbors' homes, so he slumped over the steering wheel, and for the first time in many years, felt the dampness of tears on his cheeks.

***

Gina put her leftovers into the fridge and hoped she'd remember to eat them before they turned into unidentifiable blue masses. She wondered if Alex had the same problem. His work had sounded fascinating.

She took the last can of diet soda, popped the top, and took a big gulp. Then she took her cell phone from her bag and punched in the codes necessary to retrieve the messages from her voicemail. They were almost always from the office.

"Miss Lorenzo, this is Boris Urzinsky. I think we're supposed to meet sometime soon to discuss my case, but I forgot when you said. Maybe you can call me tonight. Whenever. I am very nervous."

Gina checked the time on her watch. It was a quarter to ten. Maybe it was too late to call, but he'd said it was okay and mornings weren't the best time, either, as she left for the office pretty early and then got caught up in her case work. Rifling through her briefcase she found his client file and punched in his phone number, muttering to herself that she hoped he was home or had a machine.

The phone rang several times, and Gina chided herself for not checking her messages sooner. She was just about ready to hang up when the Russian's voice came on the line.

"Hello, Boris here."

"Mr. Urzinsky? This is Gina Lorenzo. I'm sorry to call you so late, but I just got your message. You're scheduled for a two o'clock on Thursday of next week at my office."

"Of course, now I remember. What a stupid man I am," he said.

She shook her head, though he couldn't see. "Not at all, Mr. Urzinsky. I would have reminded you the day before, but don't worry. We have a strong case. Good night."

Gina turned off her phone, kicked off her shoes, and started up the stairs. She dropped her briefcase onto her desk and plugged her phone into its charger, thinking that maybe she should have been a little more patient with poor Mr. Urzinsky, given him a bit more time to chat. He'd been fired from his job and claimed it was because he was Russian. If that was true, she would win his case. Unfortunately, however, right now all she wanted to do was sleep—and maybe be lucky enough to dream about Alex.

He'd said he liked confident women. Ironic. The only thing she wasn't confident about was how to keep a man interested.

Sleep was safe, though. She could have all sorts of fantasies without the risk. You couldn't be disappointed by your dreams, either. At least, when you were it didn't matter as much.

***

Boris Urzinsky held the phone for a while after his lady lawyer had disconnected. She'd sounded as nice as she looked. That was why he'd chosen her. He'd gone to her law office last week and watched all the people going in and out of the big glass doors. He needed a good lawyer and thought that place would have many smart people, not to mention pretty ones. He'd followed Miss Lorenzo as soon as she'd left the elevator. Not too close, just enough to observe her. She'd gone into a separate office and closed the door, that was when he'd first read the name, Gina Lorenzo, Attorney at Law.

At the front desk in the reception area he'd taken one of her cards from its small brass holder. The gold etching was very impressive. He'd smiled at the lady who came toward him, but before she got within speaking distance, Boris had turned quickly and left. He had called that very day and asked especially for Miss

Gina Lorenzo. Now, in just a few days, they would finally meet. The thought of being up close to the pretty lady excited him. He had taken the steps needed to be confident of the outcome, however. He was not a stupid man.

Chapter 6

It had been almost a week and a half since Gina's insurance company had gotten the claim form from Alex's agent. She'd assumed things were moving along in an orderly fashion, but now she regretted picking up the phone because she'd probably be late for work.

Gina fought to keep her voice down, but lost the battle. "What do you mean the repairs are going to cost over twelve thousand dollars?" The words bounced off the walls and reverberated around her kitchen.

"Ms. Lorenzo," said the man on the phone, "you do understand that the paint mixture for Mr. Bennett's car was a special blend and not a standard shade? That being the case, the entire car will have to be repainted."

"Look, Mr. Edwards—"

"It's Edward Elliott, representative of New World Insurance." The voice now had a slight edge; not exactly rude but bordering on impatient. Not that he'd started so far away from that.

"Edward, Elliott, whatever. I saw that teensy weensy scratch and I'll be damned if I'm going to pay a million times more than it's worth."

"Obviously, Miss Lorenzo, you're not familiar with the cost of foreign vehicles or their upkeep. If you want, I can send you a more detailed statement. I've already faxed one to your agent, but this isn't that unusual."

"My agent saw that tiny little insignificant scratch and he's familiar with all kinds of cars. I'm sure he was as shocked and appalled as I am."

"Well," the insurance agent replied, "Mr. Bennett has the right to have his car restored to the condition it was in before you hit it."

"Look, I didn't *hit* him. My car door scraped his. Barely. And how do I know that the dent you're talking about was made by my car? It could have been there before! I didn't inspect his vehicle prior to the alleged incident, and until this is settled, nothing is proven for either side."

"Oh my." Edward Elliott let out a long sigh. "I was so hoping we could settle this amicably. However, your insurance company has indicated that they might deny the claim, so this may be something we'll have to let the courts settle."

She had insurance, but the policy had limitations. And, really, twelve thousand dollars was ridiculous. Gina hoped she could feel a bluff on the other end of the line. Maybe she could push past it. "Really? Are you aware, Mr. Edward Elliott, or whatever your name is, that I happen to be an attorney and have yet to lose a case? With my help, I imagine my insurance company will be happy to see this go to court. If it has to."

The agent seemed unmoved. "Well, it's certainly your prerogative to offer help, Miss Lorenzo, but insurance companies have their own legal departments. And perhaps you're not aware, but troublesome clients are usually dropped from coverage."

"Mr. Edwards, that might be the policy of your company, but I've been with my company for years and if they say they might deny this claim then perhaps they have good reason. I'm late for work now, so goodbye."

Gina slammed the receiver down and ran into her bedroom to finish dressing. It was definitely a big bluff, she told herself. Alex's insurance company would never take this to court, not if they knew what was good for them. For God's sake, the scratch was so small she couldn't believe such a fuss was being made. Still, for twelve thousand dollars, she made a mental note to have her clerk research automotive accident cases.

It did irritate her, though, that this was the first she'd learned of her insurance company's possible denial of the claim. Why hadn't her agent let her know? For that matter, why hadn't Alex called her? Had they let him know? He was likely upset, but that was all the more reason for him to get in touch. He'd seemed to forgive her the night of the accident, even if she wasn't his type.

What *was* his type? Models from *Vogue*, she supposed. Models from *Vogue* who ditched hot, world-traveling photojournalists for insurance salesmen. She wondered again whom he was likely to date. And why was she so obsessive about him? Was it because she'd been in such a long dry spell? She was sure there were other guys who were just as handsome. Somewhere on the planet there must be.

Gina gave her hair one last look in the hallway mirror, punched in the code for her home security system, and hurried out the door. But as she walked to her car, her blood began to boil. She was late and it was all Alex's fault. In fact, the more she thought about it, the more it seemed likely the insurance company had called him. Then he hadn't even bothered to get in touch with her. First he'd acted like she'd dinged his door on purpose, and now his insurance agent was all over her. Just dab a spot of paint on the damn car and leave me alone, she thought.

She'd barely pulled onto the parkway before she found herself in the clutches of a horrible San Diego morning commute. If she was lucky, she could still get to the office and do some boning up before she had to appear in court, but she wasn't confident she'd be lucky. Which sucked. She couldn't count the times today's client had called previous to their first meeting. Mr. Boris Urzinsky was beginning to be a pest, and she'd be glad to be done with his case. She hadn't even wanted to take it in the first place, as the man had given her a strange vibe, but her boss had told her to just buckle down and power through. She really did want that partnership.

She chided herself again for answering the phone call that had turned out to be Alex's insurance agent. She'd thought it might be her dad, who hadn't been calling as much as he usually did, which worried her. Was he spending too much time with that redhead mother of that imbecile Alex?

"Okay, red lights. Do your thing. Turn green," she said as she approached an intersection.

It wasn't working. When she was small, her father had convinced her he was magic because he would command the lights to turn green and they would. It had been years before she figured out that he drove exactly at the speed it took to keep the lights in his favor. She couldn't even manage that little bit of magic.

Gina applied the brakes, slowing her car to a smooth stop and then drumming her fingers on the steering wheel in a frantic rhythm. Lifting her chin, she spoke with her take-charge voice, talking over the radio that she'd turned down to a faint drone. "Your Honor, I am here today to represent a hardworking man who has been unfairly discharged from a position he held for three and a half years merely because he has an uncommon surname."

Hm. Perhaps a more feminine approach would be better. She cleared her throat and repeated the sentence in a more cajoling tone, then frowned and wondered if that sounded too female and would prejudice the judge against her client. He might think she had an ulterior motive. Like—

Nah, he wouldn't think that. Mr. Urzinsky seemed an okay man, but he gave her a creepy vibe. He probably gave everyone that vibe, which was probably why he'd been fired from his job. Plus he was short, burly, and very hairy. Black hair poked out above his collar, and she could only imagine what was beneath his button-down shirt. She didn't even *want* to think about that. Not that she was against hairy-chested men. In fact, she rather liked a bit of hair. She wondered if Alex had much. Somehow she imagined him with just the right amount. Those dark curls would dust his already perfect physique—

A horn blast almost sent her through the roof, and suddenly she realized there was absolutely nothing in front of her; it had been several seconds since the car she'd been tailgating pulled away. Acutely aware of several impatient and angry drivers behind her, she pressed on the gas and sped out through the intersection before the light turned yellow. Sheesh, everyone was so impatient these days.

At work, Gina waved at the attendant as she did every morning and pulled into the closest parking spot in the garage of her office complex. Grabbing her briefcase and handbag, she beeped her car locked, then scooted into the parking level elevator before the doors closed. She didn't miss the grimace of the businessman next to her as her leather Armani satchel jabbed him just below the belt.

"Sorry," she mumbled, moving as close as she could against the elevator wall. She'd been planning to dismiss the morning's problems, but it didn't seem possible. The morning just wasn't going well, and it was all Alex's fault. What on earth had he expected? Buying an expensive car like that was just asking for something bad to happen.

Well, she reminded herself, she couldn't think about it now. She was on her way to defend the rights of a client. She had done her homework if not her presentation rehearsal. According to Title VII of the Civil Rights Act of 1964, Mr. Urzinsky was protected against employment discrimination on the basis of national origin. Not to mention race, color, sex, religion, or creepy vibe. But what about excessive body hair?

She'd barely made it inside her office before her client arrived. He peered at her through the door and grinned with stubby teeth, showing generous gaps between the upper four. She waved in return then the two of them hurried out of the building, and Gina quickly reminded him of what would go on at the hearing. She tried not to think about how frustrating her morning had been.

The courthouse was a short block from the office, and for that she was grateful. Her client took her arm and folded it in his own as they half-ran down the sidewalk. She tried to disengage, but the pace Boris set made it difficult to do more than struggle to stay upright. For a moment, Gina wondered who was in charge.

A short time later, she knew. *She* was in charge. Her arm was free, Mr. Urzinsky was as pleased as punch, and she was still at the top of her game. They had won the case. The company would be rehiring Boris, and he would garner back-salary to boot. The judge had bought all of her contentions.

"Miss Lorenzo, you were wonderful," her client enthused. "I must buy you lunch."

Gina smiled kindly. "Mr. Urzinsky, that's not necessary. I'm just glad you won." She then shook his hand and quickly made her departure, desperate to do so before he could get a hold on her arm and drag her off to some greasy spoon. She had too much to do, and the idea of sitting across from him and watching him eat was not particularly pleasant. Still, the day was looking up.

She practically sprinted to her office building and squeezed into the first elevator that arrived, its doors barely open to release the day's departing lunch-seekers. She was the solo passenger all the way to her floor. Dropping her briefcase on the edge of her desk, she sorted through the mail that had been deposited there and only looked up when she heard a voice.

"Miss Gina Lorenzo?" A young man in Levi's and a golf shirt stood in her doorway with an expectant look.

"Yes, I'm Gina Lorenzo. How can I help you?" she asked.

"I have something for you."

He reached her in three short strides, and Gina took the envelope he thrust out.

"What is it?"

"Miss Lorenzo, you've been served," he said. And with that, he turned and exited the room.

As Gina opened the envelope, her jaw dropped and her eyes widened in disbelief. She yelled after the messenger, "Wait a minute! This can't be right. I just talked to an agent this morning. Things don't move this fast."

Evidently they did.

***

Alex slammed down the phone, unable to believe his ears.

He'd been glad when his agent first suggested the car damage claim be handled through the insurance offices alone, as he hadn't wanted to deal with it personally. He hadn't even been particularly upset when he'd learned Gina's insurance company began with a totally ridiculous offer, as he'd known they would move up eventually. Or so he'd thought. His agent had just informed him that they were on their way to a lawsuit.

Things had gotten totally out of control. He didn't know if he'd agreed to anything like this, but he didn't want to sue; he just wanted his car fixed. Now his mother would probably kill or disown him. Or both. She liked Gina's dad, and this would make both parents unhappy.

To be honest, he liked Gina. Ever since that night he'd been thinking about the way he'd overreacted to the scratch and how he'd missed his opportunity to ask her out, and more than once he'd almost picked up the phone to do just that. The damage to his car was upsetting, but at the same time, Gina was the first girl in a long time that had lit a spark in him. He'd loved her sassiness, even when it was directed at him, though it had left him a bit speechless. And despite the uncomfortable date-like situation with his mother and her father, the petite girl's beauty had not escaped his notice.

He'd gone out of his way to avoid making her feel like he was checking her out, though. It was hard, because he'd liked the way Gina laughed and the manner in which she'd eaten her dinner. Though her waist looked small enough for his hands to encircle, she hadn't picked at the food the way most of his dates did; she actually enjoyed eating. Every time she'd caught him looking at her, he'd pretended he was examining her earrings. He'd figured that was appropriate, seeing as he probably wouldn't be in the country much longer.

Alex slid down into his leather sofa and let his thoughts drift back. Why hadn't he called her and gotten to know her better in the past two weeks? It might have even helped on this whole car mess. He supposed he'd been afraid she'd think he was trying to soften her up or gain some advantage. And then there had been a lot to do in order to get ready for his next assignment. The problems with the African trip were almost cleared up, and he might be leaving as soon as next week. But for the first time, the excitement of starting a new adventure seemed to be missing.

The phone rang and interrupted Alex's thoughts. He sprang off the sofa and sprinted across the room to answer.

"Hello?"

"Well, I guess I'm lucky to catch you still in the country, although if I were you I'd head out to some godforsaken island if you know what's good for you."

It was obviously a female, but he couldn't place the voice and wasn't sure he wanted to. It was an extremely angry voice. Who could be so angry at him? Was it his ex?

"Who is this?" he asked.

"This is Gina Lorenzo, attorney at law, and an excellent one at that, I might add. Just who in God's green acre do you think you are, anyway? Do you honestly think I'm going to let you bleed me dry with your trumped-up damage claim?"

Gina? "Gina! Wait a minute."

"And another thing. Are you so cowardly that you have to have your cockamamie agent call me and then serve me with—?"

"Gina, shut up a minute and I'll try to explain," Alex said, interrupting. Here he'd been thinking about her, and now she was giving him a call. It must be fate. "I had no idea they were at that stage, and I never would have let it get to that point if they'd asked me."

"You expect me to believe you didn't authorize this?" Gina's voice was several octaves higher than it started and not any calmer.

"Why wouldn't you? I don't want to sue you. I've never been involved with anything like this, so I didn't know the procedure."

"I suppose you didn't know I received a summons today, either."

"Not until a few minutes ago. My agent just phoned and told me that this can happen when one company refuses to settle or offers a ridiculously low amount." Alex hoped his tone would reflect his concern, as he really did want to get to know the girl better. He'd been imagining those dark brown eyes snapping with fiery sparks for the past week, and there was no requirement that he stay in the country just to get to know someone.

"Ridiculously low?" Gina's voice was a shriek that would have put most jungle creatures to shame. "Do you think twelve thousand dollars is reasonable for a teensy-weensy minute scratch a person can barely see?"

He felt his hackles rise. "In all fairness, Gina, there was a dent too."

"Fairness? *Fairness?* What do you or your swindling, fly-by-night agent know about fairness? I'm not about to settle anything when you and your agent are bona fide money-grabbing gougers of the worst kind. I'll see you in court."

Alex caught himself before he responded in kind. "Now just a minute, Gina. I don't think you—"

He was too late. A click came from the other end of the line.

Chapter 7

Gina sipped the last of her coffee and grimaced. *God, you'd think I could at least master this.*

After she'd stormed out of her office, she'd found herself heading home. That was force of habit, since home was where she usually went after work, though she didn't normally leave so early in the day. She'd made herself a pot of coffee and tried to find something in the fridge that could pass for lunch, but besides a few dried up strawberries and half a quart of expired nonfat milk, there wasn't anything to tempt her.

She dumped the last of her coffee down the sink and headed upstairs. Since her home computer in the small room she'd turned into an office was linked with the one at the firm, working here the rest of the day was an option. At least she might be able to read some of her emails. She sometimes worked at night from here, but seldom billed the clients for all those hours because it made her look less efficient. Besides, she didn't want people at the office to know she didn't have much of a life.

She'd barely sat down at the computer when the phone rang.

"Hello?" Gina answered in her not-at-the-office voice. Since she'd left work in a rage, it was probably the secretary checking up on her.

"Excuse me? Is Miss Lorenzo there?" It wasn't Sara. It was a male voice that sounded vaguely familiar, but her mind was racing and she couldn't think straight.

"This is Miss Lorenzo."

"Ah, you did not sound like yourself. Miss Lorenzo, this is Boris. I know you didn't have time today, but perhaps tomorrow will be better."

"Boris? Boris who?" Gina asked. Then the light bulb came on. "Oh, yes, Mr. Urzinsky. I'm sorry, what is it you want?"

"I would like to express my gratitude for your excellent performance in court on my behalf," he stated. "I want to treat you to lunch tomorrow. You pick the place."

Gina stifled a groan. Good Lord. As if she wasn't having enough problems, she really didn't want to have to deal with a grateful client. Especially not this one. "Mr. Urzinsky," she began, "that isn't necessary. I was just doing my job. I'm glad it worked out for you, but—"

"No, you don't understand. You saved my life," the Russian interrupted. "I was ready to do myself in if I couldn't go back to work." His voice was deep and gravelly. He sounded as if he might cry.

"Mr. Urzinsky, you don't mean that. It was just a job and—"

"Please," Boris interrupted again. "It wasn't just a job. It meant everything to me. Now, I insist, you must let me buy you lunch. And you must call me Boris."

A wave of uneasiness flitted through Gina. "Mr. Urzinsky, I'm sorry, but I can't call you by your given name. That wouldn't be professional, and I'm sorry but I can't have lunch tomorrow either."

"Then, dinner. Have dinner with me. Have you ever been to The Russian Palace? Good Russian food. Very...how can I say it? Uh, is upper class restaurant for a beautiful woman. Established and—"

Realizing what he was after, Gina ran out of patience. "Please, Mr. Urzinsky," she cut in. "I can't have lunch or dinner with you. Not today, not tomorrow or ever. I'm sorry, I have to go now." Then she hung up the phone and sat immobile.

A sobering thought crossed her mind, one that probably should have occurred to her the first time he'd called. How had the Russian Romeo gotten her home number? It wasn't listed, and the firm wouldn't release it—or shouldn't release it. When the phone rang again, she hesitated a minute then finally let the answering machine take the call. The machine was downstairs, so she didn't have to hear the message.

Deciding she really didn't want to stay at home, she also didn't want to go back to the office. So, maybe she would stop over and see Papá. At least there would be food there—although her appetite had decreased just talking to Boris. Boris? God, even the name sounded hairy. Wild boars were hairy too, weren't they? She shook her head and tried to remind herself to be nice. It was flattering that the man found her attractive, even if he did give her a creepy vibe and push too hard. Really? She *was* getting desperate.

Descending the stairs, she saw the light blinking on her answering machine but decided to ignore it. If it was her office…well, maybe she'd feel like going back to work after she saw her father. But it probably hadn't been her office. She had a sinking feeling it had been the Russian.

***

Boris clenched his fists, furious and surprised. The pretty lawyer lady with the dark eyes had treated him with great disrespect. Oh, she was nice when it was a matter of earning pay. She'd won the case today, and when she knew his company would be sending her a check, she'd been very friendly. But not otherwise.

"Miss Lorenzo, I think you will want to see me again. I will teach you how to treat a real man," he muttered to himself.

"Boris, did you say something?" One of his co-workers stuck his head into the cubical where Boris had just been reinstalled.

"No, I said nothing that was for your ears. I am busy," Boris spat, then watched with satisfaction as the man skittered away. A moment later he fought back annoyance. It was true his office was just one of many cubical spaces in this enormous high-rise building in downtown San Diego, but one day he would have the corner office and an executive suite. He would have his own secretary and everyone would give him the respect he deserved. Even Miss Lorenzo. He never gave up on anything, and he wouldn't give up on her either.

No, it wasn't *that* easy to get rid of him. He'd been an engineer for this scientific research conglomerate for almost four years, and yet they continued to ignore his talents. They had even tried to fire him, but he was too smart for that. With a bit of manipulation, some conversations, and other incidents he'd had the intelligence to document, he'd been able to show he was terminated from the company because of where he'd been born. His specialty was all forms of communication and the software that made it happen. He was good at what he did, and the proof of that was in his acquisition of Miss Gina Lorenzo's unlisted phone number. He could even get the President's private line if he just put his mind to it.

He picked up the phone and punched in the number of the flower shop on the first floor of the building. He would send Gina a bouquet of carnations and have them delivered to her office. Roses were too expensive. Maybe when they'd had a few dates and become close—very close—then he would buy her a rose.

"Empire Florist," a pleasant voice answered.

"Yes, I'd like to order a bouquet of carnations, and maybe a little of whatever it is you put in the vase to fill it out."

"We could add a little baby's breath or some other greenery," the voice suggested.

"Fine, fine. Just make sure they look good. I want them sent to Miss Gina Lorenzo at the law firm of Baxter, Baker and Ellis in the McPherson building. Fifth floor."

"What would you like the card to say?" the florist asked.

"There's no need for a card. She'll know who sent them. There is only one me."

"Fine, sir, the total with delivery and the vase will be $45.68. What credit card would you like to use?"

Boris gasped at the named amount. How could a few blossoms be that much? But he recited his credit card number without protest, hung up the phone and finished off the bag of chips he'd gotten from the vending machine, washing them down with a can of soda.

She will see that I can be a very romantic guy, he decided. How could she not?

***

Gina turned on her radio and tried to relax as she drove to her father's restaurant. All around her were charming old buildings that thankfully hadn't yet been leveled for new modern structures with no character. The area reminded her of her childhood. It held a combination of new and older homes. The older homes, one of which had been hers, were small compared to the newer ones, but they were all adequate and well maintained.

She liked this neighborhood where she'd grown up. Not exactly posh, it was more like a small town within the county lines of a metropolis. There was really no "bad" area, and children could actually ride their bikes to the small shopping mall where Gaetano's Ristorante was located and return to find them parked right where they'd left them.

It brought back so many memories every time she drove here. After her mother died, she'd walk with her best friend, Polly Carter, from school to the restaurant that had been her second home. Papá always had a treat of some kind waiting. Polly would stay until her mother got off work at the beauty shop in the same mall. Sometimes both Carters would stay and have dinner.

No matter how busy the restaurant was, her Papá had always taken time to eat dinner with her in his little office off the kitchen. He'd set up a card table, spread a cloth over it, and put a candle in the middle, just like the tables in the main dining room. They would discuss her day at school and sometimes he would help her with her homework, although she'd never needed much help. At eight thirty Mario's wife would take her home, tuck her into bed, and stay with her until her father got finished. Sometimes it was close to midnight, but every morning Gaetano was up bright and early to fix her breakfast and get her off to school.

Yes, it was good she was going to see Papá. He would know just what to say so that she'd feel better.

As she pulled into the parking lot, a wave of depression swept over her. This was where her problems had started. Alex and his fancy car. Why hadn't she been more careful? For that matter, why had she parked next to him? She pulled into a slot that was some distance away from the building. Better to walk a little farther than take any chance of dinging another car.

There were few vehicles parked at the moment, and the majority of those were close to the drycleaners and the pharmacy. The beauty shop was still operating, though Polly's mother hadn't worked there for a long time. Gina got out of her car and walked to the front door of her father's restaurant. Her spirits were already lifting.

The lunch hour was over and only a few patrons remained in the dining room. Gaetano sat at the counter next to the kitchen going over his accounts. Gina stood in the archway that separated the restaurant's dining room from the preparation area and the computer station.

"Papá, do you have a minute?"

"Gina! I'm so glad to see you." Gaetano slid off his stool and closed the space between them, wrapped his arms around her and gave her a huge hug. The strength of it almost brought Gina to tears. She knew he felt her mood. She could never fool him.

"It has been a long time since you've just dropped in," he went on. "What's wrong, *bambina*? Your face is all sad and somber. Are you sick? God knows you are too thin. You modern girls always working, eating on the go. No way to live."

"I'm fine, Papá, but it's been a rough day."

"Come, sit. I'll feed you lunch."

"Actually," she said, "I just wanted to talk. I'm not really hungry."

"You are too skinny. Please, it will take *un minuto*." And before Gina had time to protest further, Gaetano had hurried off to the kitchen.

He returned balancing a steaming dish in one hand with a half-filled bottle of his special red wine he kept for important clients tucked under his arm. With two fingers he plucked wine glasses from the rack above the counter, and he showed her a plate with the day's luncheon special, cheese tortellini in a rich sauce. The recipe had been handed down from generation to generation and was one of Gina's favorites.

"There, whatever you are worried about will not be so big after you eat."

"How do you know I'm worried?" Gina looked at the plate of pasta, but didn't pick up her fork.

Gaetano filled the glasses with wine and plopped down in the leather-cushioned stool beside her. "I know you are worried about something because you are doing that thing you do with your lip."

"My lip? I don't know what you're talking about."

"Gina, from the time you were a baby, if you were wet, hungry, lonely, or angry you chewed on your lower lip. So which is it?"

"Well, I'm not wet. I said I wasn't hungry. I certainly am not lonely now that I'm here, but I'm so angry I could scream. Actually, I've done that already."

"Oh, *cara*, what happened? Did you lose a case? You weren't fired, were you? If you were, it's okay. You don't need to work so hard in that big-shot lawyer place. Come work for me. You can be my manager or—"

"Papá, stop. I did not lose a case, and I might add that I never have. I am so angry because of your girlfriend's son."

"What girlfriend?"

"Alex Bennett's mother. She's a lovely lady, but her son is a jackass."

"Estelle's son? What did he do to you? Did he, you know, maybe touch you, and you had to sock him? Good for you, Gina. If a man can't be a gentleman before he's married, he should be socked."

"No, no, let me explain."

"You didn't sock him? Then I'll go sock him."

"Papá, please," she begged. "Just listen. Alex is suing me."

Gina told her father the entire story. By the time she was done, however, she wasn't sure if Gaetano was amused or irritated.

"Gina, it is a beautiful car, and I can understand how Alex would want it restored to the way it was before the accident. But why are you two children squabbling about this? Let the insurance company deal with it."

"That's just it, Papa. They offered him a settlement which he refused. Now he's suing me!"

Gaetano shook his head. "Gina, my *bambina*, surely you misunderstood. Estelle says her Alex is a very nice young man. Estelle does not lie. Your insurance will have to pay, won't they?"

She dug in her heels. "I don't think they want to, and I don't blame them. He wants twelve thousand dollars for a paint job."

"Gina, the car is worth how much? Hundreds of thousands of dollars, maybe. So, the paint is expensive, too."

"Come on, Papá, he bought it used. And, well, I don't care. Let him take me to court. I will *never* settle." She picked up the fork she'd been ignoring and jabbed two pieces of pasta. Cramming them into her mouth, she swallowed a big gulp of the red wine.

"Gina, maybe we can talk with Alex. I can call his mother, and I'm thinking this has been a big mistake. It'll be okay. You'll see."

"I don't think so, Papá," she replied. "And the more I think about it, the more I'm ready for whatever they want to bring."

She speared another forkful of food and devoured it, swiped at her lips with her napkin and folded it beside her plate. Her father glanced at her, and she could tell he'd been cooking something up, and she didn't mean in the kitchen. She waited for him to spit it out.

"Gina…I've been giving some thought to an idea that might help you and Alex find a way to come to some understanding. It has bothered me that I failed to teach you to cook while you were growing up, and I know you don't eat properly. Estelle says the same about Alex." Her father took a sip of wine and leaned forward. Gesturing with his hands and smiling broadly he announced, "So, I am willing—no, *eager*—to give you and Alex cooking lessons. Together."

Well, he had her attention. Gina frowned and cocked her head to one side. Was her father completely unbalanced?

"Are you serious? You think cooking lessons will change Alex from being a jerk and suing me? You want us around fire and knives together?"

"Cooking wonderful food can be a way to find a common ground. A family can never have too many cooks, that is what I say; it can only have too few. It will be a way for you two to learn to work together, learn new skills, find enjoyment. And, Gina, it would make your mama so happy. She rolls in her grave so many times, I can't even tell you. She sends messages to let me know I should have taught you."

"Oh, come on!" Gina shook her head. "Are you saying she haunts you because I can't cook? Papá, there are no such things as ghosts."

"Maybe not like in the movies, but every time I let the sauce stick in the pan because I forget to put the burner on simmer, that's your mamá. When I overbuy certain foods and some goes to waste, it's Rosie. She's saying to me, 'If you had taught our Gina, she would be by your side and you wouldn't mess up.'"

Gina threw back her head and laughed heartily. "Papá, that is such a crock. I never wanted to be a chef. I love my job. I'm good at it. I just don't like being a defendant. And Alex and I taking cooking classes is—"

"You laugh all you want," her father broke in, "but Rosie and I settled many problems by cooking together. You can work out a lot of anger by kneading bread or chopping onions."

Gina shook her head again. "You think cooking can solve everything. That's okay for you, but I doubt if it'd help this situation." She slid off her stool and planted a big kiss on her father's cheek. "Thanks for lunch. I'm going back to the office. I left in a huff, but I'm calm now. I've got a lot of work to do. Love you."

She waved then, and sprinting across the room she burst out the restaurant door. She did feel better. Maybe she'd been hungry after all.

At her car, Gina remembered that she'd intended to mention Boris, to see what her father thought she should do, but he probably just would have suggested a cooking class. Plus, she was just borrowing trouble. The Russian was just a lonely older man who had wanted to celebrate his victory. He was harmless, even if he made her uneasy. She wondered just how long he'd be able to stay at his company before they found some other reason to let him go, but when they did, she'd already decided not to represent him.

Sometimes, if she was thinking about it, a girl could avoid trouble.

Chapter 8

Gina sailed into her office after successfully managing to avoid any of the senior partners. They had probably heard all about her come-apart earlier in the day, which was not the impression she wanted them to have of her. Perhaps if she stayed out of sight they would forget it. If she was even luckier, maybe they hadn't heard.

As she put her briefcase down, she suddenly became aware of flowers. In a bright blue vase with a wide yellow bow, a full bouquet of multi-colored carnations sat in the corner of her desk.

"How nice. I wonder who sent them," she said and leaned over to look for the card. There wasn't any, so she buzzed the secretary. "Sara, could I see you just a minute, please?"

After a few seconds, the woman appeared. "Oh, aren't they pretty?" She leaned over to sniff the flowers. "Who are they from?"

"I was hoping you could tell me," Gina said. "Who delivered them?"

"I really don't know. I went out for lunch and when I came back they were sitting there. Wasn't there a card?"

"No, nothing." Gina's brow furrowed, and she chewed at her lower lip. "Not even a sticker or anything identifying the shop."

"They are pretty. I guess you have a secret admirer," the secretary said. "Was there something else?"

"No thanks, Sara, I guess it isn't really that important. Sorry I bothered you."

But the secret admirer quip bothered her. Gina looked again for a card, or at least for something that would identify the florist. Nothing.

Could they have been from Alex, as compensation for taking her to court? Well, fifty-dollar flowers wouldn't get him a twelve-thousand-dollar paint job. No way. She moved the vase to the top of a filing cabinet and returned to her desk to begin researching the cost of auto paint and foreign cars.

***

So, Miss Lorenzo lived in a very nice area. Boris jotted the address down on a small notepad and stuck it in his shirt pocket. Tonight after work he would drive by and see it for himself. He might even be living there in a few months. Ah, it would be nice to get out of the dump he was in. But even with the back pay he'd receive from the settlement, there would not be enough. Miss Lorenzo would need a man of means.

He leaned back in his chair and visualized how she must have smiled when she saw his flowers. She would know who they were from, and he wouldn't be at all surprised if she gave him a call before the day's end. He was a very smart guy. He knew just how to win the ladies over. Sometimes it just took longer. Then, once he convinced her he was her soul mate, they could do anything. Together they would soar like eagles.

***

Estelle straightened the flatware on the table for the tenth time and then refolded each linen napkin. She'd had an awful time trying to decide whether she should use napkin rings or just fold the cloth by the side of the plate.

"Oh, why did I ask a chef to dinner?" she complained to herself.

She left the dining room and went to check on the roast. She didn't want it to moo on the platter, but it couldn't be too well done either. What had she been thinking? Not that she was a bad cook.

She'd certainly garnered her share of compliments over the years, but inviting Gaetano to dinner had not been the best decision she'd made recently. There was a certain danger to having a culinary genius near your kitchen or sampling your work. She knew the saying about too many cooks.

And yet, she'd wanted to thank him. The past few weeks had been wonderful, and Gaetano was the one responsible. Besides being so talented in the kitchen, he was funny, thoughtful and kind. They'd spent more time together than she expected. There'd been almost daily phone calls and a pop concert in the park, where much to her chagrin he'd insisted they dance across the grass, attracting attention from all the other music-lovers. There had also been the affection. Nothing overt, just a caress here and there. And kisses that had gone from pecks on the cheek to full-blown on the lips and caused her pulse to tap dance. She'd never expected her last days to be so filled with fun and laughter.

Her last days.

That reminded her. She needed to get back with the doctor's office and make an appointment. What kind of doctor kept such bad news from a patient for so long? Maybe she'd go to the medical office and confront Dr. Bob. She had to know how much longer she had. Getting closer to Gaetano wasn't fair. He deserved to have someone with whom he could build a future. However, she was impressed with the medication she was on. Leukemia or not, she'd never felt better.

The doorbell rang and Estelle's heart quickened. She checked the table one last time then hurried to answer. Perhaps tonight she'd suggest to Gaetano that he start seeing other women, if he wasn't already. It was the only decent thing to do.

The door opened to reveal the hugest bouquet she'd ever seen, a riot of color and fragrance. Peeking through lavender irises and yellow roses were two deep brown eyes twinkling with mischief and humor.

"Gaetano, you shouldn't have. They're beautiful." Estelle took the flowers and leaned into the handsome Italian. He kissed both her cheeks and then grasped her firmly just above her elbows to pull her even closer. His lips found hers, and because her hands still held the flowers, she could do nothing but submit.

In fact, she not only submitted but responded in a way that parts of her anatomy suddenly awoke with the vigor and enthusiasm of a girl in her twenties. She certainly didn't feel like someone on the verge of death. Indeed, for the first time in ages, every nerve in her body felt as if it was doing cartwheels and back flips. Her eyes closed, and she wanted this to last forever.

"Ah, Estelle, *bella mia*, we are smushing the posies."

His voice brought her back to reality. Her eyes popped open and she met his dark chocolate gaze. He still grasped her body close to his, and she became aware of the firmness below his belt. She pulled reluctantly away.

"Oh, yes, of course. The flowers. I'll go put water on them. I mean, I'll put them in water."

He didn't release her but pulled her back to him. Estelle let go of the bundle she held. The paper unwrapped and Gaetano's floral offering fell to their feet, forgotten as her arms encircled his neck and her hands cradled his head. She laced her fingers into his crisp, dark hair and gave in to a passion that had lain dormant for too long. She heard someone moan and then realized the sound came from her.

Perhaps tomorrow she'd tell him to see other people. Or maybe next week would be better. Maybe never.

She wasn't thinking clearly. Her head was spinning, and somehow she found herself guiding Gaetano toward the hallway that led to her bedroom. Far off in the distance she got a faint whiff of beef cooking and cooking and cooking. It really didn't matter, though. Well-done wasn't a bad thing. And she did have a smoke alarm.

She pushed a twinge of guilt from her mind as they moved through her bedroom door and across the room to the king-sized bed covered with a custom-made comforter and pillows of all shapes and sizes. Holding her close, Gaetano inched his lips down her neck and then up to her ear. He finally found his way to the vee neckline of her blouse.

Estelle's heart pounded to the rhythm of jungle drums. Gaetano slid one arm around her waist, and with the other he swept all the pillows to the floor. The two of them fell—or pounced, Estelle wasn't sure which—onto the bed. Dinner was no longer a concern.

***

Gaetano moved closer to Estelle. It had been so long since he had taken a woman to bed and held her like this. He'd not been a saint all these years since Rosie's death; there had certainly been some sex, but none of those women had proven special. Not like Estelle. Nor had any of them been as beautiful.

He'd noted Estelle's lovely face at their first meeting, and she was just as beautiful now, naked and vulnerable. More so, perhaps. And she'd come to him without hesitation. While her body was not young, it was every bit as wonderful as he'd imagined. Her muscle tone was good, and thanks to his recent work to feed her there was now a supple fullness to her hips and breasts. He snuggled his chin further into the area just behind her ear and pulled her creamy soft back into his chest.

"Gaetano, are you sure this was a good idea?"

"At the moment, I can't think of one bad thing about it. Tonight was perfect for me, and I can only hope that I was not a disappointment to you."

86

"Disappointment? Oh my, no. You were...you... My God, Gaetano, I never dreamed making love could be that way. I'm not even sure if it truly happened or if I've been dreaming. No, dear man, you were magnificent. It is I who should worry. After all, this body is not what it used to be. It's deteriorated over the years."

"If your body is less, then thanks be to God, or I'd be a dead man! Oh, Estelle! I'm sorry. I didn't mean—"

"Oh, forget it. I know what you meant. But, I don't think you'd have had anything to worry about. You are a very strong man." She reached back and put her hand on his hip then let it slide up and down to his thigh, veering off course just enough to bring some of his anatomy to full attention again.

Gaetano chuckled and let his mind drift back to the event. They had both participated with all the vigor and enthusiasm of teenagers. He'd been nervous at the beginning, but his passion soon snuffed out any feelings of insecurity. He and Estelle had sailed into clouds of ecstasy as naturally as two lovers who'd been together forever. She'd responded to his touches as if she expected them, and she'd found ways to bring his body to a level of excitement he'd never known existed.

When he'd made love to Gina's mother, it had all been one-way. Rosie never made advances. Theirs had been a sweet love, but not one of great excitement. He'd adored his wife, but thinking back, their lovemaking had been mild compared to what he'd just experienced. Estelle was demanding and aggressive, yet generous and innovative. Surprising, how this fragile, ailing woman had such energy.

Estelle turned on her side and then propped herself upright. She faced Gaetano, gathering the sheet modestly in front of her, denying him any further views of her chest. "I hate to bring this up, but I think my invitation was for dinner."

Gaetano pushed himself up on one elbow but made no move to cover himself. Actually, he was hoping that the sight of his body would give her thoughts other than food. They could eat anytime, and he was pretty sure the smells coming from the kitchen were passing well-done toward charred.

He smiled and glanced downward. "I think we've had the main course, but I'd be up for dessert."

Estelle's eyes followed his. She giggled and dropped the sheet, exposing her breasts. "Gaetano, you are really bad. No, I must see to our dinner—if there's anything left, that is."

She leaned forward and kissed his forehead. Her breasts caressed his face, and the scent of her perfume stirred him with renewed desire. Then, before he could enfold her in his embrace, she escaped and left the bed, heading for the adjoining bathroom and grabbing a short, silk robe from the Queen Anne chair in the corner of the room. Slipping her arms into the robe, she turned on the small lamp on the table next to the chair and gathered her strewn clothing before disappearing behind the door.

Gaetano flopped back onto the pillow and relaxed his entire body. One thing about sex, it sure got rid of stress and tension. That's why Gina needed to be married to a good man who could supply lots of sex. And babies. His daughter was too uptight. Stressed out all the time. Always in court, and now she was going to have to defend herself, if there really was going to be a case with Alex's insurance company. She needed a husband more than ever.

Of course, Gina didn't have to be married to have sex, did she? He and Estelle weren't married. But, no. For Gina it must be marriage. It was different with him and Estelle. His lovely lady didn't have a lot of time left.

A wave of sadness washed over him, and a sobering realization that he was falling in love. He'd just wanted to ease her pain during these last days, and if sex helped Estelle forget, and brought her a bit of joy, that was the least he could do. And he'd wanted it himself. But now it was obvious that he couldn't just have casual sex with her. He wanted to be with Estelle forever.

As quickly as the sadness had come, anger took its place. If he had been totally alone and Estelle was not just in the adjoining bathroom, he'd have let loose with a string of oaths and rage that would have challenged the sounds of thunder. Instead, he doubled up his fist and walloped the pillow so hard that a few feathers burst from the cotton case.

Estelle emerged from the bathroom. She came to the edge of the bed, trailing the sweet scent of gardenias, leaned over him and smiled. "The bathroom's all yours if you want to freshen up, shower or whatever. I'll try to rescue dinner."

She kissed him then, and her lips lingered on his just long enough to push away his black mood, but she didn't stay long enough for him to pull her back into bed.

As she left the room, he admired the sway of her hips. He'd always liked the way she looked, but now that her body was less of a mystery to him, he liked it even more. He even felt a certain ownership. Not like she was his property, more like a gift entrusted to him.

A lump rose in his throat as he was reminded how very temporary their connection would be.

***

Estelle was standing at the range when Gaetano joined her in the kitchen. The roast sat on a platter…well, actually it sprawled on a dish. And while it wasn't blackened, it didn't have even a tinge of pink. Fortunately, it had been an expensive cut and many people still liked it well-done. She could only hope Gaetano was one of them.

The beautiful bouquet he'd brought was now recovering in a vase. Only a couple of the blooms had been damaged beyond repair. Those she'd cut short and arranged in a small bowl of shallow water.

She smiled at Gaetano in the doorway. His dark hair was damp and combed. The tinge of gray at his sideburns gave him a distinguished look.

"Is there something I can do to help?" he asked as he approached and slid his arms around her waist.

For a moment she couldn't say anything. These feelings he evoked in her were wonderful, and she didn't want them to stop, and yet the reality was that she had no control over the future. What were the two of them doing?

She gave herself a mental shake, pulled away from his embrace and quickly lifted the tall vase of his flowers from the counter. "You can take these into the dining room and set them on the hutch. They might be too tall for the table."

Gaetano seemed to sense her uneasiness and did as she asked. That was a relief. After what they'd shared in her bedroom, would he understand why she was trying to pull back now? He must know that they couldn't let this relationship, or affair, or whatever it was, continue. There was no point. Was there?

Estelle followed him into the dining room with the entrée. She'd already uncorked the wine and lit the candles; the salad and side dishes were also on the table. She placed the meat dish, too.

When Gaetano had deposited the flowers, he turned back and pulled out her chair for her. Estelle thanked him and sat down. She waited until Gaetano had taken the chair across from her then added, "The roast may not be very good, I'm afraid."

He scoffed. "What are you talking about? It is perfect. Everything is beautiful, and so are you. I am honored to be here."

Suddenly, she wasn't embarrassed, and as she smiled, Gaetano poured the wine, complimented her on the choice, and apologized for not bringing a bottle of his own along with the flowers.

The meal followed, and lively conversation. But as the last of the food was being consumed, Gaetano dabbed his mouth with his napkin and cleared his throat, looking uncomfortable. "Have you talked to Alex recently? What's he been doing?"

Estelle had a feeling she knew where he was headed, and she intended to be just as circumspect. "Oh, it's funny you should bring up the children. Alex is so upset right now with some misunderstanding with Gina. I was hoping you could intervene."

Gaetano nodded. "Yes, Gina mentioned something to me about him taking her to court."

"The poor boy's had to cancel his trip and is in a state of confusion. And he's not taking her to court because he wants to. He has no choice."

Gaetano's voice hinted at irritation. "Of *course* he has a choice. He could simply accept the check that was offered."

She shook her head. Her back straightened, and she squared her shoulders and tucked her chin down, leveling her gaze to meet his. Her voice was perhaps an octave higher than usual. "The check was a joke. It wasn't near enough to cover the damage. Gina should—"

"Estelle." Gaetano's voice was low and he spoke through gritted teeth. "I think we should look at both sides of this situation. I told Gina that Alex has some rights. I am being very open-minded. I think you should be too."

"I do see both sides," Estelle said. She slapped the tablecloth with her palm and startled Gaetano, but she didn't stop to apologize. "Gina is a lovely girl, but you've spoiled her. She is used to things going her way."

"Look, *cara*, I don't want to get into an argument, but it's obvious you only see your son's side." His voice was no longer low.

Critiques of his daughter and parenting were clearly not things he was used to. He leaned forward in his chair and asked, "Do you have any idea of what Gina is feeling? Maybe if you understood Gina's position, you could talk some sense into your son."

Estelle shrugged. "Alex is being very sensible. He didn't want this to go to court, and he told me so. He says Gina refuses to discuss it. What can he do if she won't talk? He has no choice."

Gaetano stopped. He took a deep breath and sat back in his chair, and the crease between his eyebrows relaxed. He then smiled at Estelle and gestured with upward palms. "Please. Let's not push this out of proportion. Our children will obviously have to come to some agreement outside of a courtroom because Gina always wins. Alex will have to accept the check that was offered in the first place."

Estelle sat up straighter in her chair. "He will not. Unless of course Gina has bribed the judge." Her tone sharpened. "I know some attorneys are in bed with judges."

Gaetano was obviously losing a battle to control his emotions. The crease between his brows returned, and it was even deeper. His dark eyes flashed not with warmth or passion but anger. "Are you speaking literally or figuratively?"

"How should I know? Maybe both," she answered, then looked down at her hands as if inspecting her manicure. She didn't want to be cruel, but Gaetano was being ridiculous. And they had been acting too close for her comfort anyway.

"Estelle! My Gina is a good girl." The veins on his temples popped out, and his face flushed dark red. "She does not sleep around. Not...not like someone else I know."

Estelle's jaw dropped, and her eyes widened in disbelief. Had he really just said that? The blood drained from Gaetano's face as quickly as it had risen, but a quiet rage replaced Estelle's sorrow. She clenched her manicured hands into fists, squinted at him, and very calmly said, "Excuse me? You…Are you saying I'm a loose woman because I let myself be lured and manipulated into bed with you?"

She didn't give him time to reply, either. Before he spoke, she stood and threw her napkin onto the table. Then, crossing her arms in front of her chest, she turned her back to him.

"Lured? Manipulated?" Gaetano's voice cracked. She heard him also stand, and from the corner of her eye she saw him clench and unclench his fists. When he spoke again, his tone was strained but had an edge of steel. "Just a short while ago it was you who led the way to your bedroom. Now I know why. You want me to intervene with Gina."

Estelle turned, shocked. Without thinking, she grabbed her wine glass and tossed the contents into Gaetano's face. "How dare you insinuate that I would use sex to gain an advantage? I think you should leave."

Gaetano looked taken aback. He wiped his face then threw down his napkin. His eyes searched hers, and a moment later sadness had replaced all anger. It was as if he were silently pleading for some kind of reprieve.

It broke her heart, but she couldn't give him what he wanted. It wasn't like they had a future, anyway. Maybe this had been a blessing, an easy escape. She didn't know how to tell him that she cared about him and didn't want to lose him. This way, she wouldn't have to. Yes, this was for the best.

He opened his mouth then closed it without saying anything. His head bent and his chin rested almost on his chest. Then he sighed heavily, turned, and left. She heard the front door open and then slam shut.

She reminded herself one more time that this was for the best.

Chapter 9

Alex slammed his front door so hard that he heard his neighbor's pictures fall off the wall. He knew this was not the frame of mind he should have when he was due in court, but it was difficult to cool off. How in God's green earth had things gotten this far? Was a car really worth it? He'd been replaced on his last assignment with the magazine when it became apparent that this whole mess was going to court and he'd said he wanted to stay. It wasn't clear whether he'd actually be called to testify, but he just wanted to be there. Though he didn't want to admit it, it was partly to see Gina in action. He definitely wanted to watch her lose.

He stormed down the stairs to the underground garage and punched in the security code. The metal door rolled up and back, exposing one cause of his frustration. The Ferrari 612 Scaglietta. It was a magnificent machine. Even in dim lighting, it made his breath catch. He'd never imagined owning such a car, and yet he no longer felt the same satisfaction it used to bring. Somehow, the image of Gina's face pushed into his thoughts and took away all joy.

He'd never have a chance with her now. She was apparently still too angry to answer his calls, and when he'd gone over to talk in person, she'd slammed the door in his face. That had been several days ago.

Now his mother was unhappy with him, too. Evidently she and Gaetano had fought over this. His beautiful car seemed to have an unpleasant effect on a lot of people. Only the auto body shop personnel seemed to appreciate its splendor. The auto-body shop personnel and him.

Alex got into the Ferrari, but when the engine roared to life, instead of feeling stimulated as he usually did, he felt as if all his energy was being sucked from his body and out the exhaust pipes.

He'd never intended to let the situation go this far.

**

Gina got out of the elevator and strode toward the courtroom. She'd felt uneasy all morning, and not just because this was a case directly related to her own happiness and well-being. For one thing, she was almost positive she'd seen a car following her this morning that had been parked on a side street near her condo. She'd purposely driven up to the second level of the courthouse parking complex just to see if it followed, but so many other vehicles entered the garage that she'd lost sight of the older model green sedan. If she found it parked near her place again, she'd take down the license number.

The other thing that niggled at her was Boris. The Russian had been leaving messages on her answering machine, had tried to set another appointment with her at the office, and now he was seated in the spectators section of the courtroom. She'd seen him in the hallway, but assumed he was here for a different case. She was definitely going to take legal action if he became any more intrusive.

Gina sat primly at one of the tables in front of the judge's bench and attempted to look calmer than she felt. She closed her eyes for just a second. A moment later, when she opened them, she saw her nemesis.

**

Alex joined his attorney at one of the front tables and stole a glance at Gina who sat alone on the opposite side of the courtroom. She looked so little, if attractively dressed in that dark business suit.

Watching her brought Alex a pang of guilt and remorse. There was something about this girl that made him want to protect her. It made no sense. Because, in reality, she was pretty capable of taking care of herself. In fact, she was doing so at his expense.

The bailiff marched to the center of the room and announced, "All rise. Court is in session. The Honorable Malcolm B. Smith presiding."

The judge appeared and took his place. The court stenographer sat at a small portable recording station, hands poised to transcribe all of the testimonies.

The preliminary instructions were read, and as this was a no-jury trial, things went very quickly. Alex's attorney gave a brief statement explaining his client's position and the amount of damages they were seeking. Then it was Gina's turn to address the court. She rose from her table and cleared her throat.

"Your Honor, normally the States Wide Insurance Company's legal representative would be presenting this case. But as a member of the bar as well as a client of States Wide, they have agreed to my representing myself and the insurance company in this procedure."

Alex wasn't really listening to what Gina was saying. He caught the tone of her voice, though, and the way she emphasized some phrases. She handed some documents to the bailiff, who passed them on to the judge. What were they? He wondered.

"So, you see, Your Honor, by the estimates I have presented, the amount that my opponent is demanding is totally inflated and out of line."

The judge shuffled the papers he'd been given, then some others, and he said, "Ms. Lorenzo, I understood that Mr. Bennett had non-regulation paint on his vehicle. I'm looking at the documents his attorney presented, and it appears therein lies the problem. Were you unaware of this fact?"

"Your Honor, I knew the paint was a special mix, but that's my point." Gina walked from behind her table and stood directly in front of it, right in line with the judge's gaze. "Since it was specially mixed and not available in touch-up amounts, the entire car has to be repainted."

Gina paused as if to let that information sink into the judge's brain; then she continued in a tone so agreeable one had to wonder why she had even made an appearance here. "I don't deny that this is the only possible solution since the paint cannot be matched. However," she went on, and here was definitely a change in tone. She was no longer so agreeable but sharp and pointed. "Nowhere is there, in any of the agreements presented to me or to my insurance company, any verbiage or instructions stating that the car has to be painted with this special mix again. The agreement was simply that the entire car should be repainted—which we agreed to do at a cost in the range of any of those estimates I presented to you in this courtroom today."

Alex stole a glance at his attorney, who sat slack-jawed and mute.

The judge leaned forward and peered down at Gina from his lofty station. "Counselor, is it my understanding that you are willing to have the car repainted, but not with the specialty paint that is on it now?"

"That's correct. Your Honor, it states in the original claim simply that the car shall be repainted in total and not just touched up. It does not state what kind of paint shall be used. Therefore, I submit that the estimations I brought into court today are fair evaluations of a full automobile paint job with any of the standard available high-grade vehicle paints."

Gina returned to her seat and sat with her hands folded in front of her. She gave him a quick, smug smile, and Alex thought she looked like a schoolgirl who'd just correctly spelled a difficult word the rest of the class had missed.

The judge leaned back in his chair, seeming to give the option serious consideration, before Alex's attorney found his voice. "Your Honor, I object. This is totally unfair to my client. He has the right to have his car restored to its original condition—and that means *with* the specialty paint."

"I am sure that is what your client intended," the judge replied, "but unfortunately that is not what was put in the claim. As Ms. Lorenzo points out, it only says the car has to be totally repainted."

"But Your Honor, any idiot should know that we're in court to have the car restored to its original state. The offer to just repaint was refused, so it's obvious."

"Your Honor," Gina rebutted, now on her feet, "I would like to assure the court that I am not an idiot, regardless of my colleague's opinion." She smiled at Alex's attorney, as if to forgive him. "No, I'm willing to do exactly what they have asked, which is to restore the vehicle to its original state. Which is"—Gina picked up a legal pad and read—"'Flash Red, code 37FS3' paint, the color and mix that was on the car when it was shipped to the United States from Italy. Every good import automotive dealer has this paint in stock, as it was a very popular shade for that model."

"That's why I changed it!" Alex bellowed.

His attorney frowned. "Mr. Bennett, please, I'll do the talking."

"Counselor, please control your client." The judge pushed aside the sheaf of papers before him. Leaning his elbows on the desk, he laced his fingers together and rested his chin upon them to say, "I think I've heard enough. Frankly, this case should never have gotten this far." Not bothering to disguise a disgusted sigh, he picked up a couple of photos from the folder on his desk and then looked straight at Alex. "I must admit, Mr. Bennett, the photos you submitted do show that the Ferrari is—or was—one of a kind. It's a beauty. I'm sure it can go pretty fast...."

For a moment, the judge seemed lost in thought, but finally he put the photos down and looked at Alex's attorney. "However, since in the preparation of the case your legal staff was not specific as to what kind of paint had to be used, I'm awarding the decision to the defendant. Mr. Bennett, you and the Trans-Globe Insurance Company are instructed to accept the highest estimate of repair offered by the defendant. If you want to pursue non-regulation or specialty paint for the vehicle, the difference in cost shall be borne by the owner and/or his insurance company." The judge cracked his mallet to the desktop and said, "Court is adjourned."

Alex slumped in his chair, shocked. What a gross miscarriage of justice! Apparently his attorney felt the same, but the man quickly recovered and pushed some papers over for a signature. He didn't even look as Alex scribbled his name, just muttered something about mistakes filling out paperwork and this being the way legal interns lost jobs and then made his way to the exit.

Alex watched Gina gather up her materials and stuff them into her briefcase. She turned to leave but then, as if on impulse, walked over to him. He remained seated, still in a daze of disbelief.

"Alex, I *am* sorry about this. I feel like I should at least offer to buy you a drink."

He stared up at her. She actually seemed sincere, but could he really believe anything she said? Part of him wanted to jump up and say, "Let's go." But he couldn't quite get around the fact that she'd stuck him with the expense of getting his car fixed after she was the one who'd ruined it.

"Somehow I don't feel like joining your victory celebration," he found himself saying. "I don't think a drink is going to make it all better."

"Oh, come on Alex. It's a car." She regarded him again with those incredible eyes, and Alex remembered again how much she'd occupied his thoughts the past few weeks. He remembered that it *was* just a car. And he was getting it repainted, just not in the original color.

Exactly. He couldn't get past what had just happened.

"You know, Gina, I'm sure you were just doing what you do best, and you won. Congratulations. I do like you, and I'm sure we could eventually find a way to get along. But, right now I can't forget that I got screwed, so thanks but no thanks." He stood, gave Gina a long look and shook his head. "Pity," he mumbled, and then he left her standing alone.

***

After leaving the courthouse, Gina drove down the freeway toward her home, but she couldn't quite bring herself to face the silent walls and empty rooms. Usually she was on a high after winning a case. She'd been smart, and now her insurance company loved her. Not only had she won the case but they hadn't even had to pay for a separate attorney. Regardless of this, she felt small and ineffectual.

She took the off ramp that would lead her to Gaetano's Ristorante. Above all things, she needed her Papá right now. He always knew how to pull her out of the dumps. She hoped she wouldn't run into Alex's mother there, though. She wasn't sure she had the courage to face another Bennett.

Why did she feel so guilty? She'd presented a good, solid case. Alex's attorneys had dropped the ball, and she'd picked it up and run it back for a touchdown. So, why did she feel like she'd thrown a party and nobody came?

She entered the restaurant and quickly scanned the interior. Satisfied that Mrs. Bennett was not present, Gina walked toward the back of the building. It was still a bit early for the dinner crowd, but there were a few people lingering over wine or coffee after a late lunch. Her dad was probably putting the finishing touches on his special sauce for the evening menu.

"Hi, Mario," Gina called out. "Is Papá in the back?"

"Oh, Gina, I am so glad you're here. I was going to call you."

"What's wrong?" The look on her old friend's face was alarming. Mario was always smiling and easygoing; no matter what happened Mario could always make the best of it. But he didn't look like he was making the best of anything at the moment.

"Your father is not here. He called and said he wasn't coming in. I say, 'Are you sick?' and he says, 'No, I'm not sick' and then he hangs up. No explanation, no nothing. Just hung up the phone! I am worried."

Gina's breath caught. "My God, Mario, what could be the matter? That's not like Papá."

"No. I think he is sick to his heart."

"He's had a heart attack? Oh my God, Mario, I've got to go."

"No," her father's friend interrupted. "Not a heart attack, but his heart. I think it's broken. For two days now, no Estelle Bennett, no phone calls, and your papá…he walks around and sighs. Big, heavy sighs. No talking, no eating, and his famous *Costolette d'Agnello alla Calabrese*? One big mess."

Gina couldn't count the times her father had served that lamb chop dish. It was one of the recipes handed down from her grandmother, and it wasn't just a meal but an experience. "What happened? He can prepare that dish blindfolded."

"I know," Mario said. "But the small rib chops should be cooked briefly to a flaming pink to hold their juices, not overcooked to a ghastly gray. The sauce should have tender but firm green peppers, onions stirred to a rich gold with fresh plum tomatoes, olives and Italian flat-leaf parsley added." Mario threw his hands up and continued, "Gaetano, he put the peppers in the skillet and then he wandered off, walking out to dining room and staring out the window. Soon, the peppers, the onions, the tomatoes—all scorched and all mushy." He put his palms to his cheeks. "What your father poured over the chops was a mushy mess. *Che Macello!* It was awful."

"How could this happen?"

Mario shrugged as if he couldn't believe it either. "Gina, do you know what he did then? He tossed everything out along with the chops. That night, no specialty dish. Gaetano is very sick man."

For once, Gina agreed. "I better go see him. Thanks, Mario. Can you handle everything here?"

It was a stupid question, she realized a moment later. Mario had been at the restaurant for as long as Gina could remember. He'd kept things going when her mother had been ill and her father was spending almost every waking hour at her bedside. Mario not only had kept the restaurant going, he'd kept Gina from feeling totally abandoned.

Moving much too fast, she reached her father's driveway in record time then took a few minutes to survey the exterior of the small but neat bungalow. She was intimately familiar with every aspect of her childhood home, yet today she scrutinized each detail as if she were seeing it for the first time. Somehow she hoped it would reconnect her with her past and maybe provide the guidance she needed to help her father.

The well-maintained yard didn't give the appearance of a home without a woman's touch. Staunch hedges stood erect, neatly trimmed, separating the property from the neighbors on either side. The flower boxes under the two front windows held blossoms of varied colors. These blooms swayed slightly in the light breeze, as if waving to everyone passing by. No peeling paint could be found on the fascia boards, and no weeds dared to grow in the circular rose garden near the front porch.

Three rose bushes stood in the small garden, each planted for a different one of Gaetano's special girls. The first, the color of pale lavender, was for Gina's *nonna,* who'd died before Gina was born. The deep red one was for Rosie, Gina's *madre,* and the last, a bright, loud yellow, was for Gina, because her Papá always said she was the sunshine in his life.

Gina got out of her car and approached the front door. She hesitated a minute and then turned the knob to let herself inside. It was frightening, and it was all Gina could do to keep from bursting into hysterics and go racing through the house until she was in her dad's arms.

"Papá, are you home?"

"I'm here, Gina, come in."

Gina's gaze scanned the living room as she moved from the small foyer into the house. She found her father seated in a chair in the corner that her mother always used to knit, or to mend the knees in Gina's play pants, sewing colorful little flowers over the holes that always seemed to appear after Gina wore them only a time or two. The drapes were drawn and no lamps were lit, even though the sun had begun to sink into the west. Dusk was not far off.

"Papá, what are you doing in the dark?" Gina hurried to his side and pulled up the footstool she used to sit on when she was a child. "Are you sick? I went by the restaurant, and Mario said you called in."

"No, I'm not physically sick, but I am very sad, Gina. I have hurt someone very special and I don't know how to fix it."

"Papá, I've never seen you like this," Gina said. Actually, however, she had. She'd seen him this way a long time ago. She'd been a bit past seven years old, and she'd come home from school to find him in this chair just as he was now. She'd sat on this same small footstool and stared up at him. Her knees stuck up a bit higher now than when she was seven, and instead of looking up at her papá she was now eye level with him.

Gina hadn't understood what death was, then. Once she'd seen a sparrow fly into the front window, and when she'd picked it up, it didn't move. She'd taken it to her father and together they had buried it in the back yard. That day he'd told her a story about angels coming down and seeing how sick her mama was, how they'd lifted her up into the clouds. He'd told her that her mama was with Jesus. He'd never really even said that her mother died, and for a while she'd thought Mama had just taken a trip and would be back to put her to bed just like always. Later she'd heard her cousins talking and realized her mama was never coming back. She'd wondered why her Papá hadn't let her help bury Mama in the back yard.

"Papá, tell me what you're talking about," she said now.

It took him a while, but finally Gina coaxed from Gaetano the story of Estelle's terminal illness. Then her father confessed that he had fallen in love for a second time, and again he would have to give up the woman he loved.

"The very worst thing is that we quarreled, and now I am denied the opportunity to make her last days joyful. I made her very angry. We fought about you, Gina, and about her son Alex."

"Oh, Papá! I am so sorry." If she hadn't felt guilty and troubled before, she certainly did now. She'd never intended for her affairs to affect her father's relationship with Estelle. Gina had to admit she was surprised to hear Gaetano was in love with Estelle. She wasn't sure how she felt about that. But if things were different, if Alex hadn't sued her, if he hadn't had a stupid expensive car, if she had been more careful and not banged his door like an idiot—

Things couldn't be worse. Today's victory in court felt empty, and she'd have traded it in a heartbeat to see her father happy.

Chapter 10

"What do you mean I'm as healthy as a horse?" Estelle sat on the edge of her chair. It seemed like the tests had been a million years ago; since meeting Gaetano, it was as if she'd been living another life.

Estelle looked at the doctor straight on. "Is this your idea of a joke? I have known my diagnosis since that follow-up visit when the results came in. I came here today to make you own up to your deception." Dr. Bob didn't say a word; she didn't let him. She took a deep breath and continued, because she didn't want him to try to deny the truth. "Stop trying to keep things from me. I know I'm dying. I heard you say so on the phone. I can take it, though. I don't have anything to live for anyway. I can go, and I doubt if I'll even be missed."

After the recent fight with Gaetano, she'd felt her condition finally start to take its toll. She'd supposed it was inevitable. At least she'd had a brief period of happiness with that handsome, kind man, even if it was now being snatched unfairly away.

"Estelle, what are you talking about? If you overheard me say anything on the phone about someone dying, I most certainly wasn't referring to you." Dr. Taylor took his glasses out of his pocket and put them on. Estelle saw an incredulous look creep across his face, a suspicious look, like the one people get when confronted with bizarre and outrageous behavior. He lowered his tone and said slowly, "Your only problem was slight anemia. The medication I gave you should have helped that. Aren't you less tired now, and hasn't your appetite increased?"

He didn't wait for an answer. Consulting the file folder in front of him, the doctor pulled out a piece of paper, ran his finger across it, then smiled. "Yes, you've picked up six and a half pounds, which you needed to do. You lost so much weight during Marty's illness, I was a bit concerned."

Estelle pulled a Kleenex out of her purse and dabbed at the tears that had suddenly welled up, threatening to smear her carefully applied mascara and run down perfectly made-up cheeks. "Are you saying I don't have leukemia?"

"Leukemia? Of course not. Good grief, woman, have you looked in the mirror lately? You're absolutely glowing with good health. In fact, I may start taking some of your meds if they have such a positive effect on everyone."

Estelle blinked, processing. Her longtime physician and friend had just told her that not only was she not dying, but to the contrary, she was in excellent health.

"Estelle," her doctor said in a patient voice, "I've shown you the results of the tests. I would have explained them to you when you were here the last time, but you left in such a hurry. What else can I tell you? What do you not understand? Leukemia? Why would you—? Oh." It was as if a light went on in his brain. "You must have overheard me talking about my dog. Sally and I just lost our cat Tootsie, remember, and I didn't want to tell her that old Barney was going to go next. Sometimes I think she loved that dog more than me!"

Estelle continued to just stare. She probably ought to show some gratitude toward Dr. Bob, excitement, or at least acknowledgment of his generous compliments about her appearance. Instead she was dumbfounded. Her illness had been the catalyst for her relationship with Gaetano, a total stranger whom she'd let him inside her thoughts, her home… *My God, my bedroom!*

"Estelle, are you all right? You act as if I have delivered a death sentence. You are happy with this news, aren't you?"

"What? Oh, yes, it's wonderful news." She lifted her chin and met the doctor's probing gaze. *He must think I'm crazy.* "It's just that I've been living as if each day was my last."

Dr. Bob chuckled. "Well, my dear lady, I've been told that we all should live that way if we want to get the most out of life. I keep telling myself to cut back and take time to really enjoy some of the good things."

Estelle's brain raced a mile a minute while her thoughts kept going back to that stupid, stupid fight she'd had with Gaetano. "So, what you're saying is that I am *not* dying. I do not have a blood disease, and I can go back to living my normal life?"

"Absolutely. But, Estelle, if I were you I'd stick to your new guide for living. It obviously agrees with you. If more people lived each day to the fullest, I doubt if we'd have so much disease and death in the world. I'm a scientist, but I also know that a positive outlook can have a huge effect on one's health."

"Yes, I'm sure that's true," Estelle allowed. "Well, I mustn't keep you any longer. I did more or less muscle my way into your office this morning without an appointment. Thank you Dr. Bob."

The physician closed the file on his desk, got out of his chair, and opened the door for her. "That's quite all right. You sounded upset, and I'm glad to clear things up. Next time, though, just ask questions. I don't keep my patients in the dark about their health."

Estelle stood and gave her friend a quick hug on her way out, then nodded at the receptionist and exited the waiting room. When she got to her car, she didn't start it up right away, however. She needed to process this news. It put things in a whole new perspective.

All she had been thinking about recently was Gaetano. She'd never have put it in words to a living soul, but secretly she'd missed him as much as Marty. Maybe more. When Marty died, she'd resigned herself to a life without him, but Gaetano was very much alive. Now she wasn't going to die, at least not in the near future. She needed to know exactly what Gaetano's feelings were for her.

Of course, the original idea had been for the two of them to join forces to get their children together. Most likely that was out. Gina and Alex probably hated each other now. She wondered if anything could be salvaged out of either relationship.

Well, she wasn't going to die and knew what had to be done. Estelle put her key in the ignition and started the engine. She put the car in gear and pointed it toward the nearest exit of the medical center parking lot, sure that the only decent thing was to swing by Gaetano's place and let him know the news. That way, if he was having any feelings of regret for being insensitive and downright rude to someone hovering at death's door, she could relieve him of that guilt. Somehow, forgiving him seemed easier now; his rudeness seemed less offensive since she'd been declared in excellent health.

That was one reason to go to the restaurant. Another was that she wanted to see him again. She wanted to touch him. She wanted to make love with him again.

Of course, he might not feel the same. He'd never said he loved her. Why should he? She'd been a dying woman and he was alive— so beautifully, sexily alive, with such wonderful talents beyond her imagination. He had made her life so much better. Not even counting the fantastic sex, they'd simply enjoyed each other's company. They'd laughed—a lot. He'd treated her like a rare treasure and seemed to delight in simply surprising her with small gifts or spur of the moment jaunts to out-of-the-way places.

It was strange, how different Gaetano was to Marty. Not that she hadn't loved her late husband. She had. Dearly. But Marty had been so serious and predictable. He'd never taken her for barefoot walks on the beach on the way to the opera. He would never have dared to leave work to pick her up and drive to the top of Mt. Soledad just to watch the sunset.

If Gaetano doesn't feel about me the way I hope he does, I might as well be dead.

It was a grim pronouncement, but one Estelle felt all the same. She put on the turn signal and steered her car toward the off ramp that led to Gaetano's restaurant. She was going to live, but did she have a future?

***

The bell rang several times before Alex opened the door of his townhouse. It was a shock to see Gina Lorenzo standing there. She couldn't be inviting him out for a drink again, could she? If so, he was going to accept. Perhaps it was time to let bygones be bygones.

"Please," she said. "Don't slam the door. I know you feel you have a perfect right to, but we need to talk." And with that she pushed past him into his living room. She looked quickly around and soon had herself seated in the one chair that wasn't covered with clothing, camera equipment, or other paraphernalia he was sorting out for his next trip; he'd gotten a call that they'd need him in Indonesia in a few days.

A wave of annoyance washed over him. "If you're here to gloat, please spare me. I've been sufficiently put in my place. At least I've been beaten by the legal system."

"No. I'm not like that. I really am sorry that things turned out like they did. I can't help it, though. When I get in a court room, I have to win."

Alex sighed. He shut the door, pushed a stack of folded shirts out of his way and sat down on the sofa opposite her. "So, if it's not to rub salt in my wounds, and you've already said you're sorry, twice, why are you here?"

"Have you talked with your mother recently?"

"My mother? Yeah, sure. I talked to her after I left the courthouse. Why?" He suddenly wondered if his mother had called Gina and said something rude. No, that couldn't be it. His mother rarely got into his business.

"Did she say how she was feeling? Did you ask her how her health was?" Gina's words were clipped and held an accusatory tone.

"Excuse me? My mother is fine. She takes good care of herself. Oh, her health went down a bit after my dad died, but she's doing better now."

Gina snorted. "A lot you know. You worry yourself silly over a stupid car while your own mother's dying. My God, what's wrong with you?"

"My mother is dying? Are you nuts? Listen, you may be a hotshot in the court room, but your idea of a practical joke stinks." He stared at her with every intention of calling 911 to come and remove her from his house, but Gina didn't look crazy. And then tears welled up in those big beautiful eyes and began to spill out through her thick lashes and down her face.

"Oh my God," she said. "You didn't know. Why didn't she tell you? I'm sorry, I just assumed...I can't believe you didn't know." She got up from her chair and sat on the arm of the sofa, reached out, and put her arm around Alex's shoulders. "I'm not very good at stuff like this. I never meant to..." Her words trailed off, and she pulled his head into her chest and rubbed his back.

Alex pulled away and looked at Gina squarely. "What do you mean, my mother is dying? How would you know and not me?"

"She's known for a while. Papá said that she'd just gotten the news the day they met."

He let Gina pull his head next to her chest again. She was muttering about how sorry she was, while he racked his brain to remember if his mother's voice had given any hint of her ill health.

She'd sounded a bit subdued, but he'd figured that was because of the argument she'd had with Gaetano.

Suddenly, it registered what Gina had said: Gaetano had known from the very first day they'd met. Her own son she'd kept in the dark, but an almost total stranger had been her confidant!

Alex jerked his head away. "Your dad told you my mother was dying? Why didn't he tell me? I'm her son, for God's sake."

"Listen, I know it hurts, but you have to understand. My father's in love with your mother and was abiding by her wishes not to tell anyone. Since their argument they haven't spoken, and he's falling apart. I went over to check on him since he hasn't gone to the restaurant for days. It just came out. It never occurred to me that you didn't really know. I just thought you were being closed up about it."

"*He's* falling apart! My God, there's no way I can leave in two days for Indonesia. My job is never going to forgive me."

Alex put his head in his hands, and suddenly the dam broke. He convulsed with sobs that shook his insides like an earthquake. His job was one thing, but there was an even more horrifying prospect on the horizon. Once again he was to become familiar with heart-wrenching pain. He was going to lose his mother.

He was faintly aware of Gina's arms holding him. Her body rocked with his, and her tears joined his in grief.

***

Across the street from where Gina had parked her car, Boris sat and watched. He'd made it a practice to watch her comings and goings. It had irritated him that she hadn't called to thank him for the flowers yet. She had to know they were from him. He hadn't seen evidence of any other suitors, and this pretty boy she'd beat in court wouldn't be sending her gifts. He'd sat in on that case to watch her in action and to give her a chance to acknowledge his gift, but she'd ignored him. And, what was she even doing here anyway?

He needed to get her attention. Boris frowned and chewed at his thumbnail. Things were not going well for him. He had his job back but was getting no more respect than before. What else could he do?

Yesterday he'd had another run-in with a fellow employee, and the bastard had probably told his side to the manager by now. Boris had left early and was seriously thinking of calling in sick for tomorrow. Let them see how much he would be missed if he was not there. He was a valuable employee, and it was time his boss gave him the respect he deserved, not to mention an increase in salary.

Boris checked the time and realized he'd been sitting in his car for over an hour. What was Gina doing in that man's house?

He also became aware of a full bladder. Did he dare step out of the car and relieve himself? No, there was too much foot traffic, people jogging or walking dogs. He didn't want to leave this spot, but he couldn't call attention to himself either. Reluctantly, he started the car and drove away to search for a gas station. He'd pick one with a convenience store and get something to eat, too, before he returned to wait for Gina.

He really had to find a way to win back her attention.

Chapter 11

Estelle paused as she grasped the handle of the restaurant door. Had it not been for a couple trying to enter behind her, she might have turned tail and escaped. As it was, she had no choice but to go in. She moved to one side and let the couple pass to the hostess station to be seated.

Hanging back, she let her gaze scan the dining room. She didn't see Gaetano, but he might be in the kitchen creating another masterpiece, or he might be in the small cubicle he called an office.

"Hi, Mrs. B. It's nice to see you. Would you like a table or a booth?"

"Oh, Debbie, I didn't see you." The perky hostess had startled Estelle. "Uh, actually I came to see your boss. Is he in the back?"

Shifting the stack of menus she was holding, Debbie shook her head. "No, he's not. Mario's in charge today. Would you like to speak to him?"

"Gaetano's not here?" That wasn't like him. Before the hostess could answer, however, Estelle saw Mario motioning to her from the dining area. "Never mind, Debbie. I see Mario."

She skirted the tables, careful not to bump any diners. The room was fairly full and gave all appearance of business as usual. Except...Estelle looked around, and though servers were delivering plates of steaming pasta, pizzas, and other entrées to the occupied tables, the restaurant seemed somehow bleaker.

Estelle's smile faded when she saw the look on Mario's face. A deep frown pinched the space between his brows, and beneath his thick mustache his mouth was drawn into a severe line.

He wiped his hands on the small towel hanging from his apron and shook Estelle's extended hand then guided her to an area near the kitchen out of the way of the foot traffic. "Oh, Ms. Estelle, it is good you came. Gaetano has not been in for three days. I call his house and all he says is 'You take care of things, Mario.'"

"Is he sick? Have you been to see him?"

"I've tried to go, but Ms. Estelle, I have no time. I'm doing all the work here. I order supplies, I cook, I manage the crew, and then on top of everything I have to make the bank deposits. I'm very tired, but I am worried, too."

"Have you talked to Gina? What does she say?"

"She was going to check up on Gaetano, but I don't hear nothing back from her."

Estelle was doubly concerned now. "Mario, try not to worry. I'll go see Gaetano right away. I'm sure it's nothing serious," she reassured him, but she wasn't sure of anything.

She hurried out of the restaurant and drove as fast as she dared to Gaetano's house. Relieved to see his car, she parked right behind it, got out, and walked to the front door. Her thumb punched the bell several times with only seconds between each push.

"*Mama mia*, what crazy nut's making such a racket?"

Estelle took a step backward when Gaetano opened the door. He resembled a snarling bear whose nap had been disturbed. His eyes were angry and hard until they focused on her. His gaze immediately softened.

"Estelle?" He opened the door wider and tried to tuck his shirt in at the same time. He rubbed one hand across his stubbled chin and said, "I wanted to call, so many times, but...but I didn't think you'd ever want to talk to me again. I'm so sorry—"

"Oh, Gaetano. I picked up the phone a dozen times to call you too. I behaved badly. I'm sorry, too." She reached out and laid her fingers on his arm.

He took her hand and pulled her across the threshold, then wrapped his arms around her and buried his head in the hollow of her neck. "Estelle, you have nothing to apologize for. I am a pig-headed, stubborn man. You have enough to deal with. Your health is the most important thing, and I didn't even give that any consideration. Please forgive me."

Estelle couldn't believe how good it felt to have his strong arms around her. Even his whiskers rubbing her neck almost raw felt like heaven.

"Gaetano, about my health—"

"No. We're not talking about anything sad. We're going to be happy, and we'll never again mention our silly disagreement either."

"Well, actually, we do need to talk just for a few minutes." She pushed gently against his chest to create a narrow space between them. "You think I'm dying."

He almost cringed. "Estelle, no. Don't even put it in words." He pulled her back into his firm grasp and cradled her head with one hand.

"Gaetano, I saw my doctor and I'm fine."

The man slowly relaxed his hold and gazed at her, searching to understand her words. "What do you mean by 'fine'? Has the medicine put you in…what do they call it? Remission?"

Estelle smiled and thought her heart was going to burst. This man truly cared for her. She didn't need any more proof than to look into his eyes. She wanted to shout with joy. Instead, she took his face in her hands and gently kissed his lips.

"No, you darling man," she said. "I'm not in remission—because I was never really sick."

"What are you saying? We can't stand here like this. Come in, I need to sit down because maybe now I'm sick." Gaetano shook his head and then reached around her to shut the door. "I am very confused."

They sat on the sofa, and Estelle explained what had happened and how it was all a big mistake. When she was finished, Gaetano jumped to his feet and stretched his arms into the air as if cheering his favorite sports team.

"Estelle, this is wonderful news! I am so happy for you. I am happy for me." Then his arms fell to his sides. He stared at her for several seconds before he spoke. "I *am* happy for me too, aren't I? Maybe I'm thinking too fast. We're more than casual friends, aren't we?"

"After that intimate evening we spent together, before our fight, I don't think casual is quite the right word," Estelle agreed. She reached out and slipped her hand into his. Her heart was so full, she wasn't sure she could say any more, and yet she knew she had to. "I didn't plan it, Gaetano, but I think I'm in love with you."

Gaetano was silent, and Estelle couldn't continue to speak, her heart pounded and her mouth dried up so much. She was not suffering from cancer, but she couldn't be sure she wasn't having a heart attack. What if it wasn't love she'd seen in his eyes?

The man dropped to his knees in front of her and laid his head in her lap. His arms reached around her and held her tight. She laced her fingers in his hair and leaned over to rest her cheek on his, and as she did, she felt her eyes filling up. Before they spilled over, she realized her face was already wet with his tears.

For what seemed like forever, they stayed clutching each other. Finally Gaetano lifted his head and got to his feet, pulling her up with him. His gentle brown eyes rested on her. His smile came slowly, as if he wasn't sure he could trust what he'd heard.

"I prayed one day I would hear you say those words, but now that you have, I am not sure what to say back."

Panic slid again into Estelle's heart. Something in her chest tightened, and she felt as if she couldn't breathe. Maybe she was having an attack after all. She inhaled as deeply as her lungs would allow and softly said, "You don't feel the same?"

"No, my darling, I don't feel the same. I feel it a hundred times more. And I don't think I'm in love with you. I know I am."

Estelle felt his arms around her and his lips on hers. The kiss deepened. His tongue explored and teased, and she wrapped her arms around his neck. Her feet left the floor. One shoe fell off and the other dangled from her toes while he carried her to his bedroom. She had a feeling this time would be even better than the last.

***

For the second time in her life Estelle had experienced passion beyond anything she'd ever imagined. This was the same man who'd made love to her before, but it was like the first time again. No, it was better. He'd awakened feelings in her that she didn't know she possessed. He fulfilled a deep hunger in her she hadn't known she possessed.

Estelle stretched out and brushed her hand over the empty pillow next to her, listened to Gaetano's rich baritone voice singing bits and pieces of several different operas in the shower. She looked around the room and was somehow comforted by the simple décor. No lacy curtains or frilly bedding. The bed was a clean design and large to accommodate Gaetano's height.

There were no vases of fresh flowers on table tops. It was definitely a man's room. However, the influence of a woman's touch still lingered like whispers from the past. A silver framed photo of Gina sat on top of an antique bureau in the corner. Next to it, in an identical frame, was a picture of a dark-haired young woman who could have passed for Gina's sister. Estelle assumed it was Rosie, Gina's mother. She was pretty, and it was obvious she'd passed her delicate features down to her daughter. Estelle wondered if Gina had inherited any of her father's talents besides cooking. If so, Alex would be a fool to pass her up.

Of course, that was all over. He had sued Gina, and Gina had won the case. Alex was enough like his father that losing was not something he handled well. There was probably nothing either Estelle or Gaetano could do to mend that fence. What was ahead for Alex and Gina was anyone's guess.

Estelle was just glad that she and Gaetano had been able to put aside their differences and get back together. Yes, she and her Italian songbird were definitely on a positive track. She wondered how her son would feel if she and Gaetano decided to get married.

A laugh half escaped her lips. This was a fine situation. She had started out scheming with Gaetano to get their children together and ended up sleeping with him! It was supposed to be the other way around. The kids were supposed to fall in love, and from all she'd been able to put together, they were now bitter enemies.

The shower shut off, and soon the scent of masculine aftershave reached her nostrils. She turned in the direction of the tangy aroma and met the gaze of the clean-shaven, tall, naked man who approached. He leaped onto the bed, burst out with another operatic volley, and playfully grabbed her. Wrapping her in his arms, he rolled her over on top of his damp, warm, muscular body.

A short time later, the shower was turned on for a second time, and this time it held both of them. They stayed until the hot water became tepid, then Estelle and Gaetano reluctantly got out and toweled off. Estelle wrapped herself in Gaetano's white terrycloth robe. The belt went around her twice and she had to roll the sleeves up three-fold, but she felt very much at home.

As usual, Gaetano went into the kitchen and prepared food. He made a huge Italian omelet, impromptu, and when he was satisfied that he had not compromised his reputation as a chef they shared it. He insisted on feeding it to her between sips of wine.

Estelle smiled at Gaetano across the small kitchen table. "I wish Alex could be as happy as I am now."

"Ah, I feel the same about my Gina. What do you think? Will they ever even talk to each other again?" A frown bunched up Gaetano's forehead; then his eyes widened and his hand clapped over his mouth. "*Mama mia*, I have to call Gina. I told her you were dying, and because we fought over her and Alex, I wouldn't be able to help you in any way. She must feel terrible. I was so sad. I guess I wanted others to feel the same."

He pushed back his chair and went to the telephone on the counter. "She told me not to worry, that she would fix things. I'm not sure what she meant."

As he punched in the numbers, suddenly he stopped and placed the phone back in the cradle. His face held a quizzical expression. "*Cara*, maybe I shouldn't tell Gina. If she thinks her actions have made me unhappy, she'll do her best to fix it. Right?"

Estelle shook her head. "I don't get it. What do you mean? She won't tell Alex that I'm dying, will she?"

Gaetano shrugged. "I'm not sure she hasn't already. You must understand, I was not myself." He returned to the table, pulled Estelle out of her chair, sat back down in his and drew her onto his lap. She curled up and wrapped her arms around him the way he liked her to do. "But, look, maybe Gina will want to make things right with Alex in view of what she thinks is happening to you."

Estelle still looked confused.

Gaetano continued. "I mean, if they settle their differences and become friends, we'd naturally want to fix our little spat. That would please them, I think. If you thought they were building something serious, that would make you happy and you would die in peace, right?"

Estelle nodded. "But I'm not dying, and I still don't understand why they must think I am."

"Because, you've never told Alex that you were dying. If Gina confronts him, he will either be very angry or he will want to protect and shelter you until you break the news to him. If it's the latter, they will probably both put up a good front for us!"

Staring at Estelle, Gaetano felt guilt rear its ugly head. It was truly sinful to keep this wonderful news from the children, but Gaetano knew his daughter, and when she wanted something, she went after it. If she set her mind to making up with Alex, the boy would succumb to her charms and all the problems surrounding the lawsuit would fade away. They had been attracted to each other from the beginning; that had been obvious to him. Gina would deny it, but that was just her way. She could be stubborn at times. With a little luck, they would find true love. Then they could spread the good news and maybe plan a double wedding. Just thinking about it excited him.

A frown settled across Estelle's forehead, and she cast Gaetano a worried look. "Alex will be devastated if Gina tells him I'm dying. Oh, if only he hadn't sued her, and if we hadn't fought—"

"And if Gina hadn't won," Gaetano interrupted, "we wouldn't have to worry and plot like this. But we do."

Estelle sat silently for several minutes. He knew she wasn't nearly as confident, but then he was an optimist. If he wanted something badly enough, it could indeed happen. And he wanted Gina and Alex together.

He grinned at Estelle and said, "The point is that they will make up, even if it's just for our sake. Then it's a matter of time until they will be truly in love. Just like us!"

Estelle rested her head on Gaetano's shoulder and let him rub her back. Absentmindedly she reached up and played with his earlobe while Gaetano continued to plot.

"We might pull this off if we don't let them catch us together until it's time. Now, how can we get them launched?" he asked.

"They need a fresh start. If only we could go back, do that first meeting all over…," Estelle said.

Gaetano jumped to his feet, grabbing her just before her bottom hit the tile floor. "I've got it! I know how to get them together again. Yes, you have to keep dying for a little while longer. Kiss me and then I will tell you the plan."

Chapter 12

Gina handed Alex a fresh Kleenex from her purse packet and took one for herself. She'd never have spilled the beans if she'd had any idea he was still unaware of his mother's failing health. Talk about non-communication! Well, at least she and her Papá were not like that. They were upfront and honest with each other about everything.

"Gina, I'm going to have a drink. Do you want one?" Alex had pulled himself together, and while it seemed a bit early for a drink, Gina conceded these were special times. She nodded.

"Alex, I'm going to call my dad and let him know we've settled our differences and suggest that he call your mom and make up, okay? I mean, if he makes her happy and loves her, it's the least we can do."

"Yeah, go ahead," he agreed. "She deserves to be happy for the rest of her life, however long that might be."

Gina pulled out her cell phone and punched in the familiar number. It was important to let Papá know right away. He could assure Estelle that they didn't have to fight over her and Alex anymore. She'd told her dad she'd fix things, and she'd at least made the first step.

She couldn't remember ever seeing her dad so upset. When Estelle's time came, she vowed to be there for him. She'd give him the same attention he'd given her when they'd lost Mama.

As she waited for her father to answer the phone, the thought occurred to her that Alex wouldn't have anyone after his mother died. He'd be totally alone. Poor guy. Being an only child wasn't all it was cracked up to be.

Well, she would be there for Alex, too. If he'd let her.

Finally, her father's answering machine picked up. Had he gone into the restaurant? She hoped that he was okay. She waited for the beep and then said, "Hi, Papá, this is Gina, and I just wanted to let you know that Alex and I have come to an agreement over our legal squabble. It's all just fine now, so I think you should call Estelle and make up with her. She needs you, Papá."

Gina hesitated. She chewed on her lower lip and then switched the phone to her other ear. "Oh, and Papá, I did a terrible thing. I didn't know Alex's mother was keeping the news of her illness from him, and I told him. He's pretty upset, so I'm going to stay with him for a while. Please don't let Estelle know. I didn't realize it was a secret. I'll call you later. Bye, Papá, I love you. I really, really do."

She flipped her phone shut just as Alex returned from the kitchen with two glasses filled with an amber-colored liquid.

"I don't know if you like Scotch, but Chivas Regal is pretty good." He handed her the drink and then shoved some stuff off the other chair and plopped himself down. "You must think I'm a big baby or a wimp or something. I usually handle bad news a little better than what you witnessed."

She shook her head. "Alex, don't apologize. She's your mom. You have every right to grieve. I just don't understand why she didn't tell you."

"Because she's my mom, and she continues to think I need protection. She kept a lot of things about my dad's illness a secret until his condition became obvious. They both were in denial for quite a while."

"Yeah, I guess that's what parents do. I don't remember much about my mother's death. Papá made life all better afterward, and frankly I don't think I missed too much." Gina sipped her drink, and while it burned her throat going down, it gave her a warm-all-over feeling when it settled in her stomach. She'd only have this one drink or it'd go to her head.

"Of course, when I was a teenager and puberty hit, there were some rough times, but I had lots of cousins and aunts, and Mario's wife was like a second mom to me."

"You were lucky to have so many people to pick up the slack. I loved my father, but he was always too busy to spend much time with me. Mom stepped in and did all the things dads usually do."

"It's pretty ironic, isn't it? You were a guy, and yet your mother was the prominent one in your life. For me it was the exact opposite."

"Another thing we have in common." He paused for a moment and then said, "I think Dad tried to be there, but the business always came first. It was as if giving me lavish presents was his way of showing love, having the best money could buy or going to exclusive private schools. He had no idea how showing up for a game or taking me fishing would have been so much better."

Alex drained his glass and stared at it for a moment. He looked up at Gina and said, "You want a refill?"

Gina was surprised to see her drink was all gone. She didn't feel buzzed or anything, just total relaxation. Still she said, "I skipped lunch so I better not."

"Me too, but I'm having another anyway."

For the first time since Gina arrived, Alex smiled. She liked his smile. His eyes were no longer puffy, and she couldn't help but be drawn into them.

He got up and reached for her glass. "Hey, I'll find something we can nibble on. I don't keep a lot of food on hand, but I'm sure I've got some cheese and crackers."

"Well," Gina allowed, "I guess if you're going to add food I'll be able to handle one more. But make it light. It's very good, by the way." Alex needed someone here that he felt comfortable with. It wasn't easy for guys to talk about feelings.

Her eyes zeroed in on Alex's absolutely perfect butt as he left the room, then she chided herself for letting her mind drift in that direction when she was here to comfort, not to admire. But the fact was Alex was turning out much better than she'd imagined him these past few weeks. His heart had to be breaking, and yet he was being kind. Hospitable. She supposed the Scotch was probably helping them both.

She'd always imagined being with a guy like Alex, back when she actually thought she could have both a career and a love life. The perfect man would be someone who would be there for her in times of need. She imagined Alex would be the kind of guy who would be there if she needed him.

Wait a minute. *She* was comforting *him*. Why did that mean he would be around when she needed him?

Well, she had caused the discomfort by blurting out the terrible news about his mother, so she supposed she owed him. But where was her prince charming on the white horse?

Oh, maybe her prince charming actually drove a Ferrari. A Ferrari that she'd failed to have repainted in its original and unique color. Well, crap, she'd screwed that up too.

Geez, Gina, no wonder you're alone.

***

Alex pulled a platter from a cabinet and arranged slices of cheese and some Ritz crackers on it. He also found an apple that hadn't gone belly up and cut some very thin slices. He balanced the two refilled glasses in one hand and the platter in the other, and he joined Gina in his cluttered living room.

She didn't notice him at first, and he took a few seconds to appreciate her face and body. The compassion she'd shown had been so unexpected after their day in court. He was discovering a wonderful, sweet side to Gina that was nothing like she'd shown him.

"Alex, what's wrong? Are you okay?"

He'd been transfixed by her beauty, and he only broke off his stare when he became aware of her voice. "What? Oh, sorry, I was just thinking…of stuff. You know." He crossed over to the sofa and put the platter down on the coffee table, sat, moved some camera equipment onto the floor and patted the cushion next to him, inviting her to sit.

Gina complied and moved next to him. She took the drink he handed her and placed a hand on his arm. "Oh. Thoughts of your mom," she guessed. "I understand. It must have been a wonderful memory, going by that smile. Tell me about it?"

"Er, no," he said, "I'd rather not. Not right now. Why don't you tell me more about your childhood and your dad? I want to know more about him. I'm still blown away that he's in love with my mom."

Gina laughed. "Yeah, me too. Do you have any idea if your mother feels the same? I guess it really doesn't matter, though, because it can't go anywhere. Unfortunately."

Alex took a quick sip of his drink, hoping the strong flavor of the Scotch would disintegrate the lump that had reappeared in his throat. Gina was right. Even if their parents were crazy about each other, how long could it last?

He looked over at Gina. "I was wondering what it will be like when she's gone. I've spent a lot of time away from home and it really never bothered me. I just assumed Mom would be around if I needed her. For a long time now, I've taken pride in not needing her."

"Oh. I would have thought you'd get closer after your father's death."

"Well, we did," Alex admitted. "I mean, we are close. Always have been, but I think we both wanted to show the other that we were okay. We weren't going to crumble or come apart at the seams. So..."

"So you each put up a good strong front?"

"Yeah, something like that. She's been a terrific mom, really, and now she needs my support, but was too proud or protective to even let me know. I feel like a real chump. I should have noticed." He shook his head and stared into his glass.

"Alex, don't be so hard on yourself. Face it, her condition isn't really noticeable. She's a beautiful woman. She looks healthy, and no one would ever know she was ill unless they were told."

"Maybe. But still, wouldn't you think I would have gotten some kind of clue? Obviously your father was able to get the truth. My mother is not one to confide in strangers, and that's what your dad was just a few short weeks ago."

"Well, my father is someone who people instinctively trust. He's kind and generous with his time and...I don't know, he makes everyone feel safe."

"I guess I should be glad he was there for her. Since I wasn't."

"You know, she could still level with you. In the larger picture, this is something one would want to take their time to tell a loved one. It's easier to talk to strangers sometimes than those so close to our hearts."

Alex took Gina's hand and said, "It's been really helpful to talk to you. I appreciate your kindness. You must possess a bit of your father's gift."

Gina laughed. "I'm glad I could help, but I don't think I'm anywhere near as kind as my dad. You don't really know me, and if you did you'd find that I'm not nearly as helpful or concerned with people—unless, of course, you're a client." She grew pensive. "I'm afraid I've put my career over individuals."

"Now who's being hard on themselves?" Releasing her hand, Alex reached up and twirled one of her dark brown curls around his finger. "You're right about one thing, though. I don't know you very well."

She grimaced. "And since what you do know of me is mostly from the courtroom, I understand why you might not be exactly impressed."

"No. I *am* impressed. Well, at least with the way you won that case. I'm fascinated, and I really do want to know more about you. Come on, Gina, give me a thumbnail sketch of the Lorenzo family."

When he grinned, Gina rewarded him with a smile that nudged his melancholy to the back of his mind. She said, "Well, let me see. My father came over from Italy as a very small boy. He helped his parents in the restaurant until they and his brother were killed in an auto accident. He was still young, then—nineteen, I think. He just kept on working, and somehow he managed to build the restaurant into the success it is today. Mario and his family helped a lot. He and my father are like brothers."

"You mean to say that the restaurant your father has first belonged to his parents? How was he able to manage? Nineteen? He was still just a kid."

Gina nodded. "I think he grew up very fast. He was barely twenty-one when he married my mother, though they held off having me for five years. Mario told me my dad took a lot of ribbing from his friends over that. They questioned his virility and his Italian heritage."

She stopped talking abruptly and reached for a cheese slice. Alex wondered if the word *virility* had embarrassed her. It certainly turned his own thoughts that way, and if times were different, he might have made a joke or two. In other times, sitting with a beautiful girl might have carried a different agenda to start with. But not today.

Following her lead, he popped an apple wedge with a cheese slice into his mouth. After chewing and swallowing he said, "I wondered about that—about you being an only child, I mean. I thought Italian families favored lots of children, especially sons."

Gina shrugged. "I think there would have been more if Mama had been healthy. I guess she never quite recovered from my birth, and then she got cancer."

"Your father's an amazing man," Alex said. "I still don't see how he did it all. I've got a good education and make an above average salary, but the idea of being a parent and responsible for someone is still a bit much for me. And I'm in my late twenties!"

"I know. I feel the same way. I don't know if I could do it. I guess my mother helped. She was also an immigrant, and she was my father's biggest cheerleader. She encouraged him to go to night school and take business classes even though she never really got the hang of English, herself. My father was so young when he came over, English was a snap for him. Of course, he never forgot his Italian."

"So…say something to me in Italian," Alex said. He sat back and let his body relax into the sofa's plump cushions, caught a scent of Gina's perfume, and tugged playfully on her curl. "Come on, say something."

She turned and looked at him, and while he couldn't be sure, he thought her cheeks were tinged with pink.

"What's the matter, can't you think of anything to say to me?"

After witnessing her behavior in the courtroom, it amused him to see her flustered. In spite of the reason that had brought them together he was fully enjoying her company. He let his hand creep up to her neck and stroke the soft area behind her right ear. Then, impulsively he leaned forward and…

He stopped and sat back. His intent had been to kiss her, but then he realized how out of place that would be in view of everything that was going on with his mom. Instead of the kiss he wanted so badly, he made himself content with fiddling with one of her curls.

"It's not that I can't think of anything." Her words came out more like a sigh. "It's just that I…don't speak Italian."

"What? You're telling me you aren't bilingual?" He fell back into the cushions and began to chuckle. For some reason, it was the funniest thing he'd ever heard. He couldn't imagine this know-it-all not knowing everything. And he meant that in the sweetest possible way.

"I knew some when I was little, but Papá made it a point to speak English more often, as it was necessary for the business. Mama wasn't exactly a chatterbox. I know a few words, but I never got fluent. Papá didn't make a big deal out of it." A grin teased at the corners of her mouth, and her dimples flickered into view as she struggled to keep a straight face. Finally, she surrendered and giggled along with Alex. "I can't even pronounce all of the Italian on the menu!"

Alex was now howling. It felt good to laugh. Just a short time ago, he hadn't known if he'd find anything amusing ever again. Then this incredible woman pulled him out of his despair and helped him escape into a state of humor and enjoyment. Their past problems were all but forgotten.

They talked and drank and told childhood stories for quite a while longer before finally both lapsing into silence. Gina put her feet up underneath her and leaned into him. Alex propped his feet on the coffee table and let his head rest on the back of the sofa. It felt good. He hadn't felt this good in a long time. Maybe ever.

***

Alex awoke, extremely aware of Gina snuggled close in his arms. They were lying side by side on his sofa, and her eyes were closed. The soft, rhythmic sounds of her breathing meant she was asleep. They'd finished off the snacks, and to his amazement, the entire bottle of Scotch. Not that it had been full, but... Well, it was fortunate that Chivas Regal was a good brand or they'd both be soon feeling unpleasant aftereffects.

He looked out the window as the last ribbon of daylight sank into the horizon, and as he did, his thoughts returned to his mother. He couldn't believe she was really dying. She'd looked so wonderful and hadn't even hinted of feeling bad. Her makeup must be a miracle product.

No, his mother's face showed none of the ravages of her disease. He wasn't sure if he could handle seeing her become shriveled and old like his father. For so long Martin Bennett had been a good-looking man, and so full of pride. At the end, he had been a shell.

Alex remembered once when he was a kid, finding a castoff snakeskin in his backyard. When he'd picked it up, it practically disintegrated. That's how his father's last days seemed: The healthy part of his dad had gone off somewhere and only the thin, fragile shell remained, until it too was finally gone. A lump the size of a tennis ball filled Alex's throat, and his eyes burned.

His gaze traveled to Gina's face. It didn't look as if she were even wearing makeup. Her skin was flawless. Besides the dimples that occasionally appeared at the corners of those full lips, there were no lines or blemishes. She did have a small beauty mark high on her left cheekbone, just below the area where her thick, curved lashes rested. Her nose was straight, with the tip tilting ever so slightly upward. She was truly beautiful.

This was the type of girl his mother wanted for him. Estelle didn't meddle in his life, but he was more than aware that she'd like for him to marry and quit roaming the world like a gypsy. He knew now that his mother had hoped that they'd hit it off that first night at the restaurant. Before the debacle with the Ferrari.

Gina stirred, and a small moan escaped her lips. Alex found himself overwhelmed with desire. Without thinking, he bent his head and brushed her lips with his own. Rather than shying away, Gina responded, still asleep, and so he deepened his kiss. She moved even closer to him, and the pressure of her breasts against his chest made his body react. Reluctantly he ended contact. He was in no place to begin a relationship, and that's what he felt was going to happen if he woke her up. A relationship that scared him more than any relationship he'd ever had because it felt so right.

Gina resumed her even breathing, and Alex gently eased off the sofa and put a small pillow under her head. He picked up their glasses and platter and carried them to the kitchen. If he stayed in the kitchen he might avoid temptation.

***

Boris was agitated. He'd been sitting in his car across from Alex Bennett's place for hours now and there was still no sign of Gina leaving. What was going on up there?

Maybe she'd left. No. Her car was still parked where he'd seen her leave it hours before.

He was getting nervous about waiting for her, though. He was getting angry, too. He had enough problems with that stuffed shirt supervisor at his office. He knew they were just waiting for another chance to fire him, and he was sick and tired of taking all the crap they handed out. But, until he and Gina were solid, he needed to pay the rent. After Gina and he were married he would start his own company, and with her knowledge of the legal system she'd be able to help him find loopholes in all those silly laws regarding copyrights and patents. In a short time, they'd be millionaires.

It was true that Gina had not spoken to him since she'd refused his dinner invitation, and somehow she'd even blocked his calls. That irritated him. If she didn't come around soon, he'd have to take other measures, drastic measures to let her know that he intended to make her his. He needed her and wanted her. Just thinking of her made his pants bulge, and so he reached down and pleasured himself while thinking of that dark-eyed beauty who would be his soon.

Chapter 13

Gaetano stepped out of the shower and wrapped a thick burgundy towel around his waist. He stood for a second and watched Estelle applying final touches to her makeup at her dressing table. She was beautiful, and he'd been staying at her house more than his own. He'd made up elaborate excuses to Gina about his never being at home when she called, but the tables had turned and now it was his answering machine taking the calls instead of hers. He found he liked that.

Estelle leaned toward the mirror and tipped her lashes with mascara, then smiled when she saw him. "Are you sure I shouldn't tell Alex and Gina that I'm perfectly healthy? It seems so cruel to deceive them like this."

He came up behind her, put his hands on her shoulders and looked at her image reflected back at him. He wasn't sure if she could pull off the charade. She simply glowed with good looks and well being.

"I know, my love, but if we come clean, they might never get their relationship going. Gina has already rushed to comfort Alex, and by now he's beginning to see what a wonderful girl she really is. If we're lucky, this will allow them to get to know each other better. Gina said they'd put that silly legal business in the past, and she urged me to call you. I still think we should be a little careful and not let them know we're back together. It's just a matter of time until they fall in love, and we can play along until that happens. Before you know it, we'll be babysitting a little Alex or a little Gina!"

"I don't know. It's not right to keep such wonderful news from them. I'm sorry, Gaetano, I'm telling Alex tonight. It's just wrong to remain silent."

"Ah, *cara*, maybe you're right. Okay, tonight you can tell them…but not immediately. It's going to be a shock, so we must handle it very carefully. Perhaps at the end of dinner."

Estelle looked relieved. "Oh, I'm so glad you agree. We should pretend that we're not quite lovers, though. Alex might be more shocked over where our relationship has gone than the state of my health."

"Okay, we'll not be too friendly. In fact, we can act like we're still angry. But, I must tell you, my beautiful Estelle, that it is going to be very hard for me to do."

He leaned over, kissed her earlobe and let his hands slide down her chest and into the top of her bra. He fingered her nipples, and a rakish smile spread across his face when they hardened. Estelle closed her eyes and leaned back against him. She might be a mature woman, but her body responded like that of a girl of twenty. His own body was feeling pretty young, itself.

He forced himself to pull away, adjusted his towel and tucked it a little more firmly around his waist. He didn't miss Estelle's smile at the growing bulge.

"Uh-uh, we can't even consider that. We are meeting the kids, remember?"

"Of course, darling. I was just window shopping."

Gaetano grinned and crossed the room. He opened a drawer and pulled out his shaver. Tonight, as far as Gina and Alex knew, was the first night he and Estelle were going to be together since their argument. He had maneuvered his daughter so well that she and Alex actually thought dinner was their idea, to show the parents that there were no hard feelings between the children, to prove there was no reason for Estelle and Gaetano not to go back to being friends. Gaetano inwardly congratulated himself for being so clever.

Estelle walked into her closet and raised her voice so Gaetano could hear her while she dressed. "What makes you think they will want to make us grandparents right away? I think Gina loves having a career. She's worked very hard to get as far as she has. She may not want to give it up just to make us grandparents."

"Well, we'll worry about that after we get them married."

Gaetano clicked off his shaver and went into the bedroom. In her closet, Estelle pulled down several garments and then placed each back on its rod. Finally making a selection, she held the hanger up in front of her and viewed herself in the mirror. She'd selected a sage green pantsuit of silk crepe which complemented her eyes.

Gaetano picked up his clean underwear that Estelle had laid out on the bed, dropped his towel, and stepped into the briefs. Then he went to the other walk-in closet where more and more of his wardrobe was collecting. "What about Alex? Can he settle down and stay in one place?"

"I guess that's another thing we'll worry about after we get them married," Estelle said, stepping out of the closet and into the bedroom.

Gaetano crossed the room and took her hand. He bowed and kissed her fingertips. *"Mama mia. Quanto sei bella, cara.* Estelle, you are so beautiful. You take my breath away."

"You are so sweet," she replied. "I don't think I've ever had my hand kissed by a man wearing jockey briefs."

"Oh, am I overdressed? I can fix that."

"Stop it, silly," she said as Gaetano stuck his thumbs into his clastic waistband. "You've got to get dressed and get out of here before Alex comes to pick me up."

Gaetano slipped on his peach-colored shirt and began to button up. It was something Estelle had purchased for him last week. He'd never worn anything like it, but Estelle had excellent taste and he'd heard secure men could wear colors that were a bit outrageous. He'd never felt more secure.

"Why aren't you meeting him at the restaurant?" he asked.

"Because I'm dying and too weak to drive that far."

"Oh yes, I forgot." He pulled on his trousers, sat on the bed, and slipped on his socks and shoes. Then he stood and accepted the tie Estelle held out. It was also peach-colored, with a fleck of beige that matched his pants and jacket. "Where is this place we're going? I don't know why we had to go anywhere but my restaurant. I know the food is good there."

"Darling," Estelle replied. "There is more to a meal than food. Gina knows where we're going, and she's meeting you at your place, so you better get a move on." She took the tie from him and put it around his neck. She deftly made the loop and slid the wide side through and then tightened the knot, picked up his jacket and handed it to him. "Now, scoot, before you get caught here."

He turned to go then reversed direction and took Estelle's hand. Bowing, he gently kissed her palm, her wrist, the inside of her elbow, and then shifted his direction to the upper portion of her breasts showing above the vee neckline of her garment. His lips lingered there for a moment, then traveled to the hollow of her neck, to her chin, and then to claim her lips in a deep, long and passionate kiss. Then he turned on his heel and left the bedroom and an extremely dazed Estelle.

Gaetano was pleased.

***

Gina cradled the phone between her chin and shoulder as she pulled the hairbrush through her thick curls. Rescuing the phone a moment before she dropped it she said, "Alex, are you sure your mother isn't going to back out? I mean, she can't be feeling that well and probably doesn't need any more stress."

"She said she'd give it a try if Gaetano was willing. What about him? What did he say when you invited him out?"

"He wanted to know why we weren't going to his restaurant. 'At least you know the food is superb there.'"

Alex chuckled at her impression of her father. "Did he sound like he wanted to see my mother?"

"Absolutely, but he's afraid she's too angry to ever forgive him for something he said. I think he may have insulted her."

"He doesn't know my mom that well then, because she's very forgiving. Speaking of my mom, I better get over there and pick her up. I told her to rest today so she wouldn't be tired tonight."

"Well, that was stupid," Gina said.

"Why? I worry about her."

"Of course you do, but you're not supposed to even know she's ill. As far as she's concerned, neither of us knows anything except she and Papá have had a tiff. Papá made me promise not to let on that we know anything about her condition. I hope you haven't blown it."

For a few uncomfortable moments the line was quiet. *Oh no, I've made him feel bad,* she realized. *Why can't I ever keep my mouth shut?* She went into her bedroom to take one more look at the dress she'd purchased that morning. Her wardrobe consisted primarily of business attire, as most of her time was spent in the courtroom or the office. At the same time she said, "By the way, I want to say thanks again for not making me feel like an idiot the other night. I could have driven home and I apologize for falling asleep on you. I usually don't do that."

Alex sounded appeased. "I'm sure the drinks had a lot to do with it. You were fine after a couple of hours of shuteye."

"Still, it was dumb. I couldn't believe it was so late when I woke up!"

"It wasn't that late. Eleven thirty? The boogie men only come out after midnight. You could have stayed over, you know. You were perfectly safe."

"I know," she admitted. "I wasn't worried about that, but I did have a big day at work and you certainly had enough on your mind. You didn't need to be bothered with babysitting a drunk."

"Come on, Gina, you were fine. You were cute, even. And I liked hearing about your family. Very much."

Gina took her dress and spread it out on the bed. She'd purchased it on a whim. Would she look okay in it? She'd never worried much about fashion. She had several really dressy outfits for the social functions of the firm but very few items that were appropriate for this type of occasion.

What was this occasion, anyway? Getting the folks together? Getting a new start with Alex? A farewell dinner for Mom? Meeting the children? Oh God, she was beginning to regret her decision to play matchmaker for her father.

Alex was recalling some of her family tales she'd told the other night. She plopped down on the bed, and cradling the phone again, removed the dress from its hanger. She wasn't sure about the color. Hot pink? She was much more comfortable in blacks and grays.

A change in Alex's tone registered in her ear, and she started paying attention again: "And, Gina, I haven't blown anything. I've always been concerned about my mother, and she likes it when I'm protective."

Gina was happy to agree. "I'm sure you're right. Now, I'll see you in a few. I have to meet my father soon and I'm not dressed yet. Bye!"

She tossed her phone on the bed then slipped into her dress. It was a warm evening, and Gina hoped she could get by without taking a wrap. The dress was a silky sheath with a flounce at the hem, and it had sleeves, if short capped ones. The scoop neck showed more of her cleavage than she was normally comfortable with, but she supposed tonight was a night to throw caution to the wind. At least a little.

***

Alex opened the door with his own key as he didn't want to disturb his mother. She didn't need to be running to let him in; he wanted her to conserve strength.

He stepped inside and quietly closed the door, and a wave of sadness washed over him as he did, letting his gaze take in the surroundings where he'd grown up. As always, the marble floor of the foyer was polished to a high gloss, and fresh flowers sat in a vase on the small table below the large oval mirror.

He took another step and surveyed the living room dominated by the white baby grand piano. The winter-white, oversized sectional curved around two walls in the corner of the large room, and above the sofa was an almost life-sized, three-dimensional alabaster sculpture of a reclining woman, only partially covered with a drape. Looking at it now, he saw the true beauty of the art instead of the detailed, voluptuous breasts and flowing locks of hair that had so inflamed his sixteen-year-old mind.

"Hello, dear, I didn't hear you come in."

Alex turned and saw his mother standing behind him in the archway that led to the formal dining room. He opened his mouth to greet her but was made speechless by her appearance. She looked beautiful. He wanted to freeze the moment in time. After she was gone, he'd remember how she looked today and hoped the memory would comfort him.

"Mother, you look wonderful. Is that a new outfit?"

"Thank you, Alex. It is new as a matter of fact. I probably shouldn't have. I mean, it's not like I need any more clothes."

Another wave of sadness swirled into his thoughts. She'd slipped. *She knows that soon she won't have a need for clothes or anything.*

He pasted a wide grin on his face and in spite of the huge lump in his throat managed to say, "Don't be silly. You should have whatever you want. You deserve to be happy." He closed the distance between them and kissed his mother's cheek. The scent of her Joy perfume teased his nostrils.

If Gaetano isn't reduced to begging forgiveness after seeing her tonight, his heart must be made of stone.

Alex wondered if his mother really cared about Gina's dad. It had puzzled him many times how devoted she'd been to his father while receiving so little attention back. She'd occupied her time by exposing Alex to the arts and taking him on trips when his father couldn't, or wouldn't, take time away from the business. She'd attended all his sporting events and volunteered on countless school committees. She'd been every bit as amazing as Gina's dad, if truth be told. The pair would be the perfect couple if they could only get past this disagreement. And if they had more time.

"Hello? Alex?" Estelle repeated. "Darling, where did you go? You looked as if you were a million miles away. Is anything wrong?"

"It's nothing, Mom, just daydreams. We had better go or we'll be late."

***

Gaetano had been fidgeting for several minutes before Gina drove up to his house.

Good, he thought, as she parked at the curb. He wanted to drive his car so that he could offer to take Estelle home. Then Alex would, of course, have to take Gina home. It was a good plan for the kids, and an even better one for him and Estelle. He had gotten very used to sleeping in her big four poster bed with the brocade spread and too many pillows. He liked the idea of holding her close to him every night and waking up with her in his arms every morning. God, it was good that she was healthy. Life was good. Love was good.

The bell rang, and Gaetano hurried to open the door. Gina gave him a quick peck on the cheek and said, "Sorry I'm late, Papá. Holy Moses, look at you!" Her eyes widened and her jaw dropped. "Papá, you look like a male *GQ* model."

"I clean up pretty good, eh?" He did a little spin and then eyed his daughter. "*Bambina*, you look gorgeous too."

"Well, I tried. I want you to have a great evening. I decided I might as well go the whole nine yards. This dress isn't something I'd normally buy, but I just want you to know how sorry I am about causing you and Estelle problems."

"Ah, Gina, you are a good girl."

He put his arms around her and pushed aside the guilt that jabbed at his conscience. He didn't like deceiving his daughter, but he also knew how stubborn she could be. Without his nudging her, she might never have spoken to Alex again. Gina would forgive her well-meaning *papá* once she and Alex were on firm footing. Forgive? She'd probably even thank him.

"Gina, we'll take my car." He drew his keys out of his pocket.

"Papá, my car is newer and I've got all my CDs already programmed."

"Don't argue with your Papá. I do not like being driven around like some old man."

"Oh, Lord, you guys and your cars. Impossible. Fine, we'll go in your car, but I get to pick the music station."

Gaetano locked the front door of the house and guided Gina toward his sedan. This was going to be a wonderful night, he suspected. He was spending it with the two most important women in his life.

He was a lucky man. In time and with a little help, Alex would be just as lucky.

***

Boris watched the older gentleman guide Gina to the sedan, and he scrunched down in his seat as the car drove past. He'd been following Gina non-stop from the time she'd left work, but it seemed like he'd caught a break. He saw no reason to follow the car she'd just left in; obviously the older man was her father. He would come back in a few hours when he assumed she would reclaim her car. In the meantime he would be able to take care of a few other things.

He was fighting the urge to become more aggressive, but not here. Not yet. Soon she would recognize his importance, and perhaps she would even want him to meet her father. That would be a grand thing. Boris smiled and fantasized about when he would be welcomed into the family.

Chapter 14

The Wayfarer Restaurant sat on the cliffs above the Pacific Ocean and gave a spectacular view of the sea and a glorious sunset. Estelle and Alex were already seated by the large windows, and Gaetano silently conceded that while he would have preferred to have this dinner at his own restaurant, this location had a certain ambience. The surf crashed upon large boulders along the shoreline.

"Here they are." Alex stood as Gina and Gaetano approached. "Gina, why don't you sit here?" He pulled out a chair then motioned for Gaetano to take the other.

Gaetano did his best to conceal his amusement at the young man's obvious unease. After all, this was not an evening of old friends getting together; Alex was likely still getting used to his mother having a suitor, and now he was expected not only to accept but encourage the relationship. He felt a brief pang about keeping the kids in the dark, but that would be remedied soon enough. It was not easy to act disgruntled toward his breathtakingly beautiful Estelle.

He grunted as if he were there under protest and took his seat. The deception was wearing, and he wasn't so good at keeping secrets. Especially not when he was so happy. He'd wanted just a bit more assurance that Gina and Alex had at least made a step toward becoming friends, though.

Ah well, I've done the best I can. I am only one man.

The waiter appeared, and drinks were ordered for the newcomers. Gaetano took a moment to gaze at the woman who sat across from him. Estelle seemed to be having as much difficulty as he in keeping up the farce. She picked up her wine glass and looked out the window.

After the waiter departed, Gaetano said in a crisp, formal tone, "I hope we didn't keep you waiting long." He was beginning to enjoy the pretense, especially since it would only last a little while longer. The children would be shocked if they knew how much closer they'd been earlier in the day.

Estelle took his lead and answered just as formally. "Not at all, Mr. Lorenzo. However, I'd thought only Gina was joining us."

Catching the worried look in his daughter's eyes, Gaetano decided to push things a bit further. "Well, I don't want to intrude." He scooted his chair back and started to rise.

"Papá, sit!"

Gina's eyes flashed, and while he found their little game most enjoyable, he recognized his daughter had just about reached her limit. Ah, that quick, fiery temper. She was definitely a Lorenzo.

But, obedient Italian girls did not speak to their fathers in that tone. He sank back into his seat and looked with mock horror at his child.

"I'm sorry, Papá I didn't mean to be harsh, but Alex and I have gone to a lot trouble for this meeting. You can at least stay until you hear us out."

"Of course, *Bambina*, I will stay—for you." He stole a glance at Estelle, but she was looking out the window again. She pressed her napkin to her lips as if to stifle a sob. She could have convinced him of her pain had it not been for that twinkle in those beautiful green eyes.

Gina continued. "Go on Alex, tell them what we worked out."

"What?" Estelle's son looked as if he'd been asked to recite the alphabet backwards. Frowning, he inhaled and drew his mouth into a tight line, clearly surprised that the burden was being dropped on him. "Well, uh, we…uh, Gina and me…"

Estelle turned from the window and leveled her gaze on him. "Gina and *I*, dear,"

"Huh? Oh, of course. Gina and I…we thought, well, actually we decided…"

"For crying out loud, Alex, spit it out!" Gina said.

By now Gaetano had nothing but sympathy for the young man. First Alex's mother had corrected his grammar, now Gina was showing little patience or respect. Gaetano realized his daughter wasn't the only one who'd reached the end of their rope.

"I would, if I had any idea of what *it* is," Alex answered. "What am I supposed to say?"

The waiter returned at that moment with drinks for Gina and her father. Alex gave him a grateful look and then ordered himself a refill, a double scotch on the rocks. He then glared at Gina with all the warmth of the ice cubes bobbing in their cocktails, drained what was left in his glass and spoke.

"I know you two had a disagreement about us, and we wanted you to know that we have decided not to be enemies." He glanced at Gina, who nodded agreement before he continued. "We're all adults, and there is no reason at all why you two shouldn't resume your friendship."

"Yes, that's right," Gina chimed in. "Alex and I have had some problems, but we're working them out now." She took a sip and then placed her drink gingerly on the table, looked at Gaetano and then at Estelle and said, "Papá I never thought about your needing a social life. Estelle is nice, and you two were getting along so well until our little problem. I think you should take our example."

Estelle smiled. "Thank you for the compliment, Gina," she said. "Our problems, Gaetano's and mine, indeed stemmed from the lawsuit that came between you two, but I think we were well on our way to becoming very good friends. I have no objection to trying again." She directed her gaze at Gaetano and pursed her lips. Then, in response to the figure that appeared at the table, she said, "Oh, here's the waiter. I do think we should order. If we're all staying, that is."

Gaetano returned the direct look she gave him and hoped no one else was watching, because he grinned ever so slightly and winked. Clearing his throat he replied, "I am a peace lover, myself, and I'm perfectly willing to let bygones be bygones. Estelle and I have many common interests, so I look forward to a new beginning."

His daughter was literally beaming as he lifted his glass in a toast. Then he took his menu from the waiter and pretended to study it in great detail while playing footsie with Estelle under the table.

The waiter soon took orders, complimented Alex on his choice of wine, and departed. Gaetano had no idea what he'd ordered, however. Estelle had slipped out of her left shoe, and her foot had traveled up to his crotch where her toes now tapped out a variation of, "I've Got a Crush on You."

***

"I thought the food was very good, didn't you, Papá?" Gina asked.

"It was adequate, but I'd like to give the chef a few tips on serving Risotto di Zucca e Vongole. One should never let the rice get too dry, and the clams should be steeped for no more than fifteen minutes. The squash was good, not too mushy, but not enough herbs."

"Papá, I don't know why you ordered Italian," she scolded. "I think you only did it so you can complain. My swordfish was excellent."

"Well, Gina." Alex dabbed his lips with his napkin and said, "This meal was good, but the dinner your father prepared at his restaurant was beyond excellent."

Gina fought back annoyance while her father beamed. "Come to my restaurant again, Alex," Gaetano was saying. "I will cook you such a meal. It will be *magnifico!*" He kissed his bunched fingertips and flung his arm into the air. At that exact moment, a waiter passed with a tray of filled wine glasses. Gaetano's fist hit the tray bottom with a deafening clang.

The waiter tried desperately to regain control. He failed. The tray flew upward, sending the glasses and their contents cascading in Estelle's direction, but thankfully most of them missed her. Nevertheless, splotches of burgundy and rosé covered the green silk of her pantsuit.

The waiter sprang into action with a bar towel he pulled from his apron, frantically dabbing at Estelle's bosom as he apologized. Gaetano, too, grabbed his napkin, and he elbowed his way between Estelle and the waiter. He patted the wine stains and at the same time added his own apology.

"I'm so sorry. It was so clumsy of me. I didn't see him."

Gina sat frozen in her chair, staring in disbelief. After a moment she wailed, "Papá, why must you always be so…so Italian?"

Alex shook his head. "Gina, it was an accident. It could have happened to anyone. It wasn't your father's fault." He rose, pulled Estelle's chair away from the table, helped her to her feet, and removed an empty wine glass from her lap.

She patted her son's shoulder and said, "I'm okay."

Gaetano opened his mouth to apologize again, but Estelle held up her hand and then turned toward her son. "You're absolutely correct, Alex. Accidents happen all the time. Sometimes people even accidentally bump car doors in parking lots."

Gina felt a moment of horror, but when she turned to Alex he looked amused. A slight smile spread over her face, and Alex downright grinned.

"Mom's right," he said, as he put his arm around Gina's shoulders. "She's been right all along. I'm really sorry for the way I've been acting. Please forgive my behavior."

Gina leaned into him and returned his hug. "Only if you'll forgive my attitude and the way I acted in court."

His daughter and Alex were holding their embrace, and the nature of their hug captured Gaetano's attention. Perhaps he and Estelle should let nature take its course, not say anything to the two while they didn't have to. They couldn't really hurt anything by keeping their secret just one more day.

He stopped trying to clean up and turned the task over to the restaurant personnel who had now cleared the floor and replaced the tablecloth with a fresh one. Gaetano gave Estelle a look that said, *It's working. Let's scoot.*

Estelle caught the signal and said, "I don't know about the rest of you, but as much as I'd like a cup of coffee, I really should get home and try to do something about these stains."

The maitre d' appeared tableside, and he was actually bowing. "Please, madam, allow the management to pay you for the dry cleaning of your garment."

"Oh, no, that isn't necessary," Estelle said.

"It's entirely my fault," Gaetano admitted.

"Then may I offer you some complimentary desserts?"

"I couldn't eat another bite," Estelle said, "but what about it, Alex? Gina?"

The maitre d' didn't wait for a response. "I'll send your waiter back with the selection tray. I think you'll find our desserts quite superb."

"I love desserts," Gina began, turning to Estelle, "but you and Alex should leave if you don't want your outfit to be totally ruined."

"Don't be silly," Gaetano interjected. "Alex doesn't have to leave. I'll take Estelle home, and I'll also pay for her dry cleaning. Alex, will you see that my daughter gets home?"

"Of course. I think Mother should go home before she gets too tired, th— Ouch!" Alex reached down and rubbed his shin.

"Sorry, did I kick you?" Gina asked.

Estelle turned to them both. "Oh. Alex, Gina, there was something I—"

"Estelle," Gaetano cut in, "your outfit is going to be ruined if we don't leave. What you have to say can wait just a little while longer, can't it?"

"Well, it's just that..." She stopped in mid-sentence, and Gaetano raised his eyebrows and jerked his head in the direction of the younger couple, neither of whom was paying them any attention. Gina was out of her chair and had Alex's pant leg pulled up to view the damage her three inch heel had done to his shin.

"I guess you're right. I'll talk to you tomorrow, Alex. Goodnight, Gina."

Gaetano didn't bother to kiss his daughter goodbye, as he was quite sure she wouldn't have noticed. She was totally engrossed in giving apologies, and Alex was just as occupied in blowing them off. It seemed like a pretty good start.

Estelle collected her purse and looped her arm through his. With her head held high, she strode across the crowded dining room in her wine-stained outfit as if it had been designed that way, so very sure of herself. That pleased Gaetano. He'd been alone a long time, and while there had been more than a few women who'd set their caps for him, most of them had been so needy that he'd started to feel suffocated after just a couple of dates. Gaetano hadn't known he could love or respect a woman again with such intensity and passion. It felt natural to have Estelle on his arm, and every day his love for her increased. There would be no limit.

He turned and looked back at the table. Gina had moved to the chair next to Alex, and they were engaged in what appeared to be a very serious conversation. The dessert tray had just been brought to the table, but the young people were seemingly unaware. After tonight, maybe they would at least be thinking about building a friendship. Maybe Gina would even be able to calm Alex down a bit and teach him to relax. If she could get herself to relax first.

Gaetano intercepted the waiter on their way out and paid the check, then took Estelle's arm and led her toward the exit.

Smiling, she said, "This evening has been lovely, even with the wine baptism. I think we got the message across that we shouldn't waste time being angry over small things. I am disturbed that we didn't share all the good news, though."

"You can tell Alex tomorrow," Gaetano replied. "But not too early. We might be sleeping late."

Outside the restaurant, they put their arms around each other and engaged in small kisses and ear nibbling all the way to Gaetano's car, and when they were on the road Estelle leaned over as far as she could and whispered into Gaetano's ear. "Drive faster, darling. I can't wait to get you into my bed."

She snuggled as close to him as her seat belt would allow, and he drove with his left hand and let his right caress her knee and inner thigh. He had a feeling that those wine stains might not get the immediate attention they needed.

***

"Well, how do you think it went?" Gina asked.

Alex folded his napkin and gave her a long look before answering. "I think it went okay. But, there was something a bit off balance. I don't mean the accident with the waiter, either. It was like they were playing parts in a play."

"You're right," Gina agreed. "It was almost as if they were trying to make things better just for us."

"Well…" Alex fiddled with the edge of his napkin. He abandoned it, propped one elbow on the table, and rested his chin on his fist. Gina's eyes looked even more beautiful by candlelight. The surf pounded the rocks in much the same way his heart thumped inside his chest. "You know they got together initially to play matchmaker for us. It's kind of funny the way things turn out sometimes."

"I was thinking about that. I mean, my dad is in love with your mother, and yet the way they acted tonight had me totally confused. They were so stiff at first. Then she was so quick to forgive his clumsiness. I don't really know what to think."

Gina fingered her gold chain necklace, and Alex let his eyes drift from the gold strand to her smooth breasts separated by that deep valley he'd like to explore. On the right side just above her cleavage he could see another beauty mark the same size as the one on her cheek. He wondered where he might find others.

"Yeah, I know what you mean. Did you catch that bit my mother threw out about accidents happening to anyone?"

Gina nodded. "Of course. And she's right, you know. It was totally an accident. So…are you going to repaint your car with the regular paint or the special mix?"

Alex sat back, placed his palms down on the table and shook his head. "I don't know. It all seems so silly now in view of what my mom's going through. I just don't understand why she's keeping it from me. Doesn't she trust me?"

"Of course she does, but she's your mom and she wants to protect you. It hasn't been all that long since you lost your father, and she doesn't want to lay her illness on you. That must be it."

"It's hard for me to believe she's dying, because she looks so good. She's not losing any weight that I can see. In fact, if anything she's put on a little."

"Maybe her medication has done that. Sometimes meds will make a person bloat. Although…I agree, your mother looks fantastic."

"Well, I guess she'll have to tell me sooner or later. In the meantime, I'm going to take a leave of absence from the magazine. Until she's…you know. Gone."

Gina placed her hand over his. "I'm so sorry, Alex. I just want you to know that I'm here for you. If you want to talk, or if you need a shoulder to lean on, you can call me."

Alex wanted to do more than talk. He took her hand in both of his and held it firmly. Then he lifted it to his lips and kissed her palm. "Thanks, Gina. That means a lot. Traveling like I do, I meet a lot of people, but they're not exactly friends."

He signaled for the waiter and was informed that the bill had been paid. Standing, Alex helped Gina out of her chair, put his hand in the small of her back, and guided her toward the exit.

"It was nice of your dad to pick up the tab," he said, "but I thought this dinner was supposed to be our idea."

"Me too. I guess Papá was trying to make up for ruining your mother's clothes."

Alex supposed it only showed that Gaetano was a nice man and suitable for his mother.

Chapter 15

The green silk pantsuit lay in a heap on the floor, its wine stains still evident and now dried into permanent blotches. Estelle rolled away from the sight and stretched her arms above her head. She looked at the digital clock on her night table. Its minute slot flipped, and the time was now six twenty-three. She reached over and turned off the alarm before the obnoxious buzzing commenced. Gaetano had wanted to get up at six thirty and get to the restaurant. He'd been feeling guilty about putting so much of the workload on Mario.

She rose up on one elbow and leaned over and kissed him.

"Mmmumff," he mumbled.

She blew softly into his ear, then smiled as he tried to brush her away as he would a mosquito or housefly. She puffed again and then nibbled on his earlobe. His lashes fluttered and then his eyes opened partway. He turned toward her and nestled his face into her breasts, taking turns sucking at each nipple then biting them just a fraction beyond gentle.

His hands slid down her hips, cupped her butt, and he pulled her naked body on top of his. She felt her passion build, and when her breath became jagged gasps, she boldly mounted him. Her knees grasped his ribcage and she lost herself and reality. Fiercely she arched and bucked as he grasped her hips and plunged deeper inside.

She fell into the rhythm he set. Her body had never felt more alive. Every nerve ending emitted sparks, and her nostrils were filled with essence of his maleness. Her chin jutted out and her eyes closed halfway. She leaned even further backward, grabbing his forearms to keep from falling. She soared through space, saturating her body with an intense pleasure and joy she'd never before experienced or even imagined existed. They climaxed together, and she heard a scream of sheer delight, realizing only after it faded to a whimper that it had come from her lips.

She slumped. Exhausted, she lay prone on top of Gaetano and then let herself slide off to his side. Wrapping her arm around his waist, she held on to him tightly until she calmed.

"You wanted me to wake you early," she whispered.

"I like your wake-up calls," he replied.

He draped one arm around her and caressed her breasts, slid his hand down her belly and lower. Her breath caught and her pulse quickened. Two of his fingers found their way inside her, and with his thumb he massaged until she came again. She moaned and squeezed her eyes shut until tears escaped.

After a moment he pulled away. Estelle lay quietly; afraid to open her eyes for fear that it was all a dream. Gaetano rolled to one side, put his feet on the floor, and then left her bed. The shower turned on just before she dozed off.

When she awoke, Gaetano was dressing. Estelle watched. She'd forgotten how good it felt to be so totally satisfied. After Marty died, she'd packed her sexuality away and buried it deep within her soul. Gaetano had awakened and released it with more power and pleasure than ever.

Just looking at Gaetano in his briefs made her moist again. She was entering the age where she was supposed to dry up and wither away. Instead she felt like a juicy, ripe piece of fruit just waiting to be picked. Her body felt like a teenager's.

Gaetano looked over and smiled. "What's going on in that head of yours?"

"Oh, nothing. I was just thinking what a wonderful orchard farmer you are."

"What? Sometimes, *cara*, you make very little sense." He slipped into his shirt then pulled on his pants and zipped them. "How long are you going to stay in bed? Why don't you come in for lunch today?"

"I don't know what I'll do," she replied. "I keep thinking about Alex. I should have told him last night like we'd planned."

"We did try, but we didn't want him to know how far our relationship had gone and then the wine accident..." Gaetano trailed off.

Estelle nodded. "We kind of had fun at the kids' expense, but I'm feeling guilty now. I've kept him in the dark too long. In the beginning, I just didn't know how to put it into words. I must find the proper way to tell him now or he'll be furious."

"*Cara*, I'm sorry I told Gina," Gaetano said, "but I was in a very bad place. I still thought you were dying and I couldn't bear the thought of never seeing you again." He selected a tie and stood in front of the mirror to put it on. "I bet Alex will be glad you're well and happy. If he does get angry, it can't last long. Then, once he knows you are fine, he and Gina can concentrate on each other."

Estelle took the pillows from Gaetano's side of the bed and propped them behind her. She drew her knees up to her chin and watched Gaetano tuck in his shirt.

Of course Alex would be glad she wasn't dying. And she'd never been happier. But, where was this relationship with Gaetano going? Had he mentioned marriage? She tried to think back, and while they certainly had talked about the future, she couldn't recall if the M-word had ever been brought up.

Gaetano picked up his wallet and put it in his pants pocket, along with his keys, comb, and a small amount of change. He winked at Estelle and said, "I'll make some coffee and bring you a cup. Don't get up."

He came to the edge of the bed. Leaning down, he kissed her passionately and once again she felt herself go weak with desire. He patted her cheek and left the bedroom whistling.

Estelle slumped back into the pillows and was suddenly depressed. What if she was making a mistake by giving herself so freely to this man? He loved her. Of that she was certain, but was that all she wanted from this relationship—just love with no rules, no ties and no commitments? Such thoughts were not making her comfortable.

Well, perhaps she was rushing. The first thing she had to do this morning was call Alex and have him come over. She would tell him everything, from beginning to end. Well, everything except that she'd been sleeping with Gina's father. That explanation was something she was still working out. Maybe she should discuss with Gaetano what his intentions were. If his love didn't mean commitment, she could decide what that meant to her. Now that she was healthy, she could handle whatever happened.

She heard footsteps approaching down the hallway. Was the coffee brewed already?

"Mother, it's Alex."

Alex? Good God, she was caught! How had Gaetano explained his presence? It had never occurred to her that Alex might surprise her with an early morning visit.

She leapt out of bed and grabbed her robe off the hook just before he tapped on her door. Kicking her ruined pantsuit under the dust ruffle, she got back into bed and pulled the covers up under her chin.

"Mother, are you awake? May I come in?"

"Alex? Uh, sure, come in, dear. My goodness, what brings you over here so early?"

"It's not that early, really," he said. "It's almost eight, and you're usually up by this time." He entered the bedroom and stood at the foot of the bed, leaning against one of the tall posts.

He wore a golf shirt and shorts and looked as if he were off for a carefree game on the links at the local country club, but the look Estelle saw on his face was not carefree at all.

Well, of course he's worried. He thinks I'm dying. Oh, why hadn't she been honest with him last night? This was getting ridiculous.

"Mother, I wondered whose car was in the driveway, and then I saw Gaetano coming from around the back of the house. He said he was returning something you'd loaned him? What did you loan him?"

Play dumb, Estelle, was her first thought.

"Gaetano was here?" Obviously he'd seen Alex in time to split out the back door. "Oh, I loaned him some…food. Uh, rose food. Fertilizer stuff that has food and stuff all together…in the bag."

Alex looked puzzled. "I thought your gardener supplied all that."

"Well, he does, of course he does, but this was something different." She smiled and really wished she'd gotten up and at least gotten showered and dressed before all this took place.

Alex shook his head. "I invited Gaetano to come in, but he was apparently in a hurry. I thanked him for dinner last night."

"Well," Estelle said. "Isn't that nice? Umm, but, Alex dear, you haven't told me what brings you here."

The thin silk robe she wore was too revealing, so Estelle kept the covers pulled up to her chin. She was getting very uncomfortable, though, and wanted to throw off the unneeded covers. Of course, trying to explain her state of undress would be worse than being overheated.

Alex shoved his hands into his pockets and began to pace from the bed to the window. He pulled the drapes open, turned around, and looked at her as if he wanted to say something.

It was clear he was troubled about her, Estelle realized. She had to tell him the truth. About her relationship with Gaetano, too. But she needed to collect her thoughts and get into some clothes first. She couldn't think straight when Gaetano's scent still clung to her body as a sweet reminder of that great sex they'd just shared.

Reversing his steps, Alex stood near the bed again. "Mom, I've been thinking about a lot of things, and it occurred to me that we've not had any real time together for quite a while."

She shook her head. "Honey, I know you're busy. I don't expect—"

"So I'm taking some time off from the magazine, and I thought we could go do something together. Maybe go to a few plays, see an art exhibit or just hang out."

"But, Alex, you had this very big assignment scheduled. You were so excited about it. Indonesia, right?"

He's taking time off from his work because Gina told him I'm dying. Now she really felt guilty. She had to tell him immediately. But as she opened her mouth to speak, another thought occurred. *I can't just blurt this out. I want to do it right since I've totally screwed it up from the beginning.*

His voice filtered into her brain.

"...some things are more important than work." Her son stared at her like she was some African animal he was getting ready to photograph, and she wondered just what he'd figured out. "Are you feeling okay, Mom? I thought you looked flushed when I first came in." He put his hand to her forehead. "Do you have a fever? You feel a bit warm."

Warm? She was sweltering underneath the blanket and spread. Not to mention the way her lover had been generating heat in her like cayenne pepper in Texas chili.

"I'm fine," she said. "Why don't you go out into the kitchen and put on some coffee? I'll get dressed and join you there. I want to talk to you, but let me get decent first."

Boy, did she need to talk to him. The guilt from her deceit was overwhelming.

As soon as he was out of the room, Estelle made a mad dash for the shower. She stood under a spray of warm water and poured a puddle of body wash into her palm, lathered thoroughly with the peach-scented liquid as if it could wash away her guilt. Then she made a resolution: She'd call Gaetano as soon as she was dressed and let him know that the lies had to stop. She was going to tell her son about everything.

***

Gaetano had barely gotten to the restaurant, put on his apron, and begun working on the specials of the day when Gina popped through the service door in the back of the building.

"Papá! How did things go with you and Estelle last night?" She pulled a bar stool into the kitchen and plopped down on it to watch him work. "Do you have any idea how much longer she has? Oh, Papá, it's just too sad. I can't tell you how torn up Alex is over this. When is she going to tell him? He already knows, of course, but she needs to explain it all to him."

"So, you really told Alex?"

"Well, of course. I left a message on your machine. Don't you play them back? I'd thought he already knew. I'd thought she was telling him at the same time you told me. I don't understand any of this, and neither does he."

"If you will slow down," Gaetano interjected, "maybe I can answer some of your questions. I don't know when Estelle will explain everything to Alex, but I'm sure it will be soon. We must respect her enough to let her handle it in her own way." He stirred the sauce he was making then scooped a bit onto a spoon and offered Gina a taste. She shook her head, and he returned the long handled, oversized spoon to the counter.

"In the meantime," he said, "she and I are taking yours and Alex's advice and we are good friends again."

He added some more herbs and seasonings to the pot, letting it all simmer on the oversized commercial stove. Picking up the spoon again, he stirred three times before he turned and faced his daughter. Gesturing with the spoon he said, "I, of course, want to be more than just a friend, but Estelle is a careful woman. She always thinks of her son first."

"If that's so, why didn't she tell him about her illness? You have no idea how hard that was for me," Gina complained.

Gaetano struggled with his conscience. He could pretend he didn't know that Estelle was healthy. Would that be so bad? Yes, it probably would. He was misleading Gina, and he should tell her the truth right now. The fact that they'd let last night pass without telling the kids was bad enough; he was honor bound to come clean.

"Gina, she was trying to protect him. All parents want to protect their children from bad things," he began.

Then Gaetano vacillated on a decision. Doing the right thing had never been such a problem. Honesty had been one virtue he'd tried hardest to instill in his daughter. Always tell the truth, he'd told her since she was a little girl. Gina was successful *and* honest. That was one of the reasons he was so proud of her.

But, if he told Gina before Estelle told Alex, that might spoil any chance of Gina and Alex developing their relationship. They'd clearly bonded over Alex's imminent loss. Gina was not an ordinary girl. She loved her independence, and for her to compromise that in any way would require a good cause. For Gina to become Alex's bride? That would take a miracle. Almost as big a miracle as her ever taking the instruction on cooking that he'd been pushing.

"I admire Estelle for all she's been through and still wanting to protect her son, Papá," Gina spoke up. "You make her happy. I think you should go for the gusto."

Gaetano glanced up. "Gina, what do you mean, gusto?"

"Well, Papá, I'm not going to draw you a picture. It's just that Alex would feel so much better if his mother was with someone she cared about for whatever time she has left."

Gaetano stared into his daughter's eyes and saw only sympathy for Estelle and hope for their relationship. He couldn't let this opportunity go by. What was a little more time of deceit? She'd just admitted she was growing closer to Alex, and this might be her last chance. At close to thirty, she was set in her ways and could easily end up an old maid. That would be worse than Cousin Lucinda, who hadn't married until she was forty-six and too old to have babies. For Gina to be like that would make Rosie toss in her grave even more than Gina not knowing how to boil an egg!

"Do you know what would really make her happy, Gina?" Gaetano asked.

"I thought it was being with you. At least, until your spat."

"Oh, me? Well, I try." Gaetano busied himself with stirring the sauce again, then put the spoon down on the edge of the pot's stainless steel lid, wiped his hands on a towel, and approached his daughter. He put his arm around her shoulders and kissed her forehead. "No. More than love for herself, what Estelle wants most is for her son to marry a good girl. She wants this more than anything in the world."

"Papá, that is the sweetest thing."

"Well, he's her only child," Gaetano explained. "She doesn't want him to be alone after she's gone. It would make it so much easier for her if she knew he'd found love. Seeing how she's going to be gone and all. Think about it. This is all the lady's asking for. One last final wish."

Gina looked ill. "I think I'm going to cry. Alex is a great-looking guy, and he's really quite nice. Once you get past his obsession about that car."

She hadn't objected to the line of conversation. That was a good first step. It strained Gaetano to keep a solemn expression when he wanted to break into a full grin and do a little happy dance. "So, you and he had a good time last night, too?"

"Yeah, we did. I think I know him a little better now, and I wish we hadn't gotten off to such a bad start. Things might be different if so. I think he likes me, but I doubt if anything serious can develop. If that's what you're getting at."

Gaetano was insulted. What the heck was wrong with young people today? "Why not? You are a beautiful and smart girl. What is the matter with him? Does he think he's too good for—?"

Gina shook her head. "Papá, don't get so riled up. Alex and I are friends, but he's busy and so am I. Relationships take a lot of time, too, something neither of us has a lot of."

"Then you make time. The lady his mother is…dying, for God's sake. Where is your compassion?" It was too late to take back the words. He was wholeheartedly lying through his teeth now, and whatever he said would only make it worse. But it was for a good cause, so he pushed the guilt from his mind and added, "At least you could *try* to fall in love with him. Maybe those cooking classes—"

"Papá!" Gina jumped off the stool and glared at him. "What is the matter with you? Am I to be auctioned off like a prized heifer? It sounds like you'd marry me off to anybody just so that I won't end up like Cousin Lucinda. And if you keep going on about the cooking classes—"

Gaetano jumped in before she could gather steam. "No, no, *Bambina*, I didn't mean it that way, but Alex is a nice young man. You are a beautiful, nice girl, and what can it hurt to think about marriage?" He went back to the stove and stirred the sauce, hung his head and tried his best to look contrite. "I admit it. I want some grandbabies to bounce on my knees before I have to have them replaced. I'm not getting any younger, either. And what is so wrong with me wanting you to know how to make a nice meal?"

Gina gave a huge huff of irritation. "Papá, I have to go to work now. I didn't mean to yell at you, but please, I can't fall in love with Alex just to please his mother. Or you. As for cooking…maybe if I end up ever having time."

Gaetano nodded, kissed his daughter on both cheeks, and watched her leave the restaurant. He had planted the seed. Just maybe, she'd let it sprout.

The thought of his scheme working out made Gaetano almost giddy. But now he had to tell Estelle not to let on that he knew she wasn't dying. *Ah, the lies I've told are going to get me in hot water,* he realized, but it didn't seem like there was an easy way to fix things.

Gaetano put the lid on the pot and turned down the burner, deciding that he'd done the right thing. Whatever it took to turn Gina's thoughts to love and marriage would be worth the effort.

Of course, it had been a close call this morning. He had agreed with Estelle not to reveal their full relationship before she could set things right with Alex. If her son had come just a bit earlier, he'd have caught them together. What was it with adult children these days? Why didn't they ever call before barging in on their parents? Why didn't they learn to cook, settle down and make happy grandbabies just like they did in the old country?

164

His cell phone rang, and he unclipped it from his belt. "Hello, my beautiful tiger lady," he said, recognizing the number.

"Gaetano, I don't have time for sweet talk. Alex is in my kitchen making coffee and—"

"I'm so sorry I didn't have time," Gaetano interrupted. "I saw Alex coming up the front walk so, quick as a fox, I slipped out the back. Pretty smart, eh?"

He heard a deep sigh. "Gaetano, I'm telling Alex as soon as I hang up this phone."

Gaetano's eyes widened, and he almost cried out. "No, Estelle, not yet! I have things almost in place." He didn't know how to tell her that he'd continued to lie to Gina, so instead he said, "The kids are getting close. It wouldn't hurt to delay confessing a *tiny* bit longer, would it?"

"But, Gaetano, there's no need now. I'm not dying."

"What?" he said, his mind scrambling. "I know, I know. But, Estelle, we both love each other and we want grandbabies, don't we? It isn't a bad thing for us to want our kids to be happy like us. It's not wrong to wish Alex would marry Gina, just like I want to marry you. Maybe they wouldn't come over so early, and I'd be able to have coffee before I have to go to work."

"What did you say?"

"Our kids need to be married," he repeated. "Just like we need to be married."

"Mr. Lorenzo, are you proposing to me?" She sounded breathless.

"Only if you agree to keep dying for just a while longer."

Gaetano heard her sigh again, and he knew he was bringing her around. "Well, my darling, I would die for another morning like the one we shared today."

"Okay," Estelle said after another moment, "I think you're crazy, but I'll go along with this for a little while longer. I love you,

Gaetano, but no more than twenty-four hours can pass without Alex learning the truth. I'm so glad I'm not really dying."

"Me, too, my angel. I hope one more day will be enough time, but I promise you, they are getting closer. These kids are not as wise as we are. It takes time for them to see we know best."

When Estelle disconnected, Gaetano turned back to his sauce, his mind full of possibilities. Maybe the restaurant would soon be renamed The Two Gaetanos' Ristorante. Maybe he would have a grandson, heir to the special recipes his *nonna* gave his papá who'd then given them to him. He'd wanted to pass them to Gina, but the girl still hadn't learned to boil water. Would she ever?

Rosie probably suffered from motion sickness with all the rolling in her grave going on.

Chapter 16

Alex clamped the phone between his chin and shoulder as he spread mustard on a bread slice. His morning had been a total waste of time. He'd brought up an art exhibit to his mother, but she'd seemed so out of sorts that he hadn't pushed. Whatever she'd wanted to tell him must have vanished from her thoughts, too. By the time the coffee had been poured, she couldn't seem to find anything to talk about but the weather.

He'd left his mother's house in a state of confusion and figured maybe Gina could sort it out for him. Of course, she'd be at work now, but maybe they could meet for drinks afterward or at least talk on the phone. He'd leave a message, since it didn't seem like she was going to pick up.

He put the top on his sandwich and took a bite just as his call was answered.

"Hello? Hello, is anyone there?" The female voice was shaky.

"Hwrphllo? Sorry," Alex sputtered as he quickly swallowed his bite then recovered. "Is this Gina?" When Gina assured him he had the right number he said, "It's me. Alex. I'm having lunch, and you picked up just as I took a bite. Sorry again. Actually, I thought I'd be talking to your answering machine."

"Oh?" she replied. "Well, I hope I didn't disappoint you."

"No, not at all. I'm glad you're there. But, why are you home?" he wondered aloud. "Shouldn't you be at work?"

She sounded upset. "Normally I'm just finishing up in court about this time, but I'm taking a personal day. Actually, something's been happening and I need to talk to someone. Are you busy?"

"Actually, no," he admitted. "I took that leave of absence to spend time with my mother. I don't know how long yet. Something's going on with her, too, and I was calling to see if you could make any sense of it. Gina, are you okay? You sound funny." He placed the remains of his sandwich on a plate and took a bottle of beer out of the refrigerator. The phone remained silent as he clamped the receiver on his shoulder again and twisted the cap off the bottle. "Gina, are you still there?"

"I'm sorry," she said at last. "Alex, I think I'm being followed. I'm probably being paranoid, but it's…it's just plain weird. Could you come over? Or maybe I could come to your place."

"What? Who's following you? Do you mean like a stalker? It couldn't be a disgruntled client, could it? Oh, I guess not, you never lose a case. Oh, but wait. Maybe it's someone you beat the socks off in court. It's not me, though. I swear."

She sounded annoyed when he chuckled. "It's not funny, and I really don't want to talk about it on the phone. I figured I'd call you because you seemed like someone I could count on, but—"

He quickly interrupted. "Gina, I'm sorry. You're right, it isn't funny and you sound upset. I didn't mean to be glib." Alex looked around his kitchen and surveyed the stack of dishes in the sink. "Listen, I'll come to your place. The maid service is due here in a little while so I was leaving anyway. Give me about half an hour."

"I'll tell you everything when you get here. I'm probably overreacting, but it's creeping me out. Thanks. I really do appreciate it."

The line went dead, and Alex wolfed down the rest of his sandwich. Gulping the last ounce of beer, he stopped in the bathroom and brushed his teeth. Then he gathered up his mail and anything he didn't want the maid snooping into and locked it all in a desk drawer.

He'd more or less stowed his equipment and suitcases. Well, actually he'd tossed them into one of the hall closets, packed, and figured he'd be ahead of the game for the next trip. Where he went on assignment didn't usually require that his garments be neatly creased and pressed.

He locked the door and headed for the garage when he saw short, chubby Sadie puffing and huffing up the sidewalk. The maid carried a bag big enough to hold a fair-sized kid or most of his camera equipment. He'd never figured out what it contained.

"Hi, Sadie. I'm leaving and in a hurry. Do you have your key?"

"What do you think? Of course I have my key. I've only been coming here for—"

Alex didn't slow down to hear the rest. The woman had been sarcastic for as long as he'd known her but was good-hearted for all that. He'd chat with her next time.

The drive to Gina's didn't take long, but it was long enough for Alex to go over all the things that somehow seemed off-kilter: his mother's strange attitude, Gaetano borrowing rose food, Gina's fear that someone was following her. Who needed an exotic day job? Compared to his home life lately, tromping around in a rainforest seemed almost boring. He'd finally found a feisty, interesting girl. Too bad he'd probably be leaving the country soon and she wouldn't want to go with him.

***

Holding the phone in one hand, Gina opened the door and motioned Alex inside with the other. She nodded at the sofa, silently mouthed a request to be excused and went into the other room to continue her conversation.

Alex sat and examined the sofa. A contemporary, but quite comfortable off-white upholstered piece, it wasn't leather, which was what he had in his place. Maybe leather was a guy thing, though. He stretched out his legs and took a more careful inventory of his surroundings.

Gina had managed to keep it simple, and yet her accessories, like that neutral-colored afghan, gave the room a cozy feel. Several nice prints hung on the walls. Van Gogh's *Café at Night* had been transferred to canvas and hung frameless on the long wall. It pulled in splashes of bright yellow and red from the throw pillows, which looked as if they had been carelessly tossed but Alex suspected Gina had purposely arranged them to look that way.

Her surroundings duplicated her persona, a contradiction of rigid order and relaxed control. Gina Lorenzo occasionally gave the appearance of a breezy, laid-back person, but underneath there were definite hints of a controlling nature. That's probably what made her such a good attorney. Even her petite size fooled people. Small but mighty. Neither he nor his lawyer had guessed that such an angelic-looking girl would play such hardball.

He clasped his hands behind his head and considered. His profession demanded an eye for detail, and he used this talent on people as much as photography subjects. Personalities could be captured in a single shot like the essence of a spectacular rain forest, and Gina was definitely more pleasant a subject than some wild species in Asia. He found himself thinking about Indonesia less and less.

Gina came into the room and put her phone back in its cradle. "I'm sorry, but I had to take care of some details at the office," she said. Dressed in a simple pair of jean shorts and a loose cotton sleeveless blouse buttoned up the front, she looked like more a twelve-year-old than an accomplished attorney. He was flattered that she'd called on him to ride in on his white horse to save the damsel in distress.

"Okay, so what is this about someone following you?"

Gina sat down on the other end of the sofa and took one of the small red throw pillows and crushed it to her chest. "I'm probably making a mountain out of a molehill, but this just doesn't seem right. A few weeks ago I had this client, Boris Urzinsky. He always gave me a weird vibe, but I just kind of pushed past that. I won his case and he wanted to take me to lunch to show his appreciation. I don't mix pleasure with business, though, so I said no."

Alex grinned. "I believe that. I sure didn't have any fun during our court business."

She didn't crack a smile. "I know you feel that I didn't play fair, that—"

Alex interrupted. "Gina, I'm kidding. I apologize for the bad joke."

Her face softened. Then a small smile crept across it. "It wasn't a bad joke. It was funny. I'm just not on the top of my game this morning." After a moment she sighed and continued. "When I declined his lunch invitation, Boris got pushy. At first I was polite, but he didn't give up. Then there were these flowers. You didn't send me flowers, did you? No, of course not. Why would you after I whupped your ass?"

"Touché," Alex said when she paused, clearly having intended the comment for comic effect. He supposed he'd had that coming. "Go on. Please."

Her demeanor sobered, and she pulled her legs up underneath her and fingered the fringe on the small pillow in her arms. She took a deep breath before she did as he asked.

"Then there were the phone calls. Somehow he was able to get my home number, which never should have happened. Anyway, I blocked the phone calls and felt sure he'd given up…" She caught her lower lip between her teeth and frowned. "It's just that lately I've been seeing this green sedan everywhere I go. For the past few weeks. I think it was even parked around here, though I'm not positive. I haven't been able to get the license number yet or I'd know for sure and report it. Right now, however, I don't have a lot to go on. Maybe it's nothing. Maybe Mr. Urzinsky is perfectly harmless or it's someone else...."

"Well, the phone calls are definitely harassment," Alex said. "But maybe the car's just someone who lives around here. How many times have you noticed it?"

"I saw it again this morning when I was on my way to see Papá. Well, I could have sworn it was behind me, but by the time I got to the restaurant it wasn't anywhere to be seen. I know that sounds silly, but it makes me nervous. To see the same car after those phone calls... I may just be getting paranoid."

When she looked at Alex with those beautiful brown eyes, he barely resisted the urge to take her into his arms and keep her safe, from a silly paranoia or from anything else in the world that might threaten her.

"By the way," she suddenly said, her face lighting up and her eyes flashing with excitement. "I think our parents are on their way to restoring their relationship. Papá was in good spirits this morning."

"Really?" Alex said. "I saw him this morning, too. He was at Mother's house returning something he'd borrowed. He seemed a bit stressed, though. Mom wasn't aware he'd even been there."

Gina looked surprised. "You saw my dad at your mother's house? That's odd. He didn't mention a thing about it. What was it he borrowed?"

"I don't know. Rose food or something. My mother wasn't exactly herself this morning either."

"Well," Gina allowed, "they both are interested in gardening, so maybe that's reasonable. I mean, if she didn't know he was there and—"

Alex interrupted. He couldn't stand it any longer. He didn't want to think of any threat to this beautiful young woman's well-being. "Gina, we'll talk about our parents in a minute. Let's get back to your being followed. I think you should report that car. You're better off safe than sorry."

"I've thought about it," she admitted, "but it seems so silly when I look at it objectively. I mean, what do I really have to report? A client was a bit enamored, invited me to lunch and maybe sent flowers and called me a few times. That's not exactly a death threat."

"No, but what if he's the one following you?"

"It may not even be the same car every time." Gina seemed to be backpedaling more every moment. "I think I got you over here for nothing. Let's talk about my Papá and your mother, instead. Do you really think your mother has forgiven him?"

Alex sighed. He really wanted to get more details on Boris Urzinsky, but he saw that Gina's mood had shifted. She had put the possible stalker behind her and only wanted to discuss their parents. He supposed he should humor her.

"I've never known my mother not to forgive," he said. "Lord knows she was always giving Dad the benefit of the doubt. I imagine if your father is acting cheerful, they probably made peace with each other. I'm frankly more concerned about her health."

"Well, of course you are," Gina said. "Her illness has to be considered, but that's even more reason for her to have some enjoyment and fun while she can. Papá says he loves her. He's never said that about any woman except my mama."

Alex grimaced, overwhelmed by reality. "Even if he loves her, where can the relationship go? It's not like she can participate in much. Well, she won't be able to when she gets sicker. What if toward the…last of her days, your father gets tired of her being ill and dumps her? She won't need to be abandoned, especially then."

Gina's hackles were raised, Alex saw. She'd put her father on such a high pedestal that he probably suffered nose bleeds. But Gaetano was still a man. From his own personal experiences, Alex knew most guys, including himself, said things that weren't one hundred percent true. He had to protect his mother.

"My father is not that kind of man," Gina said. "He was by my mother's side during her entire illness. He does not abandon."

"Gina, I'm not saying your dad isn't a good guy, but he was married to your mother. He and my mother have only known each other…what? A few weeks?"

"You're so cynical. If my father was the type of man you describe, he would never have taken the time to get to know your mother. He saw her in his restaurant and realized she was lonely and in distress. He is a kind, caring person, and actually, she's the one who will be leaving him in the end. Not Papá."

"For God's sake, Gina, the woman's dying. It's not like she has a choice in the matter."

"Well, Papá will be there for her until the very end. You can count on that. He's loyal and true and… Alex, you don't think they…you know, *do* things, do you?"

Do things? Did Gina mean have sex? His mother was having sex? Oh, my God, it was absurd. She only had a little time left, so sex would be the last thing on Estelle Bennett's mind. Wouldn't it?

He glanced at Gina and suddenly it hit him. If his days were numbered, he would be looking for sex. Sex with Gina would be great. He kind of wanted that even though his days weren't numbered. Actually, he wanted it a great deal.

Totally insane thoughts. Alex shook his head to clear it. He got up from the sofa and paced over to the window, raked his fingers through his thick head of hair, and chuckled at the idea of his mom out looking for play. His mother wasn't some young, silly schoolgirl. No way.

"Come on, Gina, that's crazy," he said aloud. "We're talking about our parents. My mother is sick. I seriously doubt if that's even occurred to either of them. My parents weren't that...er, ah, they didn't exactly engage in a lot of...*that*, even when my father was healthy."

"How would you know?" Gina asked and then giggled. "Did you spy on them? What a nasty little boy."

She was pushing his buttons again, getting him riled up so she could cut him off at the knees. But, she was kind of right. The truth of the matter was that at thirteen he'd been real curious about what went on in his parents' bedroom, especially after Bobby Renfrew invited him over and they'd surfed a few enlightening websites on the computer. After that afternoon with Bobby, Alex had started making up excuses to go into his parents' room after they retired. He'd never seen anything shocking, though. His father was usually on the phone and his mother would be propped up in bed reading. She'd reprimand him for still being awake and then walk him back to his room to tuck him in. He'd been way too old to be tucked in, but it relieved his mind to know that his parents weren't like the people in Bobby's computer.

Pushing aside those memories, Alex returned to the sofa and gave Gina a disgusted look. He even puffed through his lips like it was the most unbelievable statement ever. "No, I didn't spy on my parents! Geez, Gina, what do you take me for?"

She looked contrite. "I apologize. I was just having some fun with you. But you know, Alex, I'm having a hard time trying to figure out this relationship stuff. I mean, with our parents."

Alex relaxed and settled back into the sofa. He hadn't been a nasty little boy, but he'd been a curious one.

He glanced at Gina. She was frowning, a slight blush burning across her cheeks. "It's weird. At first, I thought Papá wanted my approval of your mom. Later, Papá told me she was very ill and that he was in love with her; he wanted our help in getting them back together after their spat. But now—get this—he's really pushing for *us* to hook up. He says if we were together, it would make your mother happy."

"Really?" Alex fought back his immediate desire to take Gina and kiss her. Instead, he tried to gauge exactly where she was going with this. It couldn't be where his head was going. "I admit I want my mother to be happy, but surely our parents don't think people fall in love on command."

Gina let her body slump against him. She was warm and smelled nice, and it seemed only natural that his arm should go around her.

"Parents can be confusing at times," he continued, letting his head rest atop Gina's. The aroma of her shampoo was almost intoxicating. Maybe he ought to ask her out? After all, his mother apparently wanted that, and he wanted his mother to be happy. One date wouldn't be a lifelong commitment, and maybe Gina was even dealing with a stalker. This way he could keep an eye on her and keep her safe at the same time. He knew he wanted to keep her safe.

"You like to dance?" he blurted. "I know a neat place with a terrific jazz trio. Let's go out. We'll eat first," he added.

"I love to dance," she responded immediately.

Alex grinned. "Okay, let me run home and change. I'll pick you up in a couple of hours."

"This is a great idea," Gina replied. "I'll be ready."

Alex disengaged himself from her, a bit sorrowfully, perhaps, rose up off the sofa and left Gina at her front door. Going outside, he gave a quick glance around but didn't see any green cars. She was probably right, then. Most likely her fears were imagined. Still, he was glad he'd broken the ice and they were actually going on a date. Even if it was partly for their parents' sake.

It was for their parents' sake, wasn't it?

***

His dirty green sedan sat parked in the shadows of several trees, and from within it, using a pair of binoculars he'd picked up at a pawn shop, Boris had watched Alex go into Gina's condo. He'd seen her face when she opened the door. Lots of smiles for the pretty boy, but not even the time of day for a real man. It made him angry.

Disgusted, Boris spat out the words, "So, Miss Fancy Lawyer Lady, you do like *some* men, eh?"

He was relieved when at last Alex left. That was good. The time had finally come for him to go into action. Gina needed to show him the respect he deserved. He'd given her plenty of chances, and this was the last. He'd done everything in his power to be nice to Miss Lorenzo, and she'd acted like she was too good for him. Well, he'd see about that. No one disrespected Boris Urzinsky. Not even pretty ladies like her.

Chapter 17

Gaetano helped Estelle clear the table and went to work cleaning the pots and pans. He'd prepared dinner for the two of them in her kitchen, a conveniently arranged space almost as well-equipped as his restaurant.

"Did I tell you that our children are going out on a date tonight?" After scrubbing it, he handed Estelle the pot he'd used for the pasta. She took it from him, smiled, and dried it with a tea towel.

"Yes, you did. Three times, actually. But don't get your hopes up for them hitting it off as well as we have," she reminded him. "They want different things than we do."

Gaetano drained the sink, dried his hands on a paper towel which he then used to wipe out the stainless steel basin. "Oh, I know, I know," he said. He didn't want her to think he was as excited as he was, but he had a feeling this was all going to work out. His Gina and her Alex were perfect for each other. Sometimes the universe conspired to make everyone happy.

Estelle bent over and put some pans away in a lower cabinet. As she did, Gaetano admired the way her slacks fit her rear. He resisted the urge to pat her bottom, but when she turned around he held out his arms and she came into them without hesitation. When he held her like this, it felt as if she had always belonged there. She was part of him. Connected.

"I just wish they could have what we have," he said. "Those kids don't realize that building a career can suck out all your energy. Then, when you're no longer young, there is nothing but the business."

Estelle snuggled closer. "You are so right. A career can bring you power and money, but it can't hold you or kiss you. Or do other things." She glanced up at him shyly.

Gaetano lifted Estelle's chin and kissed her gently on her lips. She responded by sliding her arms around his neck.

"Have you told your daughter what you're considering? If you're serious about it, she needs to know as soon as possible. We're keeping enough from both of them, and—"

"Not yet. When you suggested making Mario a partner in the restaurant, it took me a while to accept the idea. It will be the same for Gina."

"I hope she won't think I tried to influence you."

"She might at first, but Mario knows the business as well as I do and he's trustworthy. Besides, he's like a brother. Gina will see that Mario will be an asset. It's not like she wants to take over and run the restaurant."

The idea had come up when they were discussing their honeymoon and where they should go for it. Gaetano had acknowledged he'd leaned too much on Mario recently for his friend to be just an employee, and he would be taking even more time off after he and Estelle were married. Selling his part of the business was the only fair thing to do.

"Regardless of what you decide, we must tell both Gina and Alex that I am not dying," Estelle announced.

Gaetano did not reply. After several minutes, Estelle glanced at him. "Did you hear me? The twenty-four hours will have come and gone soon. I want to tell them."

"I heard, but I don't want to think about that yet. This is their real first date alone. If we want them to find each other, it's going to take time." Holding her away from him, he gazed into her eyes, which just about made him forget what they were talking about. "It won't be much longer, and I promise we'll tell them about our plans and about you being healthy. They'll probably be so excited over their new relationship that Gina won't even care about what I decide to do with the restaurant."

Estelle's expression became concerned. "What if we're being selfish and manipulative, Gaetano? Shouldn't we let the kids find their own paths? If someone had tried to push us together, we'd have resented it."

Gaetano shook his head. "Not me. I would have been overjoyed. It would have saved me all that courting and flowers and taking you to exotic places."

"What exotic places?"

"Ah, *cara*, you wound me. When I take you in my arms and smother you with kisses, do you not soar to a place you have never before been?" He began to kiss her neck, her lips, her ears and her breasts in a wild frenzy until she burst into laughter. That only made his desire for her build, especially when she returned his kisses and pressed her body closer to his. He tightened his grasp and lifted her up until she wrapped her legs around his waist, and then he carried her out of the kitchen and down the hallway.

"Did you remember to put your car in the garage?" she whispered as he laid her on the bed.

"Yes, I did—and I locked all the doors," Gaetano answered.

"Doesn't matter. Alex has a key," she murmured as he pulled her T-shirt over her head.

He unhooked her bra and tossed it aside. "Get the key back."

***

Gina was nervous about finally being on a real date with Alex. She was excited, too. She hurried through her shower but took the time to rub sweet honey and vanilla-scented body lotion all over her arms and shoulders and legs. Her skin practically glowed as she did. She surveyed her body in the mirror and was pleased to see barely any tan lines from her last outing at the beach. Her skin was olive, smooth, and perfect.

Maybe she and Alex could take in a beach day soon. Maybe they would even rent a sailboat. She'd always wanted to do that, but work had been much too crazy. Work. It seemed like she hadn't been thinking about that as much as she used to.

Gina capped her tube of cream and wrapped a towel around her body. Taking a comb, she started on her thick mop of curls but stopped when a sound came from downstairs. She froze, then listened for a moment but heard nothing more.

Shrugging, Gina shook her head and walked into her bedroom. There she found a white lace thong and matching lacy bra in the bureau, but at the exact moment the drawer closed against the wood frame of the dresser, Gina heard another sound. She was beginning to be concerned.

Quickly she stepped into the thong and fastened her bra. She moved to the walk-in closet and grabbed her shorty robe from its hook, slipped her arms into the kimono sleeves, and tied the sash in a snug knot at her waist. Then, creeping out of the closet and straining her ears for any sound she couldn't identify, she tiptoed to the bedroom door and peeked out.

The hallway was empty, the silence eerie. But if no one was there, no one would be making a sound.

What on earth is wrong with me? I'm getting way too paranoid. She chided herself for being a scaredy cat and went back to finish dressing.

She didn't know what kind of place Alex was taking her, but if they were going to dance, she thought a skirt and blouse would be more appropriate than slacks. She chose a woven jersey flared skirt in a wild black and white design, and a fitted halter of white pique that zipped up the side and plunged in the front to show a modest amount of cleavage.

When she leaned into the mirror to add a pair of black and white drop earrings, she caught a flash of movement behind her reflection. Panicked, she whirled. This time, it wasn't nothing.

"How nice you look, Miss Lorenzo. I am pleased you have gone to so much trouble for me."

***

Alex stopped in front of Gina's place and turned off the engine. He couldn't remember when he'd had such jitters. Feeling anxiety about a date was new to him, but he really wanted this time with Gina to go well. He'd changed his shirt and tie three times before settling on a casual, open-collared sport shirt and tan linen-blend slacks.

He walked toward her door. Although the sun hadn't quite disappeared, the entryway was sheltered by a small overhang, and the direction the door faced shielded it from direct light. The small porch was in semi-darkness.

I should suggest she get a dusk-to-dawn porch light for safety.

As he neared the entrance, a sick feeling stirred his gut. The house's front door stood ajar.

"Gina?" Could she have left it open for him? Not very smart, if so.

Alex gingerly stepped inside the house and looked around. The print he'd admired earlier in the living room hung lopsided on the wall, the afghan was halfway on the floor. A few of the throw pillows were askew, too.

"Gina, where are you?" Alex called, a bit louder this time. The only response was silence.

His heartbeat quickened, but he willed it to slow down so that he could think. Maybe she'd had to rush out at the last minute for some reason. Maybe her father had fallen ill. Dear God, maybe something was wrong with his mom. If so, he'd have been called, though. Wouldn't he? It was bound to be something else.

I'll call her. She may need help.

The call took a few seconds to connect. Alex heard Gina's phone ring, both in his ear and in the condo's upper level. Which made him fear that maybe Gina was hurt. Had she fallen in the bathtub or slipped on the tile and hit her head? He bounded up the stairs two at a time and quickly established that she was nowhere in sight. Her phone continued to ring from the nightstand, but he silenced it when he disconnected.

Don't just stand here. Do something.

He whipped out his cell again and punched in his mother's number. "Come on, Mom, pick up the phone."

On the fourth ring, he heard Estelle's voice, and she sounded as if she'd been napping. "Hello?"

"Mom, it's Alex."

"Darling, how are you? I was—"

"Mom, are you okay?"

"Of course, dear. As a matter of fact, I was just about to—"

"Mom, have you talked to Gaetano tonight? Did he say anything about Gina going to see him?"

"Well, as a matter of fact, dear, I fixed dinner for Gaetano and we were just…uh, finishing up our coffee. I don't think he had any plans with Gina. Let me ask him—"

"No, Mom, just let me talk to him."

"Of course," Estelle said, apparently not annoyed by his brusqueness. "Just a minute, I'll take the phone to him."

Though only seconds passed, it seemed a lot longer before he heard the Italian's voice. "Alex? What's the matter? Don't tell me you and Gina are fussing again?"

"No, actually I'm at her place to take her out."

"That's wonderful," Gaetano said. "Where are you taking her?"

Alex could hear the man's ear-to-ear grin just from the sound of his voice. It would soon vanish.

"That's just it. When I got here, the door was open and there's no sign of her anywhere. Frankly, Gaetano, I'm worried. She thinks someone's been following her, and—"

"What?" Gaetano's voice faded for a second before he bellowed, "Don't go anywhere. I'm coming right over."

Alex's news had obviously launched Gina's father like a rocket from Cape Canaveral. Before he hung up, the older man shouted a few more commands: "Check with the neighbors. Call 911. Call the FBI! I'm leaving now."

The connection was broken.

***

Soon Alex had knocked on the doors of the closest neighbors, but most of them hadn't gotten home from work yet. Those who answered didn't have anything to tell him.

He went down to see if her car was still parked. It was. Seeing that, he punched *9-1-1* into his phone, although he still felt a bit uncomfortable doing so. In spite of his misgivings, there might still be a reasonable explanation for Gina's absence. For the life of him, though, he couldn't think of one at the moment.

He was still trying to explain the situation to the 911 operator when he saw Gaetano and his mother sprinting up the front walk. Gaetano had a wild look in his eyes, and both parents looked like they'd just thrown themselves together. His mother's hair was tousled, and she didn't have on even a smudge of lipstick. It wasn't very often that his mother went out without lipstick.

"Yes, sir," the 911 operator was now saying, "we've had a separate call reporting a disturbance at that address, and a patrol car is on its way."

Alex thanked her and closed his phone.

"Alex, I called the police and told them my little girl was missing," Gaetano called out as he and Estelle came within speaking distance. As if to prove his words, a black and white pulled up at the curb.

Two uniformed policemen got out and walked in their direction. Gaetano rushed to meet them halfway. After it was established that Gaetano was the missing girl's parent, the older officer took out his notepad and addressed him.

"How old is the little girl, sir, and when did you notice her missing? Did you check with her playmates? What does she look like?"

Gaetano took a gulp of air and then began to describe Gina. "She's got lots of curly hair and beautiful brown eyes and—"

"How old is she, sir?" the officer repeated.

"What? Oh, my Gina is twenty-eight."

"Twenty-eight? Wait a minute, I thought we had a missing kid here."

"But this is not like her," Gaetano explained. "Alex was going to take her somewhere. She would not just leave."

"Fellow, I don't know what you're trying to pull, but maybe she just didn't want to go out with this dude," the younger policeman growled. Gaetano looked extremely put out.

Alex stepped between them. "Officer, I know we may be a little excited, but if you would just take a look inside her place, I think you'll agree that something is not right. The lady thought someone was following her, and—"

"Yes, who's been following my Gina? What is this about? Why didn't she tell me that?" Gaetano elbowed his way between the officers until his face was mere inches from Alex's.

The second policeman stepped close and put his hand on Gaetano's arm. "Let's just settle down a bit here and take a look inside. Even if your daughter is gone, we can't consider her missing until twenty-four hours have passed. These things usually don't amount to anything," he added sympathetically.

"I'm telling you, Gina would not leave like this. Just, poof? No, something is wrong." Gaetano scowled at both officers and then gave Alex a similar look, as if he were to blame for the situation.

"Did you say something to make her mad, Alex?" Estelle asked.

"No, Mom, we were getting along really well. I'd come over earlier, and then we decided to go out for a little dinner and maybe some dancing afterward. She was fine when I left."

"And what time was that?" The older officer took his pen out of his shirt pocket as the younger cop disappeared through Gina's front door. His hand rested on his holstered firearm.

Alex gave a full account of his earlier visit with Gina, with the times and a brief overview of their conversations, but he was careful to leave out anything that had to do with the parents since he didn't want them to know how much they had discussed his mother's imminent demise. Although, when Alex glanced in his mother's direction he had to admit she still didn't look like she was suffering from anything serious. Her color was good, and her figure looked full. She looked years younger than her fifty-something.

The young cop had reappeared. "Well, the place has a bit of disorder, but heck, it doesn't look like it's been trashed or anything. I can't see any definite signs of a struggle."

Gaetano's frustration was contagious. Now Alex had it, too. "That's because you wouldn't know what's out of place or not. The girl is a neat freak, and I'm telling you she wouldn't have anything on the floor and the picture on the wall not straight. She'd never leave it like that. Another thing. I called her phone and heard it ringing upstairs. She always has her phone."

"He's right. Gina is a nit-picker about her house. No crooked pictures," Gaetano chimed in.

"Look, folks, give me her description again and don't touch anything inside. If she hasn't turned up in twenty-four hours, give us a call and we'll do some checking," said the older officer. He then jotted down Gaetano's description of Gina, rolling his eyes only once, after Gaetano launched into a dialogue on how smart she was, expounding on her courtroom successes.

The younger of the two locked Gina's door, made a few more comments about not worrying, and then both policemen returned to their squad car.

Gaetano turned to Alex. His brow creased and his eyes were pleading. "Alex, tell me about this person who's been following Gina. Why would anyone follow her? What did they want from her, did she say?"

Estelle stepped close, put her arm though Gaetano's and stroked his hand. Alex was unsurprised. His mother was always the comforter, and even now, when she had so much to deal with, she was trying to make someone else feel better.

"I wish I knew more. Gina was vague about the details, other than a client that had become something of a pest and—"

"What client? Who? Some guy? Some crazy woman who is jealous of my Gina, maybe?"

"The client's name was…Boris something. Russian, I guess. She also mentioned a green car that had been parked near the condo, which is why she thought someone might be following her, but she never got a license plate number."

Gina's father glanced at Alex's mother. She patted his hand again and murmured something too soft for Alex to hear.

Well, Alex planned on driving around the area to see if he could spot any green sedans. He didn't want his mother or Gaetano with him, though. He didn't want to put them in any danger if there was any.

"Listen, Gaetano, why don't you take Mom and go on home to your place. Maybe Gina's car wouldn't start and she got a ride with someone…somewhere." He petered off.

"That doesn't make any sense. Where would she suddenly have gone? She's been kidnapped. I'm sure of it."

Alex agreed with Gaetano's assessment the more he thought about it, but he knew he should be strong and give the older man something to hang on to. He put his hand on Gina's father's shoulder and gave it a light squeeze. Finding words to comfort were not so easy.

"Gaetano, Mom, please don't stay here. If she had an errand to do or if she got called into work for an emergency or something, she'll contact us as soon as she can. Hey, maybe she even went to the restaurant." It seemed a long shot, but still a possibility.

"Perhaps she left a message there," Estelle offered. She slipped her arm around Gaetano's waist and began to guide him to his car. "Let's go by and see if Mario or any of the crew has heard from her. Then we'll go by your house and check the answering machine."

Gaetano's shoulders sagged and his head drooped. "Ah, I don't know. Maybe Mario knows something. The police are stupid, though. My Gina could be in danger and they think it's a big joke."

Estelle moved him, still muttering, down the walkway then glanced back at Alex. "Call us as soon as you know anything. Come on, dear, let's get to the car. I'll drive."

Alex marveled at his mother's fortitude. She was living the last few weeks or months of her life perhaps, and yet she was bearing the burden of Gaetano's weight as he leaned on her and shuffled to his car. And she would be driving? A remarkable woman, his mom.

As soon as the parents had pulled away from the curb, Alex made one more round of the close neighbors in the complex. While a few more answered their doorbells, no one could tell him anything new. He didn't have her car keys, either, so there was no way he could check to see if her vehicle was working. Finally, he fell back to his original plan; he went to his car and began what he feared would be a fruitless search. How many green sedans can there be? Green sedans of unknown make and model.

He drove routes that he thought Gina would have taken. His gut felt like he'd swallowed a pincushion, and his head pounded like a snare drum. He stopped at a small shopping mall and poked his head into various stores, hoping she'd gone for a new outfit, knowing the probability was slim. Maybe she'd taken a cab when her car wouldn't start. He should have just waited for her to change clothes and then leave with him.

Unfortunately, even as he was inquiring of salesgirls and clerks, he knew he was wasting his time. Obviously Gina had gotten a visitor. An unwelcome one. If only he had been around to protect her.

Chapter 18

Alex drove around until his gas tank was almost on empty. It had been hours since he'd left Gina's condo, and now he was punching in the numbers on his cell phone to connect with his mother's cell. Even though he didn't think he could hold any food down, he was aware of a gnawing hunger in his gut. Or maybe it was fear.

"Hi, Mom. How's Gaetano doing?"

"Not well, I'm afraid. Alex, he's beside himself with worry. Frankly, I'm contemplating calling a doctor for some medical advice."

"He's that much over the edge?" Alex asked. "Really?"

"Well, he's come a bit undone. But, then, Gina is his only child. It's no secret that he thinks she hung the moon."

Alex sighed. "Well, Mom, I'm beginning to think he has every reason to worry. I'm practically ready to storm the police station and demand some action, myself. Where could she be? It's been hours."

"Oh, honey, I wish I knew. Gaetano has called everyone she's ever known, trying to find out if anyone has seen her. No one at the restaurant knew anything. Do you have her work number?"

"No," Alex said, "but tell Gaetano I'll go to her office tomorrow and see if I can get any information on her clients, especially that Boris who's been pestering her. If not, maybe the police will be ready to start a real investigation by then."

His mother's voice softened. "They may not be too accommodating. Gaetano has called Officer O'Neal at least a dozen times. He was the older cop we met earlier. He's probably regretting giving Gaetano his card."

"So, why don't they *do* something?" Alex let out a huge breath to regain his composure. "I'm going in circles, so I think I'm going to go home and start again in the morning. I hope you'll try to get some rest. You have to take care of yourself," he reminded her.

"I'm fine, dear. I'll talk to you in the morning."

Alex closed his cell and thought again how very strong his mother was. God, it was going to be hard when she was gone.

A pang of despair joined his respect for his mother. Where was Gina? Was she being hurt? Dear God, was she being sexually assaulted? Images flashed through his mind, each worse than the last.

The only green cars Alex had seen on the road had shown females at the wheel and more times than not kids strapped in car seats behind. There really wasn't much he could do until tomorrow, and he was becoming weary if not sleepy. He made one more circle around the complex and then headed for home. This evening could have been the best, and yet it had turned into a nightmare.

***

Boris Urzinsky stirred food in the pan on the burner and glanced at Gina. "I'm thinking you will want to eat something now. I know you wanted to go out, but it was too risky tonight. This soup will be good, even if it came from a can." He looked over at her and shrugged. "I am also going to eat something. My stomach is craving food.

"Other parts of me are hungry also. You get my meaning?" He grabbed his crotch and grinned, then howled in laughter and winked at her. "I learned your papá is good cook, yes? He owns restaurant and so you must be a good cook too. Good cook is a good thing for a wife to be. Good food makes for happy husbands."

Gina would have hurled insults at him if she didn't have a gag in her mouth, and she'd have scratched his eyes out if her hands were free instead of handcuffed to the metal armrest of the futon where she'd been plopped. Her eyes searched the room to see what might help her escape. As soon as he removed the gag, which he obviously was going to do if he intended to give her the soup, she'd ask to use the bathroom and gain an opportunity to look for a weapon. Razor blades were usually in bathrooms, although Boris didn't use them much from the looks of his face and neck.

The man poured what looked like tomato soup into two mugs. He blew on one of them and put it to his lips. He took a sip and licked his lips, never taking his eyes off of Gina. Several more gulps and he tilted his head and drained the remains of his mug. He wiped the back of his hand across his mouth and sat the empty cup down on the counter. He smiled his gap-toothed grin and approached.

Gina glared at him and made an attempt to kick out with her legs, but since they were also bound, she wasn't successful in getting them too high. She'd been aiming for his crotch, but all she managed to do was give him a pretty good view of her underwear. She could tell that excited him. He grinned even wider and licked his bottom lip.

"I see you wore special things for me, my beautiful lawyer." He sat down on the battered and scarred coffee table in front of the futon and then carefully set the mug at the other end of the table.

Gina growled behind her gag, glaring. If only she could have kicked that cup out of his hands and made the hot soup burn his disgusting face.

"Now, Gina. I can call you Gina can't I? After all, you and I will soon be a wedded couple, so we should be on a first-name basis, right? I'm not sure if I can trust you to behave in the company of a justice of the peace, though, so we will have our own little ceremony right here. Afterward, when you learn how to respect and honor your husband, we will have a real wedding." The hairy man reached behind Gina, saying, "I'm going to take off the gag now, so I can feed you, and it would not be a good thing if you yell." Then he undid the knot in the handkerchief tied around her head.

The minute the gag was off, Gina drew back from his touch and yelled "Help!" at the top of her lungs.

The blow stunned her, a sharp backhand across the face. She tasted blood from a cut on her lip.

Boris's eyes filled with fury, and for the first time Gina considered the possibility that he might do her real harm. Somehow she had been thinking of him as an inept annoyance until this point, but he was not just a pest but a dangerous, treacherous beast. She fought back tears and meekly accepted a sip of warm liquid as he held the mug to her mouth.

"That's better. I don't want to hit you again, my lovely, but I will if necessary. You must learn to honor and obey just like it says in the good book."

The tangy flavor of the soup he offered stung her cut. Between sips she asked, "May I please go to the bathroom?"

"'Please?' Ah, you learn quickly. Of course. But first you drink all of this."

Gina had first thought to refuse anything he offered, but then she surmised that she would need every bit of strength she could muster if she was to fight him. It would not do to make a fuss. Until he let her into the bathroom, she would pretend she had given up. Maybe then he would relax his guard.

Boris stared at her as if reading her thoughts. "Do not yell again, pretty girl, or I will re-shackle you and you can just piss all over yourself."

"I won't yell," she agreed. "I understand that you don't want to hurt me."

"Very good. I love you, Gina. In time you will love me too. I'm not such a bad guy. You will see."

He leered at her from under those bushy eyebrows, then a moment later he said, "Okay, let me unlock these cuffs and untie your ankles. No kicking." First he untied her ankles; then he massaged them with his big hands, going further up her legs with each stroke. He rubbed her ankles and then her calves. Then he stroked the inside of her thighs. She nearly threw up the soup she'd just eaten.

Her skin crawling, Gina frantically jangled her handcuffs against the metal armrest. "Boris, I really need to go," she pleaded.

"Of course," he replied. "I just got a little side-tracked." He winked at her then pulled a key out of his pocket and unlocked the cuffs.

Gina rubbed her wrists to get the circulation going and stood up. She'd chosen a pair of medium-height sandals, since she thought she'd be dancing not being held prisoner. They'd always been comfortable, but how fast could she run in them?

Boris led her down a short dark hallway and nodded at a doorway on the left. Gina gave him a half-hearted smile and went into the bathroom.

"Uh-uh," he said as she started to close the door. "You leave the door open so I can watch you."

"What!? You won't even give me privacy to relieve myself? Are you insane?"

Boris grabbed her upper arm and she gasped. His fingers pinched her flesh as he roughly shoved her against the wall. "You either leave the door open or you can wet yourself, I could care less. You can be a stubborn bitch, you know. I don't have patience for bitchy women. Now pee or don't, your choice."

Gina swallowed, miserable. She would have liked to disinfect the whole bathroom, as it was as disgustingly dirty as Boris was hairy. She did actually have to go, though, so she slowly pulled her panties down and sat on the commode.

Finished, she used the last of the toilet paper on the roll, pulled up her panties and tried to ignore Boris ogling her from just outside the doorway. She turned on the faucet and ran warm water over her hands and looked around for soap. Not seeing any or a towel, which she probably wouldn't have wanted to use anyway, she shook her hands to rid them of excess water and then dried them on her skirt. So much for getting a weapon.

"Okay, Gina, you come out now."

Boris took her by the arm and pulled her next to him. Still holding her arm, he put his other hand on her waist and let it slide down her hips until he cupped her right buttock. Gina tensed, which for some reason amused Boris. He let out a big guffaw and slapped her bottom with his big hairy paw. When Gina jumped, he laughed again.

"You may be bitchy, but you got one fine ass."

His language was getting increasingly rough and laced with sexual overtones, as well as his behavior. Gina did not want to think about what she might be in for next, but she began to pray that someone was trying to find her. Would it be Alex? Was it possible that he could come flying out of nowhere to rescue her? She wished she'd reported Boris when this all first started. She wished she'd never taken his case in the first place.

"I think we should get some sleep. Come on, let's go to my bedroom," Boris said.

He shoved her down the hallway to a dark room and flipped on the light. Gina gasped at the view. In the middle of the room was a stained mattress without sheets and only a frayed and soiled bedspread strewn across the bottom. Two pillows were tossed at the top, the slipcases yellow with sweat and filth. There was no furniture at all in the room.

Gina's brain went into overdrive. She had to think of something fast.

"Boris, I'm beginning to see that you do care about me and have plans for our future."

Boris eyed her, and she could see that he was baffled. He'd expected her to fight and resist at this point, but her quiet and controlled demeanor was the opposite.

"Now…I *could* sleep with you," she continued, "and while that might be fun, I have always promised myself that I would go to my husband as pure as I could be. We aren't really married, Boris. You deserve the best. Let me stay pure for you until the wedding."

A huge grin spread slowly across his face. "That's a good idea. I will say a marriage vow to you, and you say one to me, and then we go to bed."

Gina forced herself to smile despite her horror. "Don't be silly. Even if we do say our own vows, we can't be truly married without a wedding. When I first met you, you were so angry that your company had promised you many things and delivered on none of them. In fact, they tried to fire you. I admired the way you made them keep their promises. I made a promise too. I would go to my future husband a pure woman. My wedding day would be special. You deserve to have a beautiful and meaningful ceremony. I want to appear for you in white. White is a sign of purity. You are a good man, a smart man, and you deserve the best. Please?"

Appealing to his overblown ego had been the right choice, even if she was lying through her teeth. Boris seemed to be weighing her words, and she prayed that he would give in. If she could get him to leave her alone tonight, tomorrow was another chance at rescue or an escape. Or later tonight. Or five minutes from now. She had to keep stalling for time.

"You have on a white shirt. That is enough," he finally decided. He began to push her into the room.

"No, wait!" Gina looked down at her top. "Look, I've spilled soup on it. It's not pure. I can't be married in a stained shirt."

He stopped abruptly, stared at her breasts. "So, what? You expect me to buy you a wedding dress? That fancy stuff is not important and costs too much money. I think you—"

"Boris," Gina cajoled, "I have a lot of money. Tomorrow we can go to my bank and I will get as much as you want. Certainly we can spend a bit on making our wedding as wonderful as it should be, seeing as we'll have the rest of our lives together."

She could see that the mention of money had stirred his interest. To be honest, she would have gladly given everything she had if he'd just let her go. Getting him to take her to the bank would be an opportunity to escape, though.

Before he had too much time to think she rushed on, "I don't need a real wedding dress, I suppose, but a clean white blouse would be nice. And, Boris, maybe we could get a little wedding cake and some food and we could come back here and I would cook you a wedding feast!" Of course, the thought of her cooking anything beyond what Boris had managed earlier almost made her laugh, and she would have if she hadn't been so petrified with fear.

"How much money do you have?" he asked. "Do you have...say, a thousand dollars?"

She stared at him, considering her chances. "I have more than that. But I don't want to go to the bank unless we are going to use it for a wedding."

"Go to the bank? You? What makes you think I won't just take your ATM card and go without you?"

Gina hadn't considered that. Her head was spinning with ideas and fear. "Well, for one thing, they don't let you take out very much at the ATM. We need to write a big fat check and cash it. But they ask for identification and they look at you, even in the drive-thru, to see if you are the person who owns the account."

Boris seemed to mull that over. Finally he said, "I never trust those sons of bitches in banks. They want to charge you for everything. I used to put my money in there, but they charged a dollar and a half for getting my money out and then wanted to charge me for calling up to complain. I called ten times one month, and they wanted to charge me a dollar each for five of those calls. So now I do everything by cash."

Gina sighed. She understood his frustration, even if she still thought he was a creep. Wait. What was she thinking? He was more than just a creep.

Boris was staring at her. It seemed to be the biggest decision he'd ever made, but finally he said, "Okay, we will wait to sleep together until after we get married. But that will happen tomorrow. We can use some money. I got fired again."

"Fired? What happened?" Gina tried for an expression that would pass for sympathetic. "Oh, Boris, I am so sorry."

"Don't worry." The Russian grinned at her and winked. "No need to be sorry. Tomorrow I'm marrying a very rich woman—and a very beautiful one."

He took her back to the living room and laid her down on the futon. Stretching her left arm above her head, he fastened one handcuff around that wrist and the other onto the metal futon frame. Then he took her ankles and tied them together and anchored them to the other end. He gave the tie a tug, then slid his hand up one leg and under her skirt.

She knew better than to protest as he fingered her lacy underwear, but it was all she could do to keep from screaming. She was relieved when at last he pulled her skirt back down over her thighs and sat back on the coffee table.

"I think we are beginning to make some progress, Gina," he announced. "I will give you what you want, and tomorrow you will give me everything I want. Including a good meal. Yes, this is a good plan. Maybe for our wedding dinner you can fix *shashlyk*. It is very good and is like…a shisha…no, it's, uh, you Americans call it *shish-ka-bab*. Tomorrow we will buy the supplies to make it. Or *pelmeni*. That is also good."

"I'm not familiar with Russian dishes, I'm Italian," Gina said.

"For you, it will be easy. I tell you what goes in and you will figure out how to do it."

Hm. The opportunity to cook something would get her near the stove and provide a chance to maybe smack him in the head with a frying pan or maybe throw hot liquid at him, Gina realized. But if that didn't happen… God, she barely knew how to turn on the oven. She should have taken her father up on those cooking lessons. How did one go about making roast Russian?

Boris interrupted her thoughts. He touched the small tomato splotch on her blouse, palmed her breast and said, "Too bad you spilled." His hand then wandered to the other side of her shirt. Fingers slipping underneath the fabric, he touched her nipple through the lace of her bra, and Gina watched in horror as he closed his eyes and began to massage the growing bulge in his crotch.

With her free hand, she grabbed his wrist and yanked his hand out of her bra. His eyes flew open in surprise.

"Boris, you silly boy, you don't want to spoil our wedding day by putting such temptation in front of me, do you?"

He looked at her and followed her gaze to his erection. There was a moment of dangerous silence. Then he laughed heartily, put his hand back on her breast and squeezed.

"You are learning, my bride-to-be. You are going to be very happy when we become one. I am a good lover. I will teach you how to please a real man. It is good you are a virgin."

Leaning over, he held her face with both hands and pressed his lips to hers, pushing his tongue into her mouth. She gagged and fought the temptation to bite down, and after what seemed an eternity, he withdrew.

"That goodnight kiss will have to do until tomorrow," he said. Then he grinned his stupid grin and left the room.

He turned off the overhead light, leaving Gina in darkness in more ways than one. She shut her eyes, and tears finally slid down her face. She was more scared than she'd ever been in her entire life.

She wondered if it was true that a man could tell if a woman was not a virgin. If so, Boris could easily become enraged tomorrow, should worst come to worst. She prayed that it wouldn't. She had to find a way to escape before that. It was difficult to hold out hope that her father or Alex would find her.

She didn't let herself fall asleep until long after she heard snoring sounds from down the hall. Then she closed her eyes and silently said a prayer that her mother had taught her as a child.

Her father wasn't around. Neither was Alex. More and more, however, she'd begun to think of him as her prince charming. If only he could be her white knight as well, arriving at the last moment to save her from the monster.

She nodded off finally. Visions of a knight in full armor but driving a red sports car played in her dreams…which quickly turned into nightmares with a hairy, rough Russian.

Chapter 19

The sun peeked through the small crack between the shade and the window casing and warmed Gina's face. She woke with a start, only to realize she was still in bondage. Her wrist was sore as hell, and her back ached from the lumpy mattress. But at least the futon was cleaner than Boris's bed. It also had the advantage of being wide enough for only one person.

Her mouth tasted like a bird had nested in it all night, reminding her of Boris's goodnight kiss. Ugh. She didn't want to think about it.

Straining to hear if Boris was up, she heard only snoring. That was good. She leaned forward as far as she could, and with her one free hand she tried to touch the binding around her ankles. It was no use. He'd tied her in such a way that the knot was beyond her reach.

Her ankles were swollen and she had to pee. She fought back tears, and immediately slammed her eyelids shut when she heard Boris stumbling down the hallway and into the bathroom. Apparently he was on the same clock as she was. Which sucked. She needed more time.

Think. She'd always been the smart kid in class, and now she needed every scrap and shred of intelligence to outwit the Neanderthal who thought she was excited about becoming his bride. There was no doubt of Boris's insanity, which could maybe work for her. Or not.

"Good morning!" came a voice.

Gina faked waking up and hoped she pulled it off. A hairy face peeked around the corner from the hall, and her abductor grinned at her with his alligator smile. She stretched her free arm above her head and tried to unknot her spine.

"Oh, Boris, good morning. What time is it?" She commanded her brain to use every bit of knowledge she possessed to get her out of this situation.

"It's a bit past seven, but I knew we'd want to get an early start. We have much to do."

He came into the room in his boxers and nothing else. That image alone convinced Gina of evolution: Boris was obviously a species that had stalled in the process. His chest and back were covered with dark black fur, and his legs were even worse. Even his eyes were bestial, resembling those of a silver-backed gorilla. She would never again be able to go to the zoo with pleasure. If she ever got to go anywhere again with pleasure.

"Boris, you must let me loose. I need to use the bathroom again. Please, you can trust me, but let me shut the door. I'm really shy."

"I'm trusting you more and more," Boris admitted. "I like shy girls. It is proper. So…okay, but do not try to pull anything. I will be close by."

"I won't," she said. "I promise. But, Boris, do you have some toothpaste and soap? I could use a washcloth and a towel, too. After all, this is my wedding day. I want to look nice for it."

At first Boris looked puzzled, as if he'd never heard of the items she'd requested. Then he brightened and grinned. "Of course. I'll get them."

He went down the hall, and she heard him rummaging around somewhere. Soon he returned with a frayed hotel towel and a small bar of soap.

"The toothpaste is in the cabinet above the sink. I don't have washcloths."

"That's okay," she said. "This will do. Can you untie me now?"

Boris leaned over and untied her feet, then went for his pocket. "Oops, no pocket," he chuckled. He put his hand inside the fly of the boxers. "Ah, just a minute, maybe there is a pocket." He grasped his penis with one hand and waved it at Gina through the opening.

"Boris, please!" She thought she was going to retch.

"Sorry, I forgot you are shy. I'll get the key."

He repositioned his boxers and then padded off down the hallway. As he did, Gina swung her legs down to the floor and scooted her body into an upright position. She maneuvered herself until her arm was no longer above her head, though still it was attached to the futon frame, then she rubbed her ankles to get the feeling back in them and pushed her hair out of her eyes.

She looked around and spotted her bag sitting on the small table in the kitchen area of the room. A small black clutch, somehow she'd been able to grab it before Boris shoved her down the stairs of her condo and out the door, and she'd put just a few items inside prior to putting on her earrings. She'd anticipated the need to freshen her makeup, so she'd taken a comb, lipstick and her pressed powder compact. She chided herself for not adding her cell phone.

Boris came back, and to Gina's relief he'd put his pants on. His hairy chest and back were still on display, however, in all their shaggy horror.

Boris's eyes widened when he saw her sitting up, but he undid her cuffs without any hesitation. She nodded her head in the direction of her bag.

"Boris, could I have my bag? It's got my comb in it."

He went over and retrieved the bag, opened it and inspected the contents. Finding the comb, he chuckled, took it out and used it on his chest. Then he glanced at her in expectation of mutual amusement.

"Ha, ha. Very funny." Gina hoped her sarcasm would be diluted by the dazzling smile she faked to keep from screaming. Then, still grinning, she crossed over and took the bag.

"What? No morning kiss?" Boris was obviously enjoying himself.

"Oh, Boris, not now. You know…morning breath."

He seemed to think she was funny. Gina scooped up the tattered towel and the small soap and sprinted down the hallway leaving him almost doubled over in gales of laughter.

In the bathroom, with the door closed, she opened the medicine chest above the grimy sink and found a miniature tube of toothpaste—and just as she'd thought, razor blades. And Boris's razor was the older kind that used double-edged blades. Smaller more compact razors probably wouldn't cut through those stiff bristles on his face. Thank God he didn't have a beard.

She remembered that she needed to relieve herself, and she did so quickly, without the benefit of toilet paper since she'd evidently used up his entire supply the night before. Then she took the wrapper off the soap and washed her hands and splashed water on her face. Spreading toothpaste on her finger, she rubbed it against her teeth, cupped some more water to drink and then swished it around in her mouth.

Replacing the small toothpaste tube, she took one of the blades from the open package on the shelf of the cabinet and slipped it into her powder compact, under the applicator pad. But at that moment, Boris banged on the door.

"What's taking you so long?"

"I'm almost finished," Gina yelled.

She snapped the compact lid shut, and after letting hot water run on the comb, she pulled it through her hair as best she could to remove the tangles. The water helped tame her curls somewhat, but it was a bad hair day no matter what.

Boris twisted the doorknob, and she knew she couldn't risk getting him riled so she unlocked the door. He pulled it open to see her staring into the mirror while applying a coat of lipstick. She dropped the lipstick and compact back into her purse.

Squeezing by him on her way back to the living room, she smiled and said, "You're out of toilet paper." Her calm performance deserved an Oscar, especially as Boris trailed after her, grumbling about it being a woman's job to keep things in supply.

He returned her to the futon where she was handcuffed again, but he let her sit up and didn't tie her feet. She found her shoes under the coffee table and slipped them on.

Boris had made coffee, and he brought her a cup in a chipped mug that had a smiley face and the words "Have a nice day!" The irony almost made her weep. Would she ever have a nice day again? She vowed to never complain about anything if she could just get away from Boris.

She sipped the coffee, and surprisingly it wasn't bad. It was strong, but she needed a jolt of something to get her mind sharp. She was anxious to get out of the apartment, and that meant "making plans for the wedding."

"Okay," she said, "we need to go to the bank."

Boris sat down at the small kitchen table and poured some off-brand cereal into a bowl, then added milk from a half-gallon plastic container. "It is too early. The banks don't open this early. You want to eat?"

The very thought of eating anything with Boris sent Gina's stomach into spasms.

"No thanks, coffee's enough. I'm not much for breakfast."

"That's why you are so skinny. You don't worry, though. After you are with me and cook for me, you will round out nicely. I like a woman with meat on her bones."

"Then why do you want me?" Gina blurted. "I'm always going to be too skinny. You need a more robust wife. Why don't I help you find someone? I don't want you to be unhappy, and—"

"No. I'll keep you," he interrupted. "I saw you one day when you went into your office, and I picked you then. You are a smart person, and I need someone with a good mind who can help me with my business. Not some dumb bitch who just wants me to spend money on her. I've had that."

Gina felt a moment's sympathy before she reminded herself of what he'd done to her. Regardless, it was to her advantage to learn all she could about this man. "You've been married? What happened?"

"It was a long time ago." Boris shoveled spoonfuls of cereal into his mouth, and as he chewed, his expression seemed to darken. His shaggy brows knitted together into a frown. Milk dribbled down his chin and fell onto his chest hair and just stayed there like drops of gooey dew on some sort of spiny foliage.

"I'm sorry, Boris, did you love her? Did she cheat on you? Did she die?"

His head shot up, and he glared at her. The mere intensity of that stare sent chills up her spine.

"You bet your ass she died. She was supposed to come over from my country and be my partner. I sent plenty of money to get her here. I worked very hard to do what it took to emigrate from Russia. I did everything legal, you know?" He pushed the empty bowl away and slammed his fist on the table so hard the spoon jumped and went clanging to the floor. "She lied to me from the minute I picked her up from the airport. She only pretended to care for me until I got all her paperwork taken care of. Then, one night, I come home and no Olga."

"Boris, I'm sorry! Where was she?" Gina knew she was pushing, but he seemed to be willing to talk.

Boris lifted his head and had such hate in his eyes that it frightened her. He clenched and unclenched his fists.

"I took off work to look for her. I had a good job then, much better than the one that just fired me. For two weeks I looked everywhere, and then my boss said he was replacing me. I found her then. Shacked up with another guy."

This time Gina didn't make any comment.

"I was very careful," Boris continued. "I waited for the boyfriend to leave, and then I grabbed her. No one really ever looked for her again. Not the boyfriend, not the police, and not me. I know where she is. In hell."

Gina's throat was dry, and her temples began to pound. She now understood terror.

A series of loud bangs outside the door jolted Gina, and her eyes flashed to the source of the noise. Boris jumped out of his chair, sent it crashing backwards into the wall.

"Whaddya want?" he yelled.

"Mr. Urzinsky, it's me, Mr. Davis, the manager. You promised me the rent money today, and the owner said if you don't pay, you'll be evicted." The banging resumed. "Now open this door and pay up. You're almost four months in arrears."

Boris looked at Gina and then grabbed a dirty towel from the kitchen sink. As he draped it over the handcuffs, he put his finger on her lips. "Do not say a word." Then he calmly went and opened the door.

Gina's knees began to shake. She feared she was going to see a murder right before her eyes.

"Mr. Davis, I am so sorry I have caused you all this trouble. I have had some problems with my employer, but things are all cleared up now and you will have the rent by this afternoon. All of it. I promise."

The manager sounded unimpressed. "I don't believe a word you're saying. You've been telling me the same thing for weeks. I'm calling the cops unless you give it to me now."

"No, no, don't do that," Boris said. "It's true this time. I'm starting a new business with a colleague, and because she believes in my ideas and concepts, she's willing to put up the front money and help me out with my personal expenses."

"Oh yeah?" Mr. Davis said. "Just where is this business partner?" Gina couldn't see, but she heard the skepticism in his voice.

"We will be going to the bank in just a little while, and if you want you can follow us in your car. I will pay you first"—Boris turned in Gina's direction, raising his eyebrows in question—"in cash?"

She nodded and wondered how much he paid for this dump.

"This is the last chance I'm giving you, Urzinsky. I'm going down to park my car right behind yours, so don't try to sneak out of here without me."

"Wouldn't think of it, Mr. Davis," Boris answered. Then he firmly shut the door. "Son of a fucking bitch."

The calm demeanor he'd displayed with Mr. Davis had vanished like smoke in a breeze. Boris seemed to have forgotten Gina entirely, and stomped back to the bedroom. Gina put her arm across her knees to keep them from knocking together. She wasn't sure if she could handle what lay ahead. It was apparent that she wasn't just dealing with a psychopath, but a murderous psychopath.

Chapter 20

Estelle was relieved to see that Gaetano had finally dropped off into a fitful slumber in his recliner. She'd been with him all through the night, and while she'd napped a bit on his sofa, he'd paced, stopping only to place an inquiring call to the police.

She hoped Alex had gotten some rest. At first she'd thought the men were overreacting, but now she was just as worried. She'd still not told Alex the news of her good health. She'd thought about it last night, but it didn't seem the right time or place. Finding Gina came first.

"What…huh?" Gaetano woke up with a start, and Estelle knew he'd been dreaming. "Where's Gina. Did they find her?"

"No, dear. There's been nothing new. But Gaetano, you must get some rest. If you don't, you won't be of any use tomorrow. The police or Alex may need your help."

He rose and began pacing again, and his face showed the strain he'd been under. "I can't sleep. I can't think. I feel so helpless. What kind of a monster would take a beautiful girl from her family?"

It was breaking Estelle's heart to watch this and not be able to supply any answers, but she felt just as helpless as he did. She checked the time on her watch and was unsurprised to see that tomorrow had already arrived. What it held was anyone's guess. She prayed it would not be horrible.

"I'm going to make some coffee and fix us something to eat," she announced.

Getting up from the sofa, on her way toward the kitchen she stopped and put her arms around Gaetano for just a moment before he pushed her away and resumed his pacing. She sighed deeply, but didn't take offense. He was grieving and afraid, and it didn't matter that Gina was a grown woman instead of seven or twelve years old. The man's child was gone, which was the worst possible thing that could happen to anyone.

Estelle thought of an old saying she'd heard after Marty died: "Lose a parent and you lose your past. Lose a mate and you lose your present. Lose a child and you lose your future."

Dear God, don't let anything happen to Gina. Please don't let her be dead.

She shivered and rubbed her arms vigorously to shake off the foreboding that had suddenly crept into her thoughts. She wiped away the beginnings of tears with the back of her hands and took the lid off the coffee canister, unwilling to let her thoughts turn morbid. She would be strong because Gaetano needed her.

Gaetano heard Estelle bustling around in the kitchen as if it were a normal morning. It wasn't, though. He felt bad that he couldn't accept her sympathy, comfort, or whatever it was that she was trying to do to help, but no one could say anything that would make this whole thing better. Words could not change the facts.

He wanted to rage and break things. Most of all, he wanted to wrap his hands around the throat of whoever had taken his baby and squeeze until that worthless piece of *stronzo* gasped his last breath.

Something interrupted his thoughts. It took a second before he realized it was the phone and he rushed across the room to answer.

***

Alex had no luck getting through to Gina's company by phone; all he got was a recorded message giving him the time the office would be open for business. He couldn't wait that long, though. He needed to look through her client list.

Calling Gaetano, he found Gina's father awake and made arrangements for them to meet at the police station. Then Alex rushed through his shower and arrived at the precinct while they were still dealing with last night's drunks, disorderlies, and ladies of the evening.

The two cops who'd been called out to Gina's originally were off duty. Alex tried desperately to convince the officer behind the front desk that a crime had been committed and was still in progress, but he was given the direction to sit and wait his turn. While he waited, Alex watched the "Law & Orde" activities taking place. Then a glimmer of recognition hit him as he watched a detective turning a handcuffed individual over to a uniform.

"Bobby? Bob Renfrew?" Alex couldn't believe his eyes. The stocky guy with the red crew cut was his childhood friend who'd introduced him to porn websites.

"Who wants to know?" The man turned and squinted in Alex's direction. "Do I know you? Wait a minute. Alex? Alex Bennett? No way!"

The two men closed the space between them and grabbed each other in a bear hug with back slaps.

"Holy shit! Alex? What the hell are you doing down here? Have you finally been nailed for something?"

Alex grinned in spite of the seriousness of his visit. He couldn't help but remember how Bobby had always been the one who got nabbed for every prank they ever pulled. For some reason, Alex had never been caught.

"Bob, it's been a while. It's great to see you. How long has it been now?"

"Geez, it must have been the high school after-grad party. Listen, you son of a bitch, why didn't you tell me that Mary Lou Denton's dad was a cop? When he caught the two of us skinny dipping in the municipal pool, I thought I was a dead man."

"Well, obviously he didn't kill you. What happened after Susie and I left? Must not have been too bad. You're on the force now."

"Yeah, well…" Bobby lowered his voice and glanced around to see who else might be able to hear. "Since Mary Lou was in the same state I was, there wasn't much he could do except make us get dressed. He put her on restriction and threatened me with a life sentence if I ever came around again."

"So how'd you decide on becoming a cop?"

"*Detective* to you, buddy. Actually, I accepted the life sentence. Mary Lou and I got married four years ago and have a little girl, Lulu. She's almost three years old and we're having a son in about five months. Sometimes things happen in life for the funniest reasons. You just gotta go with the flow."

Alex couldn't help but think of his own situation with Gina. He'd go with the flow if he could, but first he had to find her. In the meantime, he slapped his old friend on the shoulder. "Congratulations, Bob! I'm envious. Good for you."

"Yeah, thanks. It's good." The detective gave him a wide smile. "But what are you doing here? I mean, I know you couldn't be guilty of doing anything wrong—not that I can pin on you, you slippery bastard."

Alex sobered as he chose his words. He told Bob about the nightmare he feared Gina had fallen into, and gave him a brief summary of what had transpired up to and after he'd gone to pick her up.

"Gina Lorenzo? Hmmm, let me check with the desk and see if anything's been written up." Bob left Alex standing alone and went to the front desk.

The front doors burst open, and Alex saw his mother and Gaetano hurry in. "Mom, over here!" He motioned, and they veered off course and headed in his direction.

"So, is there any news? What do the police say? Did they go to the law office? What have they found out?" Gaetano's questions tumbled out one after another until Alex put up his hands to stop the onslaught.

"Mom, Bob Renfrew's on the force now. You remember Bobby Renfrew, my buddy all through school?"

"Who cares who you went to school with, what about Gina?" Gaetano sputtered.

"That's what I'm trying to tell you," Alex said. "I think Bob might be able to do some good for us. He's a detective now, and his father-in-law has been a cop forever. It can't hurt to have friends on the force because they can open doors that are closed to us. Her office client list for one."

"Of course I remember Bobby," Estelle said. "He was a bit wild as I recall. Weren't there rumors about him and some girl skinny-dipping at the municipal swimming pool? Now he's a policeman. Imagine that."

Thankfully, Detective Renfrew returned to the group before Gaetano could launch into a new tirade. Alex introduced Gina's father, and Bob acknowledged Estelle.

"You're looking well, Mrs. Bennett. It's good to see you again. I was sorry to hear of Mr. Bennett's passing."

"Thank you, Bobby. We're doing a lot better now," Estelle answered.

Alex caught her glance in his direction, and he was once again awed by his mother's strength—and hurt by the knowledge that she was still keeping her secret. But right now neither one of them could deal with anything other than looking for Gina, he supposed. He let such unhelpful thoughts go and focused on what Bob was saying.

The detective had managed to sooth Gaetano a bit. He spoke in a calm voice, but with authority: "Obviously the other two officers didn't file any official report, or if they did, it's mired in a slush pile of things that can wait before action is taken."

"How can it be put aside? This is my daughter we're talking about, not some lost piece of jewelry or stolen car. This is a person. A beautiful, special, lovely…" Gaetano trailed off. Estelle stepped closer to him and took his hand in hers.

"Mr. Lorenzo, please, I understand. I have a daughter of my own, and I can only guess what I would do if someone kidnapped her. I've just had a conversation with the captain, and I've asked him to let me take this on and see what I can come up with. After I get some more information on Gina, her work, her friends, and anything else that might be pertinent, I'll be in touch. It would be best for you to go back home. If you get a call from the kidnapper, you'll be there to take down any message or demands he might make."

"Why would the bastard call me? He doesn't know me. Are you saying he knows me?"

"Gaetano, I think Bob is telling us that the person who took Gina might demand a ransom or something. Isn't that right?" Alex clarified.

"That's right," his friend said. "I'll send a crew over to your house to set up a recorder on your phone. Try not to worry. We have several devices that are useful in cases like this."

The answer seemed to calm Gaetano, and after answering a lot more questions and giving an officer with a clipboard as much information as he could, he and Estelle left the station. Alex was glad that his mother was with the old fellow, though.

Old fellow? Until just then, Alex had never thought of Gaetano as old.

"Is there anything I can do?" he asked his friend.

"Listen, Alex, these things are best left in the hands of the professionals. We're experienced, and if you try to help, you could be injured or endanger someone else. Go home and we'll let you know as soon as we find out anything."

He was glad Bob was taking them seriously, but Alex couldn't help but resent being ousted from the investigation. They hadn't listened at the beginning, and now the police were going to take over and shut him out completely? Well, he wasn't going to sit back and do nothing.

Bobby handed his card over and said, "Call me if you hear from her." He gazed at Alex and then added with a mischievous grin, "You know buddy, maybe she just wanted to dump you and didn't know how. She just panicked and ran off."

"Yeah, sure," Alex retorted, in no mood for his friend's ribbing. "Just go find my lady, asshole, and don't stop by any donut shops on the way."

Though he had no intention of going home, Alex wanted Bob to think he was following orders, so he gave his pal a slap on the back and headed out to the parking lot. There he started his engine and pulled his Ferrari around to where he could watch the door of the station house. He planned to follow his friend and see where they went. He prayed that his flashy paint job wouldn't give him away. For once he found himself agreeing with Gina's earlier contention that it was silly and vain.

He was only sitting for a few moments when he noticed something in the rear view mirror. Behind him was a gray sedan, and seated in the passenger side was his old school chum. Bobby and his partner must have left by a different exit, and they were headed from the parking lot in entirely the opposite direction. By the time he got his vehicle turned around and headed in the right direction, Alex could find no sign of Detective Renfrew.

Worthless and helpless, that's how Alex felt. He wished there was some way he could even get a hint of where Gina might be, but he had nothing. If he were a bloodhound he could just pick up her scent and follow her trail. He wasn't, though. He was just a photographer, and one whose eye for details had been failing him in the past few days.

He felt a sudden draw to her neighborhood. Regardless of whether or not there was any logic to it, this seemed like the pull of the universe. Even if it wasn't, the investigation would probably check in there sooner or later. He supposed that when it did, he would find a way to join.

Chapter 21

Boris was in a rage, and while Gina put up a brave front, her confidence was not nearly as strong as she needed it to be. She was more scared than she'd ever been in her entire life.

"I'm sorry, Boris, but there is no way I can get any money from my bank unless we go to my condo and pick up my checkbook."

"How stupid you are to leave your important things at home."

"Look, I didn't exactly have time to pack a bag when you burst in. It's not my fault. Just tell Mr. Davis he can follow us to my condo and then we'll go to my bank. It's not far from my house, so it's no big deal."

Boris shoved his hands into his pockets and jangled his coins and probably the key to her handcuffs as he walked back and forth through the small apartment. "Okay, it's all we can do. I keep getting stupid women, and pretty ones are I guess the most stupid."

He fished around in his pocket until he found the key and freed Gina's wrist from the cuffs; then he grabbed her arm and pulled her to her feet and stuck his face just inches from hers. "Do not make trouble for me or you will join all the other stupid, pretty women who tried to screw me over."

Gina shivered.

She let Boris push and shove her in the direction of the door and tried not to stumble down the stairs to the parking area. Boris smiled at the man Gina assumed was Mr. Davis as they emerged. It must be after ten o'clock now, she realized. Her office would be calling to find out why she wasn't at work.

Boris pulled Gina with him as he leaned down to peer into the building manager's car window. In the short conversation that followed, Mr. Davis grudgingly agreed to follow them to Gina's condo. This put Boris in an even darker mood, and he didn't even try to disguise his rough treatment as he shoved Gina into the driver's side of his dirty green sedan. She hoped Mr. Davis would notice and maybe realize she was in danger.

She thought for a moment that Boris was going to let her drive, but her hopes died when he got in and made her scoot over. She entertained thoughts of making a run for it, then realized the interior latch had been removed from the passenger door. She was trapped.

Boris put a key in the ignition. Before he started the engine, however, he dropped his hand to her thigh and tugged at it until her leg pressed against his. Then Boris turned the key, the motor caught and he shifted into gear.

They drove out of the parking area. As soon as he'd executed the turn onto the freeway, he took his right hand off the steering wheel and returned it to Gina's upper thigh. She had to fight the urge to punch him and send the car careening into the median.

Gina studied her captor as they drove, trying to note any signs of confusion or apprehension. There didn't seem to be any. Boris drove the car with certainty. He knew exactly where he was going. Of course, he'd been shadowing her for weeks and had nabbed her from her condo just the evening before.

She didn't speak the entire trip, just kept her eyes peeled in case she saw a squad car or any other vehicle that might be of help. Her plan was to lay on the horn or grab the wheel or whatever it took to stop Boris then. Surely the police were looking for her by now. Someone had to know she was in trouble. Didn't they?

The thought nagged her that perhaps Alex didn't really know her well enough to recognize the signs of abduction. He knew her as a smart-mouthed, hotshot attorney who liked to win. He wouldn't think she stood him up, though, would he? For the first time, being so independent might work against her. But anyone would think it odd that she'd left her front door open, wouldn't they?

Of course, he might have decided against going out and left her a phone message instead of coming back. Maybe she'd turned him off. He might have come to his senses and realized she wasn't the girl for him; he might feel none of the things that she felt for him. In that case, it was possible that no one even knew she'd been kidnapped.

As they turned the corner onto her street Mr. Davis was right on their bumper. Boris looked in the rearview mirror and cursed, parked the car, and got out.

"He can wait here. We're not letting him go to the door with us."

Out of the corner of her eye, Gina saw a flash of bright red. Her heart skipped a beat, but she managed to stifle the gasp of air that escaped her lungs. Could it have been Alex's sports car? It had looked like his shade of red. She could only hope that Boris hadn't seen. Well, he wouldn't know that her white knight drove a Ferrari of a very different color, anyway.

Her captor grabbed her wrist and pulled her toward the driver's side of the sedan. "Come with me. Act normal."

Was he kidding? How in the world could she act normal when she was being jerked from a vehicle by her kidnapper and presented to a perfect stranger as a business partner? And yet, when Boris leaned into Mr. Davis's window to say they'd just be a few minutes, the proposition was accepted with no sign of question or disbelief. Gina was incredulous.

Boris didn't loosen his grip and began pushing her toward her home. Gina scanned the area and up and down the street but saw no sign of Alex or the police, no sign of the red paint she'd thought she'd seen from the corner of her eye. She'd been mistaken, she decided, and her heart sank. Why, oh why was this happening to her?

As they reached her front door she noticed it was shut. She knew it had been left partly open when Boris dragged her out. She also realized she'd left her keys inside along with her cell phone.

The Russian grabbed the knob and pushed to no avail. "It's locked. Give me your key."

She had a key hidden near the door under a pot of red geraniums, but she wasn't about to tell Boris that. "Uh, I don't have it. I didn't have time to get my keys when you abducted me last night." She couldn't help but feel a bit smug, actually. Served him right for kidnapping her, the big jerk.

Her satisfaction faltered as Boris let out a string of swear words, looked briefly around the small concrete slab of her porch, then reached down and moved the pot of geraniums. "I would have thought you'd be smarter. Everyone hides their spare under flowerpots. No imagination. You surprise and disappoint me, Gina. Just as it surprises me that you did not try harder to remember your spare."

Gina fought back a gasp of dismay, but Boris added nothing further. He simply slid the key into the lock, turned the knob, and then pocketed it.

"Maybe we will live here. It is nicer than my apartment, eh?"

Gina's stomach lurched at the thought of him being a permanent fixture in her condo, let alone in her life. She'd given serious thought to making a run for it at the door, but Boris never released his hold on her wrist and she knew he was not against smacking her into submission. She didn't feel like she could trust Mr. Davis to help her, either. He only seemed interested in his rent money.

"Boris, I'd really like to take a shower and get pretty," she said. "After all, it's my wedding day." She forced herself to smile while fighting back the urge to retch. She'd had a glimpse of his fury and rage. Her only chance for escape would come from manipulation.

Boris shook his head. "Sorry, no time. That idiot Davis is waiting, remember? The quicker we get to the bank and get rid of him, the better off we'll be." His lips curled into a nasty grin full of stubby brown teeth. "After we say vows, then we can shower—together." He slapped her on her behind and roared with laughter. "Is good idea, no?"

Gina yelped and rubbed her buttocks. The left cheek still smarted, and she wouldn't be surprised if she was left with a bruise from the blow his large, hard hand had delivered.

Boris took her elbow and pushed her ahead of him up the stairs. "You can put on a clean shirt, but that's all, and I get to watch."

***

His eagle eye had worked! Thank heavens that he was a photographer; he'd spotted the green sedan long before it parked, and now Alex was ready for action. He had circled the block a couple of times, quickly made a U-turn and went the other direction to keep from being seen. He had to make certain it was Gina before he called the police and alerted them.

It was. He'd watched from the shadows of the trees a bit further down the block, recognizing Gina as soon as the stocky, thick man pulled her out of the car. The abductor then conferred with someone in a car directly behind him. Which meant there were two. That made it more difficult. The one with Gina had to be the client she'd told him about, Boris. Alex hadn't figured on an accomplice.

Alex's cell phone rang, and his friend Bob Renfrew was just a block away. Alex clued him in on where he was parked and added the information about the second vehicle.

"Alex, don't get in our way on this," Bob said in a crisp, authoritative voice. "We know what we're doing, so just let us do it. Don't go charging in there like a knight on a horse."

Begrudgingly, Alex agreed. He didn't like the terms, but he also didn't want to take a chance of messing things up.

Three black and whites rounded the corner and pulled into obvious view as they parked. Alex shook his head in dismay. What were they thinking? Boris was sure to see them and panic. Worse, he'd hole up in the condo and put Gina at more risk.

He punched in Bob's cell number and waited for the call to be answered.

"Bob, what's with the black and whites? They're going to spook Boris. Get rid of them, and also get that accomplice out of his car. He's parked in the blue Honda Accord behind the green junker."

"You trying to tell me how to do my job? Trust me, Alex. I've done this a million times."

Alex muttered something and slammed his phone shut, but a few moments later he sighed with relief as the black and whites pulled off down the street and out of view. He was further satisfied when an officer got out of one patrol car and approached the Honda. After a brief conversation, the driver was escorted off to the area where the squad cars were parked.

Alex sat back to wait. After what seemed like hours—though in reality it had been only fifteen minutes—Boris and Gina emerged. Gina was carrying a shoulder bag, while Boris had a firm grip on her elbow, propelling her forward down the walkway and toward the street. Gina's hair was a mass of wildness, and while Alex couldn't make out her face, he knew she had to be terrified.

His own heart was in his throat, and he had to make a conscious effort to keep breathing. He was no stranger to fear, as there had been more than one occasion in his work where his life had been in danger. He'd almost been bitten by a cobra when on assignment in

India. Another time, he and a crew had been chased through the African jungle by a rogue elephant. But somehow those experiences weren't close to what he was feeling now.

He continued to watch as Boris and Gina moved closer to the curb. Boris looked up and down the street then turned his head to glance behind. Gina seemed momentarily confused, and at one point tried to pull away. Boris grabbed her around her waist and appeared to tighten his grip. He'd seen the officers.

Alex couldn't sit and do nothing. His hand had just reached the latch on his door when Boris spun around and from somewhere produced a knife that quickly moved to Gina's throat. The image froze Alex in place. He didn't dare make a move, because he had no doubt that Boris would slash Gina's beautiful neck at any sign of unwanted action. The idea of losing Gina was the most horrible he'd ever faced.

Obviously the police thought the same thing. They backed up, and on Boris's command they slowly put their guns down on the ground.

Detective Bob Renfrew was now in view, and though Alex couldn't hear every word, it was apparent that Bob was trying to talk Boris into surrendering. He approached the couple with careful steps, both hands held upright at shoulder height. Boris had Gina in a vise grip, her arms held tightly at each side while he dragged and half carried her with backward crablike steps that closed the distance to his car.

For a second, Boris stopped. Bob moved forward, slowly, but then Gina screamed. Boris shoved her into the cop. The detective crashed to the ground, Gina atop him, and Boris took the opportunity to yank his car door open. He slid into the vehicle, slammed the car door, and his engine roared to life.

The uniformed officers grabbed up their guns. It was too late, however, as Boris's sedan burst forward and then made a quick U-turn when the street was blocked by two black and white patrol cars. Boris almost ran down the officers before they dropped their aims to jump out of his path.

Alex watched the whole scenario in disbelief. The bastard was going to get away.

This can't be happening. The night they'd had dinner at the Wayfarer and he'd taken Gina home, they'd had a conversation about how many criminals got away with crimes—even murder. Now, this kidnapper was going to escape. Even though he'd released Gina, he still deserved to pay for the terror he'd put her through. What he'd put them *all* through. By God, someone had to do something. The creep couldn't get away.

He won't. Not if I have anything to say about it.

Alex fired up his engine and slammed the Ferrari into gear. Pulling away from his parking place, he swerved into the street just as Boris's rattletrap came barreling down on him. He didn't think about the repair bill; he didn't think about anything. Well, nothing except avenging Gina. The girl he loved.

Thank heavens he hadn't unbuckled his seat belt. Glass splintered and metal shredded, and Alex smacked hard against the door as his head slammed into the window. My bright red Ferrari, he thought stupidly. My sleek 612 Scaglietti with only one blemish, a small one-inch scrape and a tiny dent on its passenger side…

The sound of the collision echoed in his ears. He blinked once then closed his eyes and ears to the crescendo of horns and a car alarm accompanying the beat of running feet and shouts. Then Alex opened his eyes and stared into the dark chocolate irises of an angel. He smiled as the beautiful creature leaned forward and kissed him. She looked amazingly like Gina Lorenzo. He had made it to Heaven after all, and Heaven seemed to be happy with him.

He chuckled and closed his eyes then waited for his halo to arrive.

***

A short time later, Alex blinked his eyes open and took in the all-white area surrounding him. The room was white, the bed he lay in was white, and then he saw the angel who looked like Gina all dressed in white.

"I'm dead, aren't I?" He spoke to no one in particular.

"Alex, darling, you're awake. Oh, dear God, we were so worried!" Estella rushed to his bedside, Gaetano right behind her.

"Mom? What are you doing here? Oh, Lord, I am dead and so are you. Geez, Mom, I'm sorry. Did you suffer?"

"Alex, you aren't dead, and neither is your mother. You have a pretty good concussion, that's all. Thanks to your heroics." Gina stepped closer to the bed, and a moment later she put her cheek next to his face and kissed his lips. "I am so proud of you. You caught Boris. He shoved me into that cop and we both were on the ground so he almost got away. But, Alex, your beautiful car is a total loss. I'm so sorry."

Gaetano gently took Alex's hand while avoiding the IV attached to it. "Alex, your quick thinking and brave action saved my Gina. Thank you."

As Gina's father ended the pseudo handshake and slipped his arm around Estelle, pulling Alex's mother closer, Gina eased down onto the edge of the bed and dangled her feet off the side. Alex started to shake his head but then stopped when it felt like everything from the neck up was connected with rubber bands. His thoughts were a blur.

"Wait a minute. I don't know what you're talking about. The last thing I remember is getting ready to take Gina out for dinner. And…Mom, I have a confession. I know you're dying. Gina told me, and I'm so sorry I am not the son you feel you can trust enough to tell me that kind of news. I've always tried to—"

"Oh, Alex, honey," his mother interrupted, "you don't have to apologize for anything. It's really a long story, but you're not up to it now. I'm really fine, though, Alex. Don't worry. Certainly not about me. Gaetano and I are going to go now so you can get some rest."

"That's right," Gaetano said, patting his shoulder gently. "They said not to stay too long, so we'll leave you and Gina alone and come back later. You're a good man, Alex," he added.

Estelle leaned forward, kissed his forehead and smiled. "We love you, dear." As she and Gaetano retreated to the door, she threw him one last kiss before the pair of them disappeared.

Alex fixed his gaze on Gina and took hold of her hand. She was alive! They both were alive. For a moment he said nothing, just took in all the loveliness before him. Her mouth was tilted at the corners revealing her dimples; her curls lay obediently around her shoulders and the lace blouse she wore dipped provocatively to display a deep valley between her two perfect breasts. Those rose and fell with each quick breath she took.

He lifted his gaze to her face. Though his ears were buzzing, he found the strength to do something he hadn't yet managed while she was awake, something he felt was a long time in coming. Slowly, with his unencumbered hand, he pulled her head down until their lips connected.

He kissed her deeply. Passionately. With all the crazy love he felt in his heart. Sometimes, as his friend Bobby Renfrew had said, things happened in life for the funniest reasons. You just had to go with the flow.

They both moaned, but not with pain.

Chapter 22

"Gaetano, I think I should have told him in there. He still thinks I'm dying. Oh, I just get shivers when I think of what could have happened to him." Estelle looped her arm though Gaetano's as they exited the hospital and walked toward the parking garage.

"There will be time for that, and he will be just as thrilled later as he would be now. If you had told him, he might not even have remembered, so better to tell him when his brain is all connected again."

"Maybe so," Estelle said and sighed.

Gaetano patted her hand. "I just keep thinking about that beautiful car. *Mama mia,* it may make him relapse when he sees it."

"Oh, you men. Cars! What's important is that Alex is going to be okay. And that Gina is safe."

"Of course, of course, my love, but a Ferrari 612? That is not just a car. That is a work of art."

"Gaetano, you're a piece of work," Estelle retorted. She swatted his backside with her clutch bag.

He stopped abruptly and turned to face her. "And you, my love, are going to be the most beautiful bride, a work of art far surpassing any hunk of metal."

He wrapped his arms around her and kissed her right in the middle of the parking garage, and curious bystanders and passing cars slowed to gape at the handsome couple, but they noticed not. They were lost in a world of their own.

"So, your place or mine?" Estelle asked a short time later as they drove out of the hospital parking lot and headed for the freeway on-ramp.

"I really should go to the restaurant. Even before all this kidnapping business, I was letting Mario shoulder most of the load. With all of that's been going on, Mario has been on his own for much too long. I have been out of the restaurant for the past three days now! I should go in and give him the day off."

"You're absolutely right," Estelle agreed. "Poor man. Have you given any more thought to taking him in as a full partner?"

"*Mama mia*," Gaetano muttered. "I knew there was something I forgot to tell him. And Gina for that matter. I've gotten in the habit of being so close-mouthed, I haven't told anyone anything!"

"Ha!" Estelle responded. "You think you've been keeping secrets? I don't know how my son is going to react. First I must tell him I'm in perfect health, and then we need to tell both children about our wedding plans."

"I know, I know. But I also know they're going to be so happy for us." Gaetano glanced over at her with a devilish smile. "Listen, what do you think of this? As soon as Alex is released from the hospital, we'll have one big party at the restaurant. It'll be to celebrate Alex's bravery, Gina's return to us, your good health, and our engagement. We'll break all the news there. How does that sound?"

"It sounds wonderful, but don't you think I should tell Alex tonight? I can go back to the hospital in a bit, and he and I can have a heart-to-heart talk. I think I should tell him everything now, including our impending marriage."

"Ah, but that would spoil the surprise," Gaetano grumbled. "What will a few hours or a day matter?"

He was in such a joyful mood Estelle hated to bring him back to reality. She still wasn't sure a continued deception was a good idea, but it was hard not to get caught up in his excitement. A celebration would be fun, and it had been so long since she'd felt like celebrating anything. She supposed she could give in this once. Just like she had the several times before.

"I'll invite all the policemen who helped save my Gina," Gaetano said, and when Estelle nodded he grinned at her and added, "What's the name of that cop friend of Alex's?" He emphasized his comments with wild arm gestures as he drove down the freeway. "You tell me who you want to come, your doctor for sure, and all our regulars at the restaurant. We'll shut the doors to the public and throw one huge party. Maybe hire a band. We'll dance and drink and then we'll make love…but maybe we'll go home before that."

Estelle laughed. She couldn't resist the spontaneity of this crazy Italian, and she found herself nodding in agreement with every idea he suggested. It was a good thing she had some connections from all her charity work, because she could probably get a band or at least a combo if they chose a weeknight for the party. Midweek would be better for the restaurant. Certainly better than closing it down on the weekend.

She scooted as close to Gaetano as the seat belt would allow, resting her head on his shoulder. To be a bride again? She couldn't wait to tell Alex. But Gaetano was right. He needed to get his strength back.

They arrived at Gaetano's Ristorante, and while Gaetano and Mario busied themselves in the kitchen, Estelle sat on a barstool at the small counter near the office at the back. She thumbed through an issue of *Brides* magazine. All of the photos showed young girls with perfect bodies and smooth complexions.

What am I thinking? I'm not young and beautiful like these girls. I look more like a mother of the bride.

Warm breath stirred the hair on her nape, a breath tinged with a pleasant aroma of tomatoes, basil, and just a hint of garlic. Estelle smiled and turned slowly to meet Gaetano's lips. In his embrace, all her concerns vanished. She let her mind drift and just enjoyed the passion of her lover's deepening kiss. When he touched her like this, she felt as young as any of those pretty models in their glossy magazine prints.

Gaetano pulled away, and with his arms still around her waist he gazed into her eyes and smiled.

"So, have you found the perfect dress for the perfect bride?"

"Not yet," she said. "And I'm not sure we ought to make a big fuss. It's not like we're doing this for the first time."

"But, *cara*, it is like the first time, only better and newer and even more wonderful."

She laughed, embarrassed despite his enthusiasm. "Perhaps, but maybe I shouldn't wear white. I mean, I'm not exactly a virgin. I have a son who's almost thirty years old."

"Ah, but before you met me, you were like a virgin. So delicate, and so untouched for so long. I think you were…uh, what is it called? Ah, yes, a 'born-again virgin,' and if you want to wear white, it is okay."

She shook her head and giggled. "I'm not so sure. Since I've met you I've become a trollop."

The extraordinary sex they'd shared had not only managed to awaken her hormones and activate her libido, it had shaken them into a hungry, wanton frenzy every time Gaetano got her naked. Which was more often than she'd ever dreamed possible. Her carnal appetites had increased tenfold, along with her appetite for his food. His culinary art had managed to increase her petite size four to a well-rounded eight, and he seemed to love every pound she'd gained.

As proof, even now she felt his hands slide down and cup her bottom in a loving caress. He nuzzled his chin into her full bosom, delivering kisses that threatened her composure and control.

"Gaetano, stop," she scolded. "You mustn't. If you haven't noticed, we're in the dining room and it's beginning to fill up. Go cook something and leave me be."

Her beloved chef swatted her bottom and kissed her on the forehead. "Okay, I'm going," he said. But he left whistling Wagner's "Wedding March" from *Lohengrin*.

***

Gina insisted on staying with Alex after he was released from the hospital. She'd thought his mother would insist on taking him to her house, but Estelle hadn't said a thing when they'd spoken on the phone. All either of the parents said was how blessed they were to have their children safe again, and that they were throwing a big party to celebrate their good luck.

Since the nightmare of Boris and the accident, Gina had become more and more aware of how much her thoughts were of Alex. When he'd kissed her on that hospital bed, it sent her into a place she'd never before visited. Her whole body had responded, and it was all she could do to keep from crawling into that narrow cot with him. Along with those thoughts were hints of wanting what she was pretty sure her father and Estelle had. She could see herself finding that with Alex. Long term. But did Alex feel the same?

Gina propped Alex up on one end of his sofa with a pillow under his head, and positioned herself on the opposite end. She looked at him and, given her thoughts in the last few minutes, couldn't help but smile. He made a very nice view.

"What? Why are you staring at me?" He'd looked up from his magazine and caught her staring.

"Nothing. I was just daydreaming and thinking about how much you sacrificed for me. I owe you so much."

"Oh, come on. Don't butter me up. But if you really want to repay me"—he grinned—"how about getting me a beer from the fridge?"

"Did the doctor say it was okay to have alcohol?" she asked. The last thing she wanted was for anything else bad to happen to him. He was her white knight. Her white knight in a red Ferrari.

"Of course. I'm fine!"

"Okay, but just one. Are you still on painkillers?"

"I only take them before bed."

Mollified, Gina left the sofa and came back with two bottles of Samuel Adams. She handed one over and settled back into her corner.

Alex tilted his bottle toward her and smiled. "So, do you really want to go to this bash your dad is throwing at the restaurant for us next week?"

"I don't see how we can get out of it...though he wants me to invite my boss. Can you imagine that? I appreciate that the firm is giving me an extra week of paid vacation to get over the trauma Boris put me through, but that's not enough. I mean, I told Mr. Baxter after my first meeting with Boris that I thought he was creepy, and he implied that I was prejudiced. He told me I should just buckle down and power through. I don't want to party with Mr. Baxter. Ever." She wasn't even sure she wanted to keep working for the man. Not unless he gave her the partnership she deserved. Actually, the more she thought about it, the surer she was that she could turn this situation to her advantage. After all, she'd never lost a suit. She doubted that would change against her own employer, assuming they were dumb enough to contest what she'd more than rightfully earned.

When she made a thoughtful face, Alex rewarded her with one of his drop-dead gorgeous smiles. Shivers ran up and down her spine, and she realized again how lucky she was that they'd met. He was indeed the white knight of her fantasies. She enjoyed talking to him. She enjoyed just sitting next to him on his sofa drinking a cold beer. She wanted to do all of this a whole lot more in the future, and she cursed Boris for having ruined their chance at a first date. Still, at least they'd kissed. That was a beginning. And what a beginning! Just remembering made her warm all over. It made her feel happier than even the idea of that partnership.

To get herself back in control she said, "It's getting close to dinnertime. Do you want me to call in a pizza order?" For the second time in recent memory, she wished she knew how to cook. Her father had offered her and Alex cooking lessons, had pushed them, even, and in the back of her mind the thought nagged that it would be nice to serve a husband a nice meal if she ever married. Not that she was thinking about marriage. She wasn't. Was she?

Alex shrugged. "I'm feeling well enough to go out. Why don't we surprise your dad and pop in on him at his restaurant?"

"Are you sure?"

"We can make it an early evening, and I promise not to drink too much or dance on the tables."

She kind of wanted to see him dancing on a table.

***

The dining room hummed with activity as regulars greeted Gaetano with hearty back slaps and good wishes on the return of his Gina. The news had been splashed across television screens and the Web, so the Ristorante had received a fair amount of publicity— which wasn't bad for business.

Estelle stood next to him, and she seemed to be basking in the overflow of joy that exuded from his very soul. He could not remember a time when he'd felt this happy. He looked down at his beautiful bride-to-be, overcome with the need to share his good fortune with anyone and everyone he could.

"Excuse me for a minute, my dear," he said, and walked toward the kitchen. Instead of going in, however, he passed it and continued on to the chamber where the chilled wines were kept. There enlisting the help of several employees, Gaetano returned with an entourage carrying trays full of glasses holding his very best Prosecco.

"Attention! Attention, everyone! Thank you all for your wonderful comments and support regarding the difficulties we have been through the last few days. For those of you not aware," he explained, "my daughter Gina was kidnapped, but she's safe now, and thanks be to God, unharmed!"

Gaetano took two filled champagne glasses from the tray and handed one to Estelle, keeping the other for himself. "To celebrate that good news, I want to make a toast. The champagne being passed around is on the house."

His announcement brought a murmur of surprise and appreciation from the room. A smattering of applause accented the clinking of the glasses being delivered.

Gaetano smiled down at Estelle and raised his voice above the buzz of conversation now filling the room. "This lovely lady standing beside me is Estelle. Some of you have met her. It was her son, Alex Bennett, who rescued my Gina."

An increased amount of applause erupted, and Gaetano beamed. He pulled an empty chair from one of the tables and climbed up on it. "But that is not all of my good news."

"What are you doing?" Estelle whispered, pulling at his trouser leg.

"I'm going to tell them we're getting married and invite them all to our party next week," Gaetano whispered back.

"Gaetano, that's a bit much, isn't it? I mean, do we really want to make a public affair out of our engagement announcement?"

He laughed. "Why not? It is wonderful news, and I'm the happiest man in the world. I want to shout it from the rooftops. I'm going to do that right now."

He raised his glass of champagne above his head and motioned for Estelle to do the same, then cleared his throat and smiled out at the crowd. "Dear friends, please join me in a toast to my daughter's safe return—and to the beautiful Estelle, who's not only the mother of a hero, but the future Mrs. Gaetano Antonio Lorenzo."

***

Alex and Gina got out of her car and walked toward the restaurant entrance. As they did, a wave of concern filled Gina. She knew Alex was tired, but she also knew how much the coming days would mean to Estelle. She didn't want him to regret anything.

"Alex, let's try to indulge our parents. They want to throw a party for us? Let's go along with that and help them with the plans. It might be fun to kick up your heels after what you've been through."

He sighed, but his words cheered her somewhat. "Don't worry, Gina, I won't be a grump. It may be the last time my mother will feel like partying, so you bet I'm going to indulge her. I hope she doesn't overdo it."

"Well, Papá will watch her," Gina assured him. "They've become pretty close. And he's so grateful to you that he'll do anything to make you and your mother happy."

She looped her arm through Alex's, and he covered her hand with his own. When he smiled down at her, her heart did a double somersault. It was amazing the effect he had on her. What did it mean when she found being with Alex was more exciting than winning a case or becoming a partner? Not that she wanted to give up her career, but she certainly saw the benefit of having her own full-time knight in shining armor. Maybe she'd always seen the benefit of that. She just hadn't met the right one.

Alex chuckled, bringing her out of her reverie. "I think your dad would have thrown a party in the hospital if the doctors would have allowed it. Of course, you'd had a rough twenty-four hours and certainly enough excitement for a while. *Boris.* God, I was so afraid you'd been hurt by that creep. At least you won't have to worry about him anymore. He's already charged with kidnapping, and with the information you gave the police, they're very interested in finding out what happened to Olga, his Russian bride. Boris is going away for a long time."

She eyed him gratefully, shaking off her awful memories of the kidnapping. "You were worried about *me*? What about you? You took a pretty good blow to the head. The doctors insisted we keep the excitement to a minimum."

"Well, I don't think you succeeded. I was pretty excited when I woke up and saw you standing by my bed."

Alex opened the door for Gina but stopped her as she made to move forward into the restaurant. He leaned down, cradled her face in both hands and kissed her softly on the lips. Her heart took off once again like a gymnast doing back flips.

Still buzzing from the kiss, they walked past the reservation podium and into the main dining area. Laughter and conversation was everywhere, making the room sound much like an active beehive. All of the customers were holding champagne glasses in the air, and their attention was directed toward the back.

Gina's gaze followed the crowd's, and she saw her father standing on a chair. Cocking her head she caught the last few words of the announcement...and froze. Had she heard correctly? Gina looked at Alex, and his face reflected the same emotions as she felt. Shock and disbelief.

"Did Papá say 'the future Mrs. Lorenzo'?" She whispered. Her mouth gaped, and her eyes widened.

Alex shook his head. "My God. I can't believe it. What on earth is she thinking? How could Mom be considering marriage in her condition?"

"My father has gone mad," Gina agreed.

"Come on, we've got to get to the bottom of this."

Alex took her by the arm, and they elbowed their way through the crowd and around the tables. Everyone was applauding. Gaetano had come off the chair and had Estelle in his arms. She was smiling up at him. In fact, their parents were so wrapped up in each other they paid no attention to Alex and Gina standing right in front of them.

Estelle's gaze finally flashed over and then she did a double-take. She immediately pulled out of Gaetano's grasp.

"Alex, you're here!" Smiling broadly, she hugged him. Then she looked more closely at the two younger people. "Gina? What's wrong? Oh, well, you both must be wondering what's going on."

Gaetano grabbed both Gina and Alex in an unexpected hug. He planted kisses on both their cheeks and stood back grinning widely. Gina just stood speechless.

It took Alex a few minutes to recover. "That's an understatement, Mother. Isn't there something you're leaving out here? What about your health, remember? You're dying, for God's sake. How can you get married?" Alex's mouth twisted to one side and his words were bitter. "Although for some reason you didn't think that was something I needed to know."

"I'm sorry, Estelle, but I told Alex," Gina spoke up. "He did have a right to know. He's your son and he loves you."

Alex continued his tirade. "Obviously Gina and her father were taken into your confidence, but you chose to keep me in the dark. Your own son. I guess you didn't feel the need to share such important news with me? Were you ever going to say a word, or was I going to learn when I found you drawing your last breath?"

Gaetano spoke in a soft voice that contrasted with Alex's harshness. "Please, Alex, you misunderstand. We are in love and—"

"Papá." Gina broke into her father's explanation. "Love does not make everything okay. Estelle is a wonderful person, but do you know what you're doing? This doesn't make any sense."

"Gina is right," Alex began again. "I don't think either of you have—"

"Now, just a minute," Estelle commanded, fists on her hips. "Everyone stop talking."

All three turned to stare at her, surprised by her strident tone.

"First of all," she tried to whisper, but it came out raspy, "we are moving out of the dining area. We're the center of attention here."

"Fine," Alex said, glancing around at their rapt audience. "Mr. Lorenzo, may we use your office? I'd like to speak to my mother. Alone."

Gaetano gestured to the room beyond the kitchen. "Of course. But—"

The two didn't wait; Alex herded his mother off and she seemed more than willing to go.

As soon as they left, Gina turned to her father, grabbing him by the arm. She maneuvered him to the hallway separating the kitchen from the main dining area and hissed, "Papá, I can't believe you would carry on like this in public."

He glared at her. "In the first place, I wasn't carrying on. I was sharing my good fortune with all my friends who have come to my restaurant for many years."

Her father was angry, and she wished Alex was there to take some of the heat. She loosened her grip on his arm and said in a calmer tone, "Papá, I know you care for Estelle, but are you sure this isn't coming from pity? I mean, your whole relationship is based on the fact that she's dying. Wanting to make her last days happy is not a good reason to rush into marriage. How long have you even been seeing each other?"

Gaetano shook his head. "I'm old enough to know what I want, Gina. And we've been trying to tell you. Estelle isn't dying. It was one big mistake. Yes, in the beginning I was very sad for her. But as we spent time together, we found we have much in common. I fell in love again, *Bambina*—and she's as healthy as you are. Maybe healthier. She knows how to relax. And even if she were sick, sometimes you just have to take a chance."

Gina couldn't believe her ears. "She's not dying?"

Gaetano just took both of her hands in his, brought them to his lips and kissed them.

Gina continued processing his words. "What mistake, Papá? Did you really just say Estelle isn't dying? Why not? I mean, how do you know for sure?"

"She misunderstood the doctor. Estelle found out the wonderful news just a little while ago, so now there is no reason we shouldn't be married. Be happy for us, *Bambina*. If you weren't, I don't think I could bear it."

Gina shook her head, flummoxed. Then she looked into her father's eyes and knew she could never deny him what made him so obviously happy. "Oh, Papá, that *is* wonderful news. I'm just surprised. I guess I knew you and Estelle were getting serious, but not *that* serious…and so quickly."

"Besides your mama, Estelle has made me happier than I ever imagined any woman could."

Gina smiled and wrapped her arms around her father, determined to believe he was doing the right thing. Like he said, sometimes you had to take a chance.

She was still embracing him when Alex strode out of the office and whisked past.

"Alex!" she called after him. He paid her no attention and continued toward the exit.

"Papá, I'll call you later," she said. "I'd better see what's wrong with him. But if I don't come back, tell Estelle I'm happy for both of you."

***

Alex paced back and forth in his living room. Every time he thought he could let it all go, a new wave of resentment swept over him. He still couldn't believe his mother had kept him in the dark all this time. Lied to him, jerked him around, made him feel like a fool. He'd thought they were close, especially after his father's death. She'd respected his independence but consulted him on everything important. Now he felt as if he didn't know her. His old mom certainly wasn't that giddy female he'd seen in a crowded restaurant embracing a man she'd known only for a short time and who was practically a stranger.

"Alex, give it up," Gina said. She'd followed him to the car and driven home with him in silence, but now she sounded exasperated. "Your mother and my father really don't have to answer to us. They aren't children."

"That's the whole point! They acted like impulsive, selfish children. How could she be so cruel?"

Gina looked confused. "Are you mad because she didn't tell you she was dying, or because she told you she isn't?"

"Don't be ridiculous," he snapped. "Of course I'm glad she's okay, but don't you think she could have given me an indication what was going on? The health issue is one thing, but your dad's another! She lied to me about that, and about the fact that they've been carrying on this whole time. They weren't even upset with each other for very long."

Gina looked affronted. "'Carrying on?' What is that supposed to mean? They're in love. Doesn't that mean anything to you? Haven't you ever been in love? In love enough to do something stupid. To marry and take it all on faith that things will work out?"

"Have you?" he snapped, turning to face her. He was tired of being put on the defensive. He'd always felt his mother deserved more than she'd ever gotten from his father, but he'd never imagined she'd have a serious relationship again. And was this going to get her what she wanted? To be honest, he was scared for her. He supposed that was what this was all about.

Gina had settled herself on his sofa. Her feet were drawn up under her, and she was staring at him with those deep brown eyes that were capable of swallowing him up. A blush covered her cheeks. "I think I was close once. Sort of. Maybe not head over heels in love, but I liked him. A lot."

"See? You're no better judge about this than I am. So don't give me any more grief."

His words only got her ire up. "Well, if neither of us has a clue about love, what business is it of ours to say whether they love each other or not? Whether or not they should get married."

Alex stopped pacing and slumped onto the cushion next to her. "Because…she should have told me sooner."

He'd wanted to make a point but sounded like a petulant, spoiled adolescent. "I mean, don't you think she was at least inconsiderate?"

Gina sighed. "Maybe. Maybe she was also excited and full of joy about being the center of someone's world. Maybe finding someone who cares about what she thinks, what she says, how she feels, and all the other wonderful things that love is, made her forget to tell you." She dipped her chin and seemed absorbed in inspecting the polish on her thumbnail. In a soft voice Alex had to strain to hear, she added, "Whatever it was, I hope I find the same thing someday."

Alex grimaced. "I suppose everyone has that hope. Even me." When he looked at Gina, he caught the hint of a grin tugging at the corners of her mouth. "But how can anyone be sure if they've found it?"

Her smile vanished and was replaced with open irritation. "For crying out loud, Alex, I'm not a psychic. How does anyone know anything? You take chances. Of all people, you should know about risks. You've told me about the dangerous places you've photographed for that magazine. Are you positive you'll get great shots every time you take a picture? Are you always sure you'll come back?"

"No, of course not—but that's different. That's not putting anyone at risk but me. This is my mother we're talking about."

"And my father!" Gina reminded him. "You act like he's an unsavory character instead of the decent, loving man he is. If he says he loves your mother, he means it. You should be glad they're together. We should be rooting for them, not picking out reasons they should fail."

Alex suddenly felt silly. He stole another glance at Gina and his pulse quickened. How beautiful she looked. Flushed pink cheeks, her dark eyes snapping like bolts of lightning…

"I'm sorry, Gina. I didn't mean anything against your father. Actually, I'm feeling rather foolish right now. Maybe I'm just jealous. Besides my dad, I've been the only person in my mother's world. She's always done everything expected of her. Gaetano brings something out in her that I don't understand. My dad would never have made a spectacle of himself by climbing up on a chair and expressing his emotions like that. This late-in-life love thing throws me for a loop. They act like they don't have a care in the world."

Gina nodded. "But just because you don't understand what's happening doesn't mean it isn't right."

"So you're saying I should be ecstatic?"

"At this point she'd probably settle for your not acting like a jackass. I know I would."

He gave her a wry glance. "I suppose I could try."

He moved closer to her and put his arm around her shoulders. She turned and looked at him, her face just inches from his. It seemed only natural that he should kiss her. He took her lips, gently, then deepened the kiss when he sensed her pulse had increased as much as his own. They broke contact only to reconnect in an even more passionate kiss.

He stroked her back while his lips left her mouth and found the soft area beneath her ear and finally the hollow of her neck. His right hand slowly migrated to her breast and the top buttons on her blouse. He heard her gasp as she took in air, and a slight moan escaped her lips. She pulled away for a few seconds, grasped his knitted shirt, and quickly pulled it over his head.

His fingers worked furiously to undo the remaining buttons on her blouse as she nibbled on his neck and earlobe. Tossing the garment aside, he leaned close, feeling her warm, full breasts against his bare chest. Their passion accelerated at Mach speed, shutting out all awareness, all sounds, everything that was reality. His arms lifted her onto his lap, and with strength he didn't know still existed after his accident he stood.

"Gina, are you sure about this? I am. I really think we might have something, and I'm willing to try it. Let's let bygones be bygones and do this right. Let's take a chance."

Gina wrapped both arms around his neck and grinned. "I've been thinking of nothing else since I met you. Now hurry, before you drop me."

Alex chuckled. She still liked being in charge. Somehow, he didn't mind. She was feisty just like he loved, and he hadn't felt this good in a long time. Even his wrecked car didn't seem important. *Especially* his wrecked car didn't seem important. It was probably time to get something more practical anyway.

He hesitated only long enough to kiss her one more time before slowly carrying her to his bedroom.

Chapter 23

Estelle peeked out of the bride's room at Saint Phillip's by the Sea church, giving herself a good view of the altar and the center pews filled with guests. Everyone she'd invited had come. They likely wanted to see what had gotten into their normally sensible friend.

Out there, up at the altar, her groom fussed with his cravat and tugged at his cummerbund. That just made Estelle surer that she was making the best decision she'd made in a long time. It tickled her to see Gaetano so flustered and fidgety. He'd put up a real fuss about getting dressed in a "monkey suit," but Gina had taken care of that. She'd been a tremendous help with the wedding plans too. She couldn't ask for a better daughter-in-law. If only she'd eventually be Alex's wife as well.

***

Gina snagged Alex and pulled him to one side of the hallway outside the room where his mother was waiting and straightened his boutonniere. He leaned over and kissed her. She beamed but cautioned, "Watch it. We don't want to tip our hand just yet, do we?"

"I guess not, but it's hard to keep my hands off you."

Gina giggled and squeezed his hand. He was so handsome in his tux, and the cut on his head had healed completely. "I think we should keep our secret until after our parents get back from their honeymoon. I mean, we don't want to give our parents the pleasure of knowing they got us together yet, do we?"

"We'll keep it if we can," Alex said, though she could see the sparkle in his eye. "How do you feel about a honeymoon in Indonesia?"

Gina's heart raced. *What?* Was he saying what she thought? "Indonesia? When? Why? Is it even civilized?"

His expression grew nervous. "They have some nice hotels, and it's really quite beautiful. I've been offered an assignment to go there. I'm not sure just when, but I'm not leaving you behind. I thought we could tie things up before the trip, and maybe you can take some time off.... I finally figured out what love is, and I'm not taking any chances. Assuming you want to come. Uh, we can have a long engagement if you want, but do you want a wedding like this? It's, like, really big."

Gina couldn't believe her ears. "Are you *proposing*? If so, the answer is yes—and no, I don't want a big fancy do. I love you, too, Alex. I'll go wherever you want, stay in five-star accommodations or in hovels, unlike that last girlfriend. And I promise to learn to cook for you. No, I don't know how to cook. Shhh, don't say anything; I know I'm an Italian who doesn't know how to cook. Maybe we both can learn to cook. My dad asked me to take lessons, and he suggested you and I... You really did just ask me to marry you, didn't you?"

He leaned down and kissed her again, grinning widely. "Yes, I sure did. Sorry, I thought a smart girl like you would have guessed it was coming."

Gina shook her head, dazed with pleasure. Then she realized, "Oh, damn, I've forgotten your mother. It's time to start or my father is going to have a stroke. Then we won't get our cooking lessons." She gave him a hug and hurried off to alert her soon-to-be twice-over mother-in-law. How ever was she going to keep this a secret? She supposed she would have to. Today was her father's day. And

Estelle's. Plus, hadn't they been keeping secrets themselves? She supposed turnabout was fair play. Especially when it was good news.

***

"Estelle, it's time."

Estelle turned to find her soon-to-be stepdaughter. Gina had never looked more beautiful.

"Alex is waiting for you out in the hallway. Mario will escort me down first. You and Alex follow when the Bridal March begins."

Estelle's eyes misted. "I think I remember. Thank you for being so helpful and wonderful."

Gina pushed a Kleenex into Estelle's hand before giving her a hug, clearly careful not to crush her bouquet of pink and white roses. "Thank you for making Papá so happy. I haven't seen that sparkle in his eyes for a long time, and you're the one who put it there. And Alex and I may have thanks to say of our own when—"

"Gina, come on," came a whisper from beyond the door. It was Mario. "The wedding boss lady is giving me the signal. We have to go. The best man and best girl are supposed to walk down the aisle now!"

"I'm coming, Mario, and it's 'maid of honor' not 'best girl'."

Estelle followed Gina out the door and into the hallway. Grinning from ear to ear, Gaetano's daughter took the older man's arm and winked at Alex who stood nearby. Estelle looked past the couple to her groom waiting at the altar. She saw Gaetano's gaze focus on his daughter, and his hand went to his chest as if she took his breath away. Estelle blinked back tears and smiled. The girl was indeed lovely. Perfect for her son, if they ever got things together.

The first official pair began to walk down the aisle: Mario and Gina. The older Italian man struggled to walk in time to the music, but of course he failed. He laughed, took two small steps and then hurried to catch up with Gina's metered pace. Estelle laughed too.

Her son moved close and kissed her cheek as they waited for the best man and best girl to make it all the way down the aisle, and Estelle couldn't help herself from speaking up. "Gina is absolutely beautiful, isn't she, Alex? You know, you might want to give some thought to you and her making this little trip yourselves. It's obvious you two have feelings for each other."

"Yes, she is stunning," her boy agreed. "But don't you think we ought to get *you* married off before we start worrying about me?"

He'd been wonderful since the night at the restaurant. He'd come over to her house after he'd cooled off and they'd had a good long talk. He'd been sweet and understanding and was truly happy she'd found love the second time around. He'd also met with Gaetano and given his blessing, which made Gaetano very happy. She wanted so much for him to have what she and Gaetano had. She didn't want to push him into anything he didn't want, but she just *knew* the two kids would just make the most perfect couple in the world. Why else would the past few weeks have played out as they had?

She kept her response to: "I only said she was beautiful. Still, you could do a lot worse, you know. She certainly comes from a good family."

"I guess she does at that. But doesn't this little event make her my sister? And did you know she doesn't even know how to cook?"

"What? What are you talking ab—?"

Trumpets sounded, and everyone in the church rose, all eyes now on the couple at the back. Alex gave her a grin and nodded. "Sshhh, Mom, we're ready to roll. Let's save my relationship till this is all over, and we don't need to worry if Gina can cook. We have more than enough cooks in this family, and *you're* the one who needs to be happy today. And every day hereafter." He tucked her hand through his arm and guided her down the aisle.

Estelle stared straight ahead as she walked. Before her, Gaetano waited. He looked entranced. She knew he considered her the second love of his life, that he was grateful that she "put up with" a crazy Italian whose aftershave was often co-mingled with the scent of garlic and basil. But it was so much more than that. She felt so much more than tolerance. She loved Gaetano, in a very different way than she'd once loved her first husband Marty, but she loved him just the same, and now she loved his daughter just as much. The fact that he was eccentric would only add spice to their upcoming life.

Alex smiled at her as they reached the altar, kissed her once more, and then placed her hand in Gaetano's outstretched one. Her soon-to-be husband's eyes were full of love, and it was all Estelle could do to keep the giggles inside as she contemplated what life held in store for her.

Something spontaneous, something exciting, a life full of fun and laughter. Something always unpredictable. That's what she was taking a chance on today. And, no, she'd never guessed she might be this lucky.

ABOUT THE AUTHOR

As soon as she learned to hold a pencil, Shirley Ann Wilder started writing stories. As a wife and mother of four, her dream to write books was put on hold while she devoted herself to the family, but she had regular columns in community newspapers, authored a monthly column "On the Wilder Side" in a special-interest magazine, and published in college literary magazines. When the children grew up, she joined Romance Writers of America and began her career of weaving characters into full-length tales of romance. *Too Many Cooks* is her first published novel.

SYNOPSIS

Gaetano Lorenzo was the sweetest man that the widowed Estelle Bennett had ever met. That morning began terribly, with awful news, but now the owner and head chef of a local San Diego *ristorante* was offering up Italian delights: red wine, delicious food, walks on the beach, laughter when she'd never thought she'd laugh again.... Estelle felt twenty-five. She and Gaetano had found the recipe for love, and a simple variation might just get their adult children to settle down, too. A scoop of sugar, two ladlefuls of lust, a pinch of deception and a whole 24 oz.-can of danger—Suddenly, ingredients were coming from everywhere! But kitchens are crazy places, and variety is the spice of life. And for anything to get cooked, things have to get hot.

Did you enjoy this book? Drop us a line and say so! We love to hear from readers, and so do our authors. To connect, visit www.boroughspublishinggroup.com online, send comments directly to info@boroughspublishinggroup.com, or friend us on Facebook and Twitter. And be sure to check back regularly for contests and new releases in your favorite subgenres of romance!

Are you an aspiring writer? Check out www.boroughspublishinggroup.com/submit and see if we can help you make your dreams come true.

www.ingramcontent.com/pod-product-compliance
Lightning Source LLC
Chambersburg PA
CBHW061613170626
46811CB00001B/423